Praise for In Search of the Magic Theater

"Karla Huebner's debut novel offers a sophisticated meditation on the idea of art, mythology, theater, and music (classical and jazz) as two women, separated by a generation and divided by a cultural shift—from 60s to post-60s—negotiate sexuality, love, regret, grief, and above all forgiveness, all done in a style that's deceptively simple at first but grows on the reader and quietly lures him inside the magic theater only to discover that all lies within - the actors, the script, the theater, the magic. A treat for the denizens of the world of art and intellect."

–Moazzam Sheikh, author of *Café Le Whore and Other Stories.*

"Exciting… A sophisticated, queer-friendly, and feminist take on Hesse's *Steppenwolf.* Although loosely set in the late 1990s, Huebner's meditation on repression, instinct, and the creative drive is fresh and timeless."

–Gabriella West, author of *Time of Grace* and *Once You Are Mine*

"Through the voices of two women with overlapping lives but diverging paths, Karla Huebner explores the tension between control and surrender, reason and ecstasy, dreaming and choosing. This engaging, erudite, yet accessible novel takes us on a cultural journey spanning millennia, from Greek mythology to Jimi Hendrix, from Elizabethan lyric poetry to performance art, revealing along the way the joy of self-discovery."

–Julie Wittes Schlack, author of *This All-at-Onceness*

"Huebner sets us up for a climax of dazzling theater that combines Keats's romantic poetry, Greek drama, music and dance, a production that leaves the reader excited and fulfilled by the magic one can experience with good art. And, yes, a sense of adventure in our unforeseeable future."

–Margaret C. Murray, author of *Spiral* and *Pillow Prayers*

"At some point every life should have a disquieting blast of Kari. She's a down-but-not-out whackadoodle, the perfect foil to serious young Sarah in this page-turner fugue between two women whose views of music, men, and even the meaning of existence couldn't be more out of sync. Karla Huebner's lyrical prose has the ring of a bold new showtune with a message about how to suffer joyfully and artfully. And even if 'you don't always know what you want, and you can't always get what you need,' *In Search of the Magic Theater* will give you reasons to sing along."

–Jan Alexander, author of *Ms. Ming's Guide to Civilization*

"Two women, a generation apart though their lives intertwine, tell us in their most intimate voices of their quite different, sometimes comical and mostly but not always disappointing adventures with men. And careers, and cellos, and dope. When the quest for satisfaction of the elder and more pro-active of the two takes the stage, we are treated to a simultaneously comical and erudite 'magic theater' production, in which we see their present dilemmas as repetitions or reflections of the ancient myths of Endymion and the goddesses, with pictorial and poetic references through the ages. In this tale of two women, in which the men are also treated very sensitively, Karla Huebner calls on her deep knowledge of European of classical paintings and verse for a story of desire denied, delayed, and sometimes precariously fulfilled."

–Geoffrey Fox, author of *Welcome to My Contri*, *A Gift for the Sultan*, and *Rabble*

IN SEARCH OF THE MAGIC THEATER

Karla Huebner

Regal House Publishing

Published by
Regal House Publishing, LLC
Raleigh, NC 27587
All rights reserved

ISBN -13 (paperback): 9781646031917
ISBN -13 (epub): 9781646031924
Library of Congress Control Number: 2021943787

All efforts were made to determine the copyright holders and obtain their permissions in any circumstance where copyrighted material was used. The publisher apologizes if any errors were made during this process, or if any omissions occurred. If noted, please contact the publisher and all efforts will be made to incorporate permissions in future editions.

Interior layout by Lafayette & Greene
Cover images © by C. B. Royal

Regal House Publishing, LLC
https://regalhousepublishing.com

The following is a work of fiction created by the author. All names, individuals, characters, places, items, brands, events, etc. were either the product of the author's imagination or were used fictitiously. Any name, place, event, person, brand, or item, current or past, is entirely coincidental.

Printed in the United States of America

For Frank Lupo, in honor of Consuelo Sandoval

SARAH

My aunt takes in renters. Sometimes this seems very irritating; why can't we have enough money to keep her house to ourselves? But we don't, and besides, I think she likes having renters. It gives her someone besides me to be interested in and keep an eye on, in an inoffensive, auntly way.

A while ago she took in a new one, a woman named Kari. Kari must have been around forty, we eventually realized, although she looked younger. That is, she seemed middle-aged to me, because it was clear she was older than I am, but she wasn't awfully middle-aged like some people, and my aunt thought she was young. She was slender, with wire-rimmed glasses and an exhausted, slightly strained look that I didn't like; was she going to be one of those characters who look normal on the surface and then turn out to be a little unhinged? People who rent rooms have to be careful about their renters, after all; it's not enough that they can pay the rent on time. My aunt isn't always careful enough about this, so I have to watch out a little on her behalf—the household is too normal to attract real bohemian types or druggies, but sometimes we get people who aren't as normal as they seem at first, who turn out to be obsessive-compulsive or have unstable boyfriends or think it's okay to eat our food without asking. Once we had a guy who turned out to be seriously paranoid and ended up trying to sue us for being anti-Semitic, which was ridiculous but very unpleasant.

Anyhow, I was not sure that Kari was the right person to rent our room, even though she was neatly dressed in a plain blue shirt and off-white pants with plain brown clogs, and even though she was friendly enough. I could tell something wasn't quite right with her, and what if it turned out to be something that would bother us? My aunt, however, is more open and forgiving than I am. I think it's something to do with her feelings toward my mother, who was her little sister and for some reason her responsibility. She liked Kari right away and immediately invited her to move in.

"Why'd you do that?" I asked her after Kari had gone; after all, usually we try to interview at least three potential renters so that we can pick the likeliest one.

"She needs a place," said my aunt.

"That's silly," I said. "Everyone needs a place to live, and we don't take all of them. Are you going to check her references?"

"Oh, I suppose," said my aunt, which meant that she didn't really intend to bother. "Kari needs a calm, clean, orderly home."

"Well, don't let her make any problems," I said. "I don't want any more fragile types with abusive boyfriends, or manic-depressives who start screaming in the middle of the night or want to slit their wrists in the bathtub. We don't need to live with people like that."

"No, no," said my aunt reassuringly. "Kari will be just fine."

Since Kari did strike me as intelligent and a fundamentally nice person, even if potentially a bit unstable, I put up no more arguments, and in retrospect I grant that my aunt was, on the whole, right. Kari didn't cause us any real problems during her stay. Instead, she roused my curiosity to an unusual degree. Normally, I try to keep my nose out of the renters' business and hope that they'll have the courtesy to return the favor, but I grew abnormally curious about Kari. I think my aunt did as well.

I suppose in part it was that she had an outward appearance of being very quiet and fairly conventional, yet radiated something thoroughly and unsettlingly untamed and unconventional. That was why I was put off at first, fearing that she'd suddenly crack and be troublesome. Maybe I'm hypersensitive about that sort of thing, but my mother was all the trouble I ever felt I needed. Unlike my nice, solid, sensible, kindly aunt, my mother had been a wild child. She had felt some sort of unaccountable need to run off and be a hippie and live in communes and have lots of sex and drugs. We think my father was a Jewish poet named Eli, but we don't actually know this for a fact. While I'm fine with the idea of having a Jewish poet for a father, I was never fine with not knowing who he was, or whether he was really my father, or with really anything at all about my mother and her life. I like being a quiet, normal, non-hippie who plays the cello and reads books like *Jane Eyre*. I like living with my aunt, who listens to trashy pop music from her youth—maybe even her childhood—like "Calendar Girl" and "Downtown" and "Windy" and who mainly reads books that sound sappy to me. I prefer to have renters who have regular nine-to-five jobs and are mainly in the house to sleep, who say hi when they see us, and whose lives don't prompt my interest, because usually when I have to take an interest in a renter, something has gone wrong. My aunt does take more of an interest in them, because she likes to know things like whether they have brothers and sisters or are divorced or have an unreasonable boss. But that's because she's determined to take an auntly interest in nearly everyone who crosses her path.

We didn't, however, really learn this sort of detail about Kari Zilke. In fact, until I saw her rent check, I thought her name was Carrie Silky, which sounded like a dumb name, but when I commented on the spelling of her first name, she told me that it was spelled the Norwegian way because she was half Norwegian.

"Which half?" I asked, but she only joked, "The right half." The left half, she claimed, was German. Other than that, she didn't volunteer much information about herself, although now and then something would slip out.

Instead, what we knew was that when she moved in she brought a couple of suitcases of clothes, a box of books, and a box of LP records. There were a few other things, like a phonograph to play the records on, but not much else. Other than the records, which seemed pretty old-fashioned considering that most people had switched to CDs in the eighties or at least the early nineties, I have to admit that this was a fairly standard setup, as people who want to rent a furnished room in a house like ours are either too young to have acquired much stuff or have put most of it in storage while they figure out what to do with their lives. My aunt and I automatically put Kari in this latter category, although we didn't actually know for a fact that she had anything other than what she brought to the house. I think, however, that perhaps she really didn't have anything else. As I got to know her, to the small extent that I did get to know her, she struck me more and more as a person who jettisoned things she considered inessential.

Kari's books and records marked her as a more intellectual and cultured person than usual, which was part of what prompted my interest in her. As I say, I play the cello and read books like *Jane Eyre*—classics—but I didn't recognize most of the books or records she had. She didn't seem to read much of the American or British literature that I knew, but for some reason favored foreign writers. I had heard of Marquez and Günter Grass, but I hadn't read them. There were a lot of unfamiliar Spanish-sounding names like Cortazar and Calvino and Borges. She had a well-worn copy of *Andersen's Fairy Tales*, which I thought was peculiar for a grown-up, and a book of Japanese tales by Lafcadio Hearn. About the only American writers were Toni Morrison and Carson McCullers, although, strangely, she had a copy of *Rubyfruit Jungle*. Was our renter a lesbian? I didn't really think I should ask about her sexual preferences.

Eventually I did ask her about some of the books, and whether she thought I would like any of these authors; she looked at me intently, then glanced away and said literary preferences were very individual but that I should read some of these writers and see what I thought. After a while I did read some of them and I could see that they were good writers, but mostly not really my kind of thing. Not my cup of tea, to use an old-fashioned phrase. I like stories about real people, with events that could really happen, so I didn't exactly take to these crazy South Americans or Günter Grass. I thought Carson McCullers was pretty good, although her characters were a little freakish. When I told Kari that, she laughed and said the world was full of writers I would like.

"I don't know about that," I said, a little insulted. "I don't think it's that easy to go to the library or the bookstore and just find something I really like. I don't like just any old bestseller."

"No," she hastened to say, "but I think you'd like a lot of the classics. People like Hawthorne and maybe Dickens and Balzac." She came up with a list of authors I might enjoy, and she was right, I did like some of them. They weren't writers she was into when she lived with us, but she knew about them.

At night, I could often hear her playing peculiar music—not loudly, but really odd stuff, like a plaintive, folkloric thing about the murder of someone called Sir John Barleycorn, which she later explained to me was about making whiskey, of all things. I know a lot of classical composers, of course, and it turned out that she did too, but she didn't have all that many classical records—mainly things like the *New World Symphony*, the *Peer Gynt Suite*, and *Scheherazade* and *Pictures at an Exhibition*. When I asked, she claimed that if she wanted to listen to classical music, she could turn on the radio or go to a concert.

"Well, but isn't it the same with the popular music you've got?" I inquired. I don't care much for popular music, which tends to be vulgar and inane. Once I discovered classical music—my aunt is ignorant about it but she liked to watch the Boston Pops on TV when I was little—I knew that that was my music.

"To some extent," she said, "but popular music is more subject to fashion. If I want to hear Bach or Beethoven, it won't be long before they come up on the radio. If I want to hear Van Morrison, I could wait a long time unless he's just come out with a new album."

I had to grant that this was true. Evidently she didn't need to hear very much Van Morrison, because the only album she had was one called *Moondance*. It looked pretty ancient. Then there was the even older copy of *Rubber Soul* that still had a green sticker indicating she had bought it used for fifty cents. Most of her records were even more eclectic than her books. She had one of Swedish folk fiddling, one of African mbira music, one of Peruvian flute music, one of Gregorian chant, and one of Javanese gamelan. This was before so-called World

Music became such a popular category, and I thought this was very bizarre stuff. I kind of liked her Alan Stivell records, but I didn't really care for some of her British folk music; I agreed with her that there were interesting rhythms in some of the Martin Carthy songs, but the lyrics were often too grotesque for my taste.

This seemed to amuse her. "You don't like hearing that 'the slobber that hung from between their mouths would've tethered a two-year-old bull'?"

"Good god, no, that's gross," I said. "I can't imagine why anyone would ever want to do a song about two monstrosities marrying. Or why anyone would want to listen to it."

I'm sure she thought I was sheltered; after all, plenty of people in my generation were out getting full-body tattoos and genital piercings and were listening to rap music or something. But I wouldn't say I'm sheltered; I just didn't feel like telling her about my mother the hippie. I like living with my aunt and soaking in her middle-of-the-road Middle American tastes and comfortable values. My aunt grew up in the fifties, and she knows exactly what was good and bad about that time. My aunt is very real and very grounded, and we knew that was part of why Kari Zilke wanted to live with us.

KARI

I sit about in my godforsaken room, a blessed island of wild disorder in my landlady's spotless, well-maintained, almost suburban house, and feel all the discontented achiness and creaking of my fortyish state. What on earth possessed me to rent a room in a place like this, and how long will it be before my landlady tires of my craziness and kicks me out? Well, I suppose that even in my wildest excess, I'm not drawn to live in squalor; there must be an underlying order to my disorder, a bourgeois backdrop to my bohemian tendencies. I'm a Bad Girl, but bad only to a point. My landlady will tolerate me awhile, I think, because first off, she's a good-hearted person, and secondly, I sense that buried in her past was just a little taste of hippie-dom, an unsatisfied craving perhaps for the Summer of Love. I envision her as one of those Nice Girls of the Sixties who wore her hair up in an attempt at a beehive and felt like she was being terribly fast when she dared put on a bit of green eye shadow, but who secretly thought those hippie chicks in art class with the long hair and beads were very, very exciting and lucky. She does, after all, wear a touch of black eyeliner in a highly unbecoming but tellingly sixties manner.

And then there's her little niece, who's actually not little at all but close to six feet tall and very disapproving in her well brought up way. I hadn't thought young people were so polite to their elders anymore, but this one is a model of decorum and plays the cello diligently for several hours a day, which I gather makes finding renters more of a challenge despite the fact that she plays very well. The difficulty in living with a musician, of course, is not so much bad playing as that you will hear the same passages repeated numerous times, possibly even in more than one key if the player is getting playful. We'll see if it bothers me; I've spent a good deal of my own life practicing music, though not as seriously, so I like to imagine that the niece's cello will mitigate the white slipcovers tarting up the dining room chairs. Ah, bourgeois life; cleanliness and order are always in style, although sometimes more insistently than other times, but décor has its fashions. No more the bowls of plastic fruit of my childhood, or the orange, brown, and then the avocado green and mustard of my teens; now we've reached the point where every well-appointed middle-class home is decked out in a color scheme of dark green and a sort of drab pink. My landlady has dutifully swathed her sofa in cabbage roses in these shades, matching her curtains and valances, and she's wallpapered the living room in green stripes with roses (if it weren't for the photos of her family, we could be in a hotel), but I gather that white slipcovers are the new direction. I'm working in the opposite direction by stringing up the kind of India print gauze I never had when I was younger; my landlady took a look inside my room, a sort of double take, and then assured me that this "retro" look was very imaginative of me. I don't suppose it will last long; I don't suppose I will bide here very many months.

Where was I in my life before I came here? Oh, that's really asking for it. I could go on at length about the disgusting, stifling trap I'd crawled into—though it wasn't a trap made by anyone but myself. In my twenties, I was passionate about everything. Men, career, everything. If I couldn't be passionate about it, I had no interest in it. And then I had one of those unhappy loves that never even develops, but which leaves the one who loves in a state of utter desolation, utter misery, floundering along near suicide. I realize that such loves are typical of a certain romantic variety of sensitive person, of whom I was just another one in a long line of Werther-esque beings, but there it was, I was desolate, howling at the moon. I wallowed in my agony. Yet only half of me was made in that wild mold; half of me is practical, sensible, balanced, responsible, and boring. And this practical half of me was repelled by this madness and by so much careening about on the dark side of the moon. The practical half got a practical job in an office and next thing you know, I had managed to enchant a poor guy who had no concept of what he was in for.

Oh, he's a good sort, a solid, reliable kind of person, gentle, mild-mannered, extremely trustworthy. All of these things were in his favor; I've never cared for mean or violent or trouble-making men. But they mustn't be too domesticated either. They need a streak of wildness.

And this one, I'm afraid, had just enough of that wild streak to take to someone like me, but not enough wildness to answer it. I can tell you that this had never before happened to me; no domesticated men had ever taken to me, only wild ones who had the wrong mix of passions and soon ran away. I knew this one was not right for me, but I was worn out, burned to the core, so I ignored that and let him woo me. I suffered from that stupidity common to women of thirty: What if no one else ever loves me? What if this is the best it will ever be?

Reader, I married him, and if ever a less romantic union existed, it can only have been one of the commercial variety, and not one involving the affections. For I did care for him, just not in the way that he cared for me.

And so I sank into a severely domesticated existence that partly satisfied that practical, traditional, nearly housewifely side of me. Temporarily united in the cult of frugality, we were shocked to find that our wedding would cost nearly five hundred dollars at a time when the average price was, I believe, twenty thousand. Not actually being in love, I had no ambitions of glamorous dresses, elegant surroundings, an entourage of attendants, or an exotic honeymoon. No, a nice little gray dress from the thrift store seemed like the most suitable gear, for I was too depressed and bitter to imagine anything more flamboyant, even though I appeared cheerful and happy. We weren't planning to have rings, but ended up getting them at the last minute in case it wasn't legal to marry without them or some such thing. The only things we went a little crazy on were music and flowers: we both loved those, so we had a harpist and some vases of calla lilies. The so-called honeymoon was a weekend in a chain-hotel suite, which my poor spouse imagined would be the height of luxury and which I consented to experience because I wanted to make him happy.

In describing this relationship, I have the persistent sensation of telling a story about people who lived a hundred years ago, and not about something I myself chose to endure in the 1990s. It is hard for me to imagine that anyone, anymore, marries "on the rebound" in a state of near apathy and enters into the married state purely on the important but rather limited grounds that the other person is kind, hardworking, and shares some common interests. One likes to imagine that everyone, these days, marries for love, even if their notion of love is poorly formed to the point of monstrosity and their concept of compatibility is based largely on a shared liking for cheap beer.

And yet, when I stop to think about it, I am aware that there is plenty of evidence that other people, even today, marry for reasons not quite worthy of being called love. We need not bring up instances of family alliances in India or among the world's royalty; all around us in North America, people are marrying on the grounds that they feel they shouldn't be single and that someone nice enough, suitable enough, and complaisant enough has happened along. Often these matches even turn out well, and this, I suppose, was what encouraged me to persist in my attempts to make my marriage a success.

But what was going on during all those years of attempted marital bliss was, in fact, a complicated bid for takeover by my dull, practical, bourgeois side. Perhaps this side of me even encouraged my long-suffering spouse to become even more placid and unadventurous than would otherwise have been his nature. He was already capable of sitting at his desk, working quietly for twelve hours at a time with scarcely a break; I too became more and more able to sit at my desk and produce the required work without actually having a complete breakdown and running into the street screaming. We talked about wanting to have some nice pieces of furniture, but we couldn't afford much, so we got used to the ugly combination of things we had acquired through inheritance, garage sales, and discount stores. We believed we should put away money for our retirement, but my spouse argued that it was unwise to gamble our savings, so we put everything into an account so risk-averse that it averaged a two-percent annual return when I suspected we might want to try to beat inflation with something more like twelve. Interest rates were, after all, vigorous. We've been having, I hear, the longest period of growth in U.S. history, although now people are muttering that so-called Y2K computer problems might throw us into a state of savagery and barbarism come the year 2000. We'll see, New Year's Eve.

At first I was glad that my spouse was both hardworking and uninterested in wealth; these fitted with my morals, which had been thoroughly inculcated in a staunchly Norwegian-Lutheran fashion. After all, one would not want to be around someone who was lazy, and while thrift was important, it would be dis-agreeable to live with someone who thought too much about making money and piling up the worldly goods. But before long the wilder and more flamboyant side of me began to get bored with all this modest rectitude. Surely we could be hardworking and live a little less ascetically?

My friends, too, had gotten married, but they were having children, or leaving their lovers because the lovers didn't want children, or they were going to fertility clinics or adopting Chinese and Romanian babies. They weren't pursuing their passions either. Actually, after my marriage I didn't see much of them anymore. The effort of being married and keeping in touch with people just seemed to be too much. Still, I heard from some of them now and then, or met this one or that one for lunch. Some of them were on Prozac. Some had gone into technical writing or had positions with medical firms that involved writing reports about endoscopes and rotating biolog-ical contactors. I got Christmas cards telling me about going to hotel management school, or becoming a veterinary technician, or teaching piano to second-graders. I had the feeling that my most exciting friends had dropped off the planet and had no time to keep up with the likes of me, a person who no longer made phone calls, who no longer traveled, and didn't yet have email.

Sarah

I got to know a certain amount about Kari Zilke while she lived at my aunt's; not much, but a little. She seemed to be a rather antisocial person; she rarely talked on the phone and didn't seem to seek out friends. I didn't actually spy on her, but I was curious about the peculiar sorts of music that she played on her antiquated phonograph—after all, the nostalgia for "vinyl" hadn't yet seriously begun—and I was curious what had brought this relatively cultured person into our house. And what possessed her to hang gauze Indian-print fabrics in her room, for heaven's sake? When I saw those, I thought, Oh my god, she's one of those closet hippies, next thing you know she'll be burning incense and putting up a poster of Ganesha or some kind of Tibetan mandala with copulating gods. How icky.

When I mentioned this to my aunt, she looked mildly concerned for a moment, and then said, "Sarah, Kari's too young to be a hippie."

"Who are you kidding?" I said. "Kids my age are hippies. Being a hippie is back in style."

My aunt sighed and said, "Kari's both too young and too old to be a hippie, I think." This was, as it turned out, precisely the case, but I had no way of knowing it at the time. Having my own personal anti-hippie stance, for which I think I had very good reasons, I was blind to the nuances of hippie-dom and weekend-hippie-dom and wannabe-hippie-dom and latter-day hippie-dom. I envisioned every hippie in the shape of my mother, who seemed like the quintessential historical hippie girl: long-haired, granny-skirted, barefoot or sandaled, draped in beads, ever attired in Indian gauze and Mexican blouses, constantly breathing inanities like "wow, man," and "trippy," and referring to her latest beau as "my old man." My mother, who was allegedly an intelligent person, went through life reading

Kahlil Gibran (despite the scorn of my putative father the poet Eli), making decisions based on the *I Ching*, and listening to sitar music. My mother, in short, set herself up to be a cliché, and my early years were those of the hippie baby playing in the dirt who can't start kindergarten on time because she hasn't been vaccinated. It's no wonder my grandparents gave up and died of cancer in their fifties, leaving my aunt to deal with the hippie baby sister and baby sister's hippie baby daughter. Why our renter, or anyone else, would want to drape a bedroom in nasty old Indian-print gauze reeking of import-store incense was really quite beyond me.

My aunt, however, looked at me and merely said, "I think you're overreacting."

KARI

The India-print gauze tacked to my walls gives me a sense of excitement, of starting a new life. Or at least a new part of my life, one in which new possibilities open up. I'm too bourgeois, especially after my domestic phase, to run off and join an ashram or even take up Zen; the fascination with Eastern religions that gripped the older half of my generation has no real hold on me. I just like the exotic trappings, which is no doubt regrettable. Well—not to put myself down, or others either for that matter—but while I respect Hinduism and the various forms of Buddhism, I've never felt the slightest inclination to become a Hindu or a Buddhist, and I've always had the suspicion that quite a few of these religions' Western adherents were just lost souls looking for something trendy to join that had a little more substance and truth to it than the various cults that attracted the more confused. No, I admit I just like the look, coupled with the feeling of being simultaneously in a clean, unimaginative, bourgeois, household but having an orientalist counter-culture fantasy in my own little corner. My landlady has her nice little house, which I simultaneously respect and want to defile with gauze print hangings. If she had pictures of sad clowns and big-eyed children, I don't think I would have been able to stand being in the same building, but while her tastes are uninspired, at least they aren't repulsive. This is good, because I like her, and I like going down to her kitchen and making a cup of tea in the presence of her shiny white electric mixer, her toaster with its quilted fabric dust cover, and her ceramic canisters for flour, sugar, coffee, and tea.

Sarah

I find that I'm wandering a certain amount in my attempt to convey my impressions of Kari Zilke. Why on earth should I go on and on about my mother of all people, who wasn't really anything like Kari? If I worried initially that Kari might be a hippie in disguise, and bring all kinds of repugnant things into my aunt's house that would remind me of my mother—incense, dope-smoking, self-indulgent rock music—those fears weren't, as my aunt recognized, terribly realistic. It's true that Kari had more of the hippie in her than was evident at first glance, but I quickly realized that she had an intellectual, or at least literary, aspect to her, as anyone who looked at her books would certainly figure out. She seemed mildly depressed, yet at the same time there was an undercurrent of feverish excitement that seemed to be awaiting an outlet. This had made me wary of taking her in as a renter, but it made me more interested in her as a person, because I began to realize that there was something deep about her, and even though I meet some intelligent people through my cello lessons, I wouldn't say that most of them are all that deep. Or if they are, they're too busy competing to let on that they have any other side to them.

When I say there was something deep about Kari Zilke, I don't mean that she philosophized or pontificated. Instead, I mean I had the impression that she had had a variety of experiences in life—certainly more than my aunt or I had ever had or wanted to have—and that this had made her thoughtful. I had the feeling that she was always searching for the meaning of the things that happened to her and the significance of the choices that she and other people made. This impressed me, because in my experience most people either take the life that has been given to them and go along in that path, or they make choices which can be either foolish rebellious ones like my mother's, or carefully considered ones. Hardly any of them, wise or foolish, then bother to think much about their path in life unless to say they're content or that they've made a mess of it. My aunt has taken the path that was given to her, and she claims to be content with it. I've chosen to learn my cello and see if I can learn it well enough to be a teacher, but I don't have very many thoughts about it. I had the feeling that Kari, however, had made both good and foolish decisions and that she looked at life as a network of interconnecting paths, some taken and some not taken, but all of which continued to exist in some sort of tantalizing form even after she had taken a different path that seemed to erase the one not taken. I had the feeling that she looked at the people around her and secretly or not so secretly assessed their paths and whether their paths were interesting or dull, and whether they were suitable or unsuitable. I had the feeling that she looked at my aunt and regarded her path as dull but suitable; that she looked at me and saw that I was too young to make judgments about, because I would require more watching.

I didn't know anyone else who seemed to approach life in this way, which made it strange but intriguing. My cello teacher assessed me regularly, but in a purely professional sense as to my technique and not as to whether I was destined to become a cello teacher. We didn't entertain fantasies that I would become a famous cellist, or even that I'd play in a major orchestra; we simply took as our goal that I could become good enough to play in local ensembles and earn a living passing on what I knew. We didn't worry about whether I would get along with other performers, or if I would make useful contacts, or whether aspiring composers would ask me to premiere their works. I did know young musicians who were more ambitious, but I wasn't impressed with their goals. I didn't see why anyone would aspire to be first flute in a major orchestra, or want to be involved with performing new works by composers who probably weren't very good. Yet I was intrigued by Kari Zilke's need to see patterns and significance in people's lives and choices.

And that must be why I find that I keep throwing in so much

about myself when I don't really want or intend to; when I don't think of myself as an interesting person or even a person who has any need to be interesting, and certainly not a person who has an unusual psychology or a life that will matter to anyone but those immediately around me. I see myself as a normal, ordinary person—not average, admittedly, or like everyone else, but straightforwardly set in my course and not terribly unusual—an ordinary intelligent person who happened to encounter someone less ordinary. If I were used to hanging around geniuses, I suppose that someone like Kari Zilke would seem mundane. She might not seem interesting enough. Her fondness for coming down and making cups of tea in my aunt's kitchen might seem terribly dull. But in my world, which consisted mainly of my aunt and my music studies, Kari was interesting. She seemed to hunger for something, but we didn't know exactly what, and it seemed very unlikely that she was going to find that something in my aunt's house, where she was only satisfying her taste for a modicum of fundamental quiet order and decency.

What was she like, then? Oh, that's such a difficult question! And here I have to make a confession. Though she lived with us for several months, suddenly she moved on, and happened to leave behind a kind of diary. This manuscript gives some clue to her personality, but at the same time it doesn't really show the side of her that my aunt and I came to know.

Clearly Kari Zilke was properly, even religiously, brought up, but that didn't satisfy her. Well—we could see that in her, but we saw her quieter side, her more domesticated side, even though it was obvious that she didn't value that side of herself as highly as the other side, which she tried to avoid making too evident to us. There was something rebellious in her, but she kept it in check in our household. And as to her personal history, we knew much less than even the small amounts she revealed in the manuscript. We had no idea she had ever been married.

Around us, then, she lived fairly quietly. Before long it became clear that she had no regular job, although she did take in publishers' manuscripts to edit, and kept stacks of what she called "galleys" sitting on her table full of Post-its and scribbles. I did ask her about these once, but she rolled her eyes and said they were terribly boring and mostly were enough to make lab rats eat their own tails. Occasionally she got self-help manuals, which were apparently better in that they at least induced fits of mad laughter. Usually, however, she sat around reading books of her own choice, mainly from the library. I was unsure whether she had some plan to her reading or simply had a long list of books she had been meaning to get to someday; there was a binge of Germans, with names like Goethe, Novalis, Döblin, Mann, and Böll, and more books whose authors had Spanish names, and on and on. Some of them were by Russians and others had authors whose identities I would have had to look up because their nationalities were completely obscure to me—they could have been African or Yugoslavian for all I know. This intense reading program made me feel kind of illiterate, even though I do like to read and my tastes are reasonably serious. But I also recognized that Kari must be more of an expert, so that comparing my knowledge with hers was sort of like comparing the knowledge of a diligent high school student to that of a college professor. It made me wonder what my alleged father, the poet Eli, read. What did he like, if he thought Kahlil Gibran was stupid? One day this question bothered me to the extent that I actually got up the nerve to ask Kari what she thought a poet was likely to enjoy reading.

Kari looked at me with a slight bemused smile, in which I could see irony at war with compassion. "What kind of poet?" she asked.

That threw me, although I should have expected it. Naturally poets must vary as much as any other kind of writer. "I don't really know. He was a poet my mother used to know," I said, being careful to keep this ambiguous, "and he had a low opinion of Kahlil Gibran."

"That doesn't give us a lot to work with," said Kari. "What was he like otherwise?"

"I don't know," I said. "He was Jewish, he was a poet, he was a hippie. That's about all I know."

"Where did he publish?"

"Well," I admitted, "I don't know if he was a published poet. He might have been a beginner. I don't suppose he was very old when my mother knew him—he might have been about my age."

"I don't think I have an answer for you," said Kari. "This is much too nebulous. He might have liked Neruda; I think Neruda was popular with a lot of young counter-culture writers. He might have liked Rilke. Maybe Rimbaud. But I don't know much about poetry and I don't know your poet, so for all we know he might have had a thing about Siegfried Sassoon or Ezra Pound or even Robert Frost."

I felt simultaneously discontented and reassured by this answer. I was discontented because she hadn't given me the kind of answer I was hoping for but had to recognize couldn't be given, and I was reassured that Kari, who answered my question seriously, might know more than I did but all the same was no expert on poetry.

"Who's Neruda?" I asked, picking the name of the likeliest-sounding object for Eli's admiration.

"He was a South American Communist," said Kari, "Chilean, I think, but he took his name from a nineteenth-century Czech writer, so people sometimes confuse Jan Neruda with Pablo Neruda. I haven't read him, but he was much admired by romantic young revolutionaries in the sixties and seventies."

"Was he good?" I persisted.

"Well, you're hardly asking the right person, but he's very much loved. People who oppose his politics like to point out that he supported Stalin, but I don't suppose that supporting Stalin would make him a bad poet."

"I don't know how anyone could possibly have supported Stalin," I said, thoroughly disgusted. "It's hard to believe anyone could be a good poet and support Stalin."

Kari looked very much amused. "There's the problem. How

does talent coexist with unpalatable politics? And how do we know to what extent Neruda was a misguided idealist or a knowing supporter of show trials and executions?"

I didn't have answers for these questions; I don't think much about politics. But I felt honored to be included in such a discussion.

We didn't have such conversations with any great frequency, but the fact that we had them at all added a new dimension to my admittedly rather self-limited existence, and I began to look forward to them. Most of the time, however, Kari Zilke and I kept to ourselves and didn't impinge on one another. I practiced my cello for several hours each day and went to lessons and rehearsals, and Kari read, marked up her galleys, and occupied herself in ways that I was less aware of. Her hours were fairly irregular, which struck me as peculiar in someone who clearly had a well-disciplined mind. She didn't really cook, which she once explained as being the result of not liking to clean up the results or keep track of the leftovers, but it was not very evident just what she ate. In the morning she made herself a cup of strong coffee and poured half-and-half in it, which seemed simultaneously austere and extravagant; my aunt and I normally made a pot of weaker coffee which we drank with skim milk and plenty of sugar, and we usually ate cereal as well. My aunt remarked to me early on that half-and-half was very fattening, so surely the only way Kari kept slim was by eating so little of anything else. This may have been true, but Kari was entirely capable of eating a big plate of spaghetti or Thai food when the mood struck her, so I think that she was simply one of those people with a fast metabolism, while my aunt is inclined to be roly-poly, just as you would expect an aunt like her to be. Not a skinny, bony, querulous aunt, but a roly-poly, short, and welcoming aunt.

Kari also got some of her calories from alcohol, which I thought was very questionable. The idea of a person sitting in her bedroom drinking a brandy or a gin and tonic all by herself seemed like a sure sign of alcoholism, but when once I made a remark about that, she laughed and said she didn't think she was in much danger of *that* anymore. Anymore? How could you stop being in danger of alcoholism unless you simply didn't drink at all, or limited yourself to the occasional glass of wine at dinner? This was another of those areas in which my aunt was more relaxed than I was. While she shared my concern that Kari might drink too much, she pointed out that she had known quite a few people who drank a bit without being out-and-out alcoholics.

"Your grandpa was very fond of his beer," she said, "and he certainly wasn't a drunk. Mama never worried about it a bit other than that it gave him a gut. And all the kids your mother and I knew in high school used to drink themselves sick on the weekends, but most of them have turned out just fine."

I remained skeptical, but let it ride; after all, if Kari didn't cause us any problems with her drinking, it was really none of our business. We had had one renter who let beer bottles accumulate in the room, causing a sour, disagreeable odor from the evaporating dregs, but although Kari sometimes let bottles accumulate, she closed the tops; she seemed to detest stale smells as much as my aunt and I, and believed the best way to avoid them was to open the window, even though we suggested she might be more comfortable with a good air freshener than a drafty window.

"No, I don't think so," she said. "If I get cold, I'll put on a sweater." She indicated that if only she weren't so lazy, she'd hang her bedding out the window to air as the Europeans do, but I told her I didn't think the neighbors would appreciate seeing a lot of bedding hanging out the window. That fussy Mrs. Smith across the street would probably come knocking on our door and tell my aunt that we were dragging down property values by having renters and letting them hang things out the window like a lot of slum-dwellers.

Yes, Kari Zilke was a bit of a character, and not quite our usual renter. It never occurred to me, though, that she was as different as the papers she left revealed.

KARI

I had gotten pretty depressed about my life's direction, or rather its lack of any. I'd been drifting for the past ten years—how else can I explain my marriage?—and was getting more and more acclimated to some variant of conventional bourgeois life. A frugal, stripped-down version without the usual consumer trappings, to be sure, but nonetheless conventional and unadventurous.

I'm not precisely sure how my husband envisioned our life. He's a modest, kind, unassuming, unambitious person who doesn't see himself as conventional. And indeed he's not exactly ordinary. He plays piano pretty well, in a way that would have been very much appreciated back in the days when that was an important parlor skill—he can rattle off all manner of show tunes, Billy Joel songs, and old standbys like "In the Gloaming" and "Bill Grogan's Goat" that he must have learned from his grandmother. He does this as a break from working—he programs databases, which doesn't pay as well as it used to—when he doesn't just crawl out to the living room and fixate on the TV. He plays in a showy, facile manner quite at odds with the rest of his demeanor, and can break into a ragtime or boogie-woogie passage out of nowhere. If he has any shadow of an ambition, it lies in his secret longing to write a musical. At one point he tried to convince me that I should write a libretto, and I did consider the idea, but had to conclude that musical theater is simply not my métier. Other than performing in my high school's annual summer musical, which I won't deny was lots of fun, I really have no interest in musicals. I don't like opera, I don't like operetta, and I don't really care for musicals either. This may be a character flaw in me—I recognize that *West Side Story* is good, but I wouldn't care to watch it often. And *West Side Story* is much more serious than the kind of musical my husband hankered to write. As he tends to be a very serious person, not drawn to any kind of fluff in any other medium, I can only conclude that his fondness for show tunes and lightweight musicals is some desperate form of compensation for an excessively sober personality.

So he is not, strictly speaking, a conventional person, because hardly anyone these days hammers out show tunes on the piano (a poor-quality old upright, because he didn't see any need to indulge himself with anything better), and he doesn't adhere to conventional ideas about the importance of money and status and possessions. But I would never have married someone who had such ideas, any more than I would have married someone who beat me or wasn't intelligent, so for me he induced a sensation of excessive conventionality. It was not he, himself, but what he prompted in me.

Indeed, another person might have found him liberatingly unconventional. Another person might have rejoiced in his Spartan habits, and might have embraced his musical interests as a gateway to an excitingly cosmopolitan world. They might have gotten involved in community theater together and had a wonderful time being on the bohemian fringe of the bourgeoisie. I don't say this satirically, but quite truthfully. My husband is a man who simply needs the right wife and has not found her.

Had I been an entirely extreme character, altogether focused on my ambitions and on experiencing an intense existence, I believe he would not have been much drawn to me. He might have been somewhat attracted, but I am sure he would have recognized that I was not at all for him. It was my peculiar and temporary combination of ambition, intellectual tendencies, and forlorn emotional state that rendered me possible for him to like and desire. He does not like or trust ambition, but he admires talent and self-direction; he is an intelligent and somewhat meditative person, which causes him to approve of those who use their minds; and like me he was in a state of forlorn sadness which he had begun to accept as his fate. Thus, it was perhaps natural that we found ourselves lunching together and began to keep company.

Certain of my memories of this period are pleasant; for the most part we got along well, and neither of us was inclined to fight. But I moved along in a dull, submerged, suffocated way. I accepted too many things about his way of life, while he accepted too many things about mine, which ended up making each of us angry that we had tolerated things we did not like and which were not natural to us. None of these things were particularly bad things, merely habits and ways of doing things and ways of thinking about the world. For instance, despite his interest in musicals, he had a low opinion of actors. Not of ordinary people who enjoyed acting as a pastime, but of true actors. He saw them as people who don't know who they are inside, who try on different characters because they have no identity. Akin to this, he rejected the idea of "trying to be something you're not." Nothing could be so false, he implied, with a slight grimace.

I have no particular admiration for actors either—unlike most people, I pay little attention to who has appeared in which play or film, I do not follow the Academy Awards, I do not venerate acting as a profession. On the other hand, I take acting as something amateurs enjoy and professionals excel at, and as something that should be well done. I like people who have some degree of a desire to perform, and if real actors try on different roles because they have no identity of their own, then I think it is an excellent thing that they have found a way to make use of their disability, one that provides pleasure to nearly everyone. As for trying to be something you're not, I believe that the only way to become what you are not is to make the attempt. We learn by simulation as well as by being true to ourselves.

Thus, I saw no reason to denigrate actors when we didn't even spend time around them, which would probably have given us all the cause we needed to satirize them. But my husband is not a satirical person, and for him there would not be humor in the preening and self-aggrandizement and bombast and public display of the actor's life.

He, I believe, was content or thought he ought to be content with his life as it was. He wished life to be entirely satisfactory as experienced in the moment, humbly, without annoying longings and desires. I, on the other hand, have always been subject to a parade of longings and desires. The Buddhists would, I suspect, find me woefully unevolved. Nonetheless, I have not wanted to be free of these longings and desires, but to use them. It is not that I am opposed to living life in the moment—I believe one must—but that part of my moment involves longing and striving and violent emotion. I am too contemplative as it is, so I feel a great need to balance this with intensity. I've always wanted to be totally immersed, but somehow I've lost my connection to that and float helplessly on the surface, cold and numb and experiencing little if anything of interest. Contentment—well, contentment is a fine thing in its way, and we should all feel contented some of the time, like after a good meal, or while watching a fine sunset, or petting a cat, or after writing or painting or composing or performing well, or after good sex. But contentment must be intermittent, even at times a reward. Too much flabby self-satisfaction is another matter, as is dull plodding along in neither pain nor joy. And I can take only so much dull plodding and insipid existence before I start to explode, or implode.

So—there I was starting to implode, longing for strong emotions and sensations that were simply not to be found in my tame domesticated married life. I wanted action, but became increasingly inactive and withdrawn. Had you offered me real action and adventure at that time, I would have been quite unable to partake of it. I would have said, "I don't have the money to do it," or "I can't take the time off work," or "That would really bother my husband." But no one was offering, and I wasn't out looking. Even had I taken it into my head to look for the cliché adventure of an affair (affairs need not be cliché, but affairs undertaken from boredom and dissatisfaction tend that way), I had no real opportunities. I would have had to chase after some acquaintance or coworker and persuade him to be naughty with me. I assure you that there was once a time when this did not require any persuasion and such adventures welled up naturally. But no such thing welled up during my marriage; I evidently gave off an odor of unavailability and unattractiveness, which was what both my husband and I pretended to want. No, the closest thing to an affair occurred one day when we were making dinner together—back when we still did this and food was not yet an area of hostility—and discovered that there was not enough spinach. I had to run to the store and get more, and in the parking lot, clutching the spinach, I was accosted by a man.

"I'd really like to get to know you," he said, to my complete bafflement. "Could we have coffee sometime?"

"Um, I have to get home," I said. "My husband's waiting for the spinach."

"I'd really like to have coffee with you," my interlocutor persisted. "Are you free tomorrow morning?"

"No," I said. "I mean really, I told my husband I'd be right back. We're in the middle of making supper and I don't have time to talk."

"I'd really like to get to know you," the stranger continued, as if nothing I said was getting through to him at all.

"Well, I'm going home," I said. "It was nice chatting with you." I plopped myself into the car, slammed the door, waved, and departed. If my only visible opportunities for adventure, sexual or otherwise, lay in crackpots who accosted me in supermarket parking lots, it can hardly be any surprise that I was leading a life devoid of adventure.

Yet earlier in my life I had sought and attracted adventure. Not just sexual adventure, by any means, but certainly including it. Life in general was an adventure, even if certain aspects of it (mainly the need to make a living) struck me as loathsome and a complete waste of time. In the evenings I met with a small group of friends, in bars not far from the offices where we worked. We spoke of our ambitions in literature and theater, read over manuscripts, drank copiously of our chosen beverages, and analyzed our mostly doomed romances. From five-thirty or so until eight or nine we sat rooted at our favorite tables, picking through the nuts and crackers in the bowl, calling for yet more wine and yet more gin, and saw ourselves in a most romantic light, as the latest in a long line of loquacious, hard-drinking, fiercely determined aspirants. We were always nicely dressed, because our jobs required it, but we saw ourselves as kin to Thomas Wolfe, Eugene O'Neill, Jack Kerouac, and other larger-than-life characters of an earlier day. Unlike the Brontë sisters, we did not adulate Lord Byron, but this was only because he had been born too long ago and was not precisely present in our minds, although we were certainly well aware of his fame. Byron and Marlowe were interesting but historically distant, as were Keats and even Ibsen. We could not aspire to die in wars or bar fights or of plague or TB; we wanted to be part of a new generation and form its vision, but we were born at the end of a generation that had already formed a vision that was not really ours. People our age were always somebody's younger brother or sister, and even when they weren't, there was always the weight of everyone else's older brothers and sisters setting an example or providing a cautionary tale. To be our age was to have sisters or cousins who had been homecoming queens at a time when that was actually a big deal; to be our age was to be just too young to admire Twiggy or listen to the Beatles before they broke up; to be our age was to hear endless scary lectures about how marijuana led straight to heroin addiction and how people who took LSD went mad and killed themselves.

And so we had no clear sense of how we would fit into history, other than that we were part of this amorphous generation of the big brothers and sisters yet did not truly share its experiences or concerns, and other than that we were anxious to make our mark individually. We sent off our manuscripts to magazines and theaters, drank another for the road, and staggered out into the cool night streets to gaze in wonder at the tall buildings around us and look for our buses home.

This was not perhaps very adventurous behavior, but it gave us the sense of living intensely and of being young and brilliant in a big city. With other friends, I went to punk rock concerts or to experimental theater and performance art. I went to parties full of writers and artists and composers and actors, people who made their livings as messenger boys, massage therapists, proofreaders, and bookstore clerks. We were a seething mass of ambitious, cultured youth. Any person under thirty working in a bookstore or art supply store was almost certain to be a desirous soul with a bedroom full of manuscripts or canvases. We knew that this was how to seek our fortunes. But gradually our places were taken by aspirants of another generation, people ten or fifteen or twenty years younger, as our cohort became magazine columnists, bookstore buyers, technical writers, computer programmers, marketers, and mental health professionals. Gradually some of us married, and a few, as I have said, even had children.

Sarah

It is hard for me to imagine Kari Zilke as a married woman; my aunt and I both thought she was one of those resolutely single people who simply don't need or want a mate. If she were a man we would have said she seemed like a confirmed bachelor, but I guess even now it sounds bad to describe a woman as a spinster. People have tried to reclaim a lot of disagreeable and impolite words and make them positive, but I don't think they have even bothered to try this with "spinster." It wasn't insulting enough; it wasn't supposed to be impolite, but everyone knows it makes you think of skinny old menopausal ladies with gray hair in tight buns, wearing dowdy clothes from about 1940. We all saw pictures of them in kids' books when we were little. And obviously Kari Zilke didn't fit this stereotype, even though you sometimes do meet people who pretty much do. Kari Zilke had only a few gray hairs, and her hair was too short to put in a bun (besides which these days it's mostly younger women who wear them, messy buns with wisps sticking out). She never looked dowdy; some days she looked sleek and well dressed, and other days she looked like any other average person on a day off, in jeans and T-shirts or something. She looked very unremarkable, although there were things she never seemed to wear, like sweatpants or tennis shoes or running shoes. She looked like someone who would attract as many men as any other woman her age, but she didn't seem like someone who needed to or cared whether she did. My aunt and I are well acquainted with women who are anxious to meet men; they talk differently and send off different signals. Women who are anxious to meet men talk constantly about how all the good men are taken, and how all the attractive men are gay, and what was wrong with the various ones they met through this or that dating service. My aunt and I must have heard every variation on this theme, and while my aunt is sympathetic, I get bored and want to tell them to go get a life. I was glad not to hear Kari Zilke adding to this chorus of complaints, but I was truly astonished to discover that she had ever been married. Usually women whose marriages have just ended, or even whose marriages ended quite a while ago, want to rehash how badly they were treated or how they can't believe he left them, or whatever the situation might be. Even when they're glad to be out of it, they usually like to tell you this—what a slob the husband was, or how demanding, or how he spent all his time out in the garage or wouldn't buy them enough shoes. I personally don't find this information all that interesting.

KARI

While my friends and I used to go to concerts and performance art and exhibitions and so forth, I found only a small percentage of these events really stimulating. Unlike some of my friends, I did not thirst to keep track of all the latest artists or writers or bands or films. I never had the energy to keep truly up to date, especially since in order to do so I would have had to go to more shows than I could afford and considerably more than would have held any interest for me. I was particular. I sought out work that pierced my heart or that took me into some new world. It could be about mundane events and mundane people, but it couldn't be mundane in itself. I wanted mythic intensity, heart-stopping beauty, an art of transfiguration.

Of course, there was very little of this to be found. We weren't living in the heyday of surrealism or in the psychedelic sixties. Most playwrights treated us to tense dramas about unimpressive people getting angry with their parents or their mates or their children; typically there were several scenes setting up the situation, and after the intermission everything built to a tedious climax in which these banal people accused one another of various things, shouted a certain amount, and eventually someone committed suicide or walked out or sat down on the edge of the stage in a gesture of utter frustration. Every time I saw one of these plays, I asked myself why I bothered to attend. Just because some people behave this way in real life doesn't mean we need to make it a theatrical norm. A few plays of this sort would be enough to ensure we were representing that aspect of life.

Now, it may be that a majority of the population behaves like this in their private life. Certainly, most of us sooner or later find ourselves in some difficult situation with one or more people in our lives. But even if most of the population has no concept of civilized ways of handling their problems, or is obliged to partake of someone else's unpleasant drama, surely it isn't necessary to enact this sort of thing on every theater stage in North America four or five nights a week. Surely, when dealing with unhappiness, there are other ways of presenting it. Some lives are tragic; can't we have tragic theater? Some events are tragicomic; can't we have some works that veer back and forth between making us laugh and weep? Yes, many plays are alleged to do that, but doesn't anyone want to fill the audience with awe and wonder?

But all right—I'm out of step with the pleasures of the masses. I don't like blockbuster films, I don't worship musical theater, I get bored at Disneyland and its imitators (though I do like a good rollercoaster), I dislike most of today's popular writers and find self-help books absolutely ludicrous, the thought of going on a cruise fills me with ironic laughter—I don't say these things are bad, I merely say they aren't for me and that I don't understand their appeal. This was one reason some of us took to punk rock. It wasn't beautiful, it didn't necessarily mean we hated all the extravagant rock opera that preceded it, but it lashed out in a fury against anything middle of the road. Of course, in North America we didn't have the same reasons to like punk as the British, so our liking was paler and trendier, lacking the searing rage, but all the same we got something out of pogo-dancing and slam dancing and chanting "Mongoloid, he was a mongoloid, living in the USA!" I only ventured into the fringes of punk and only had a few friends in bands, but still it was something crazy and untamed and special to people my age. It wasn't the music I would have chosen to represent myself, but it represented a part of me.

So, one evening, contemplating my old search for performance and literature that went beyond the banal and partook of a mythic dimension—and admittedly there had been times when I found it—I felt I had to get out of my nice quiet little rented room and roam the streets.

It was dusk and drippy out. Not raining, but misting. I wandered into parts of the city that I did not know well, older parts, and looked idly into the doorways and into shop windows filled with repulsive-looking furniture that someone had once bought because it was cheap and had now intelligently consigned to the secondhand dealer's. Chairs with ripped orange vinyl seats; rusting TV trays; couches with missing cushions.

As I walked, I remembered an incident from my childhood that I had almost forgotten: my family was traveling in Germany, back when few Americans went to Europe except to man our military bases, but when college students, who all looked like hippies to me, were beginning to discover Europe in a curiously updated, down-at-heel version of the Grand Tour. They congregated in specific cities and haunts, like flocks of birds; you didn't see just one or two, you saw fifty or a hundred draped around a public square or fountain, sitting with their backpacks and sleeping bags, smoking and taking in the scene. They were barefoot or wearing sandals, and preferred battered blue jeans or granny skirts. Their hair was long and untidy, and I was torn between despising them and wanting to be like them.

It never occurred to me to wonder whether any of these were the same young artists who could be found in nearly every German city painstakingly drawing enormous scenes on the pedestrian thoroughfares in colored chalk. We always liked to watch them work, and I always assumed that this was what German art students did. With amazing patience and skill, they recreated the *Mona Lisa* with a ten-foot-tall head, or produced thirty-foot-long landscapes, all in clear vibrant colors against the blacktop. To have artists drawing giant murals on the street impressed me as a uniquely European pleasure, akin to having castles and cathedrals scattered generously about the landscape. It was all there for my benefit, and the benefit of everyone else who passed by. It was all magic.

One afternoon as my family wandered down a busy street in some German city—Munich, perhaps, as there was a subway under construction and you could stand on the sidewalk and look down brand-new escalators that didn't yet run—a troupe of actors in giant masks strolled by beating a drum and tooting a horn. They passed out flyers to all and sundry, and my father took one. "Magic Theater!" exclaimed the flyer, which was bedizened with sketches of giant masks or puppet heads like those worn by the actors and which looked most mysterious and droll. There was to be a performance at seven, so my father made sure to get directions, just in case our map might not prove helpful. We went about our business for the rest of the day—whatever it might have been—and after supper set out to find this Magic Theater and its performance.

We walked and we walked, until finally, on a deserted side street lined with big sooty buildings that I assumed to be really old but which were probably erected no earlier than 1880, we found what seemed to be the address.

There was no sign on the door suggesting that any theater of any sort was within.

We walked back and forth and verified that we were indeed on the correct street. We went back to the door and loitered irresolutely for a moment, and then my father pushed open the door, which was one of a pair about eight feet tall and with dirty glass on the upper portion. We stood in a cool, dusty vestibule leading to stairs both ascending and descending. There was no immediate indication here either that any theater might be within, only a vague booming sound.

Then, just as he turned to go out and give up, my father caught sight of a scrap of paper taped to the down staircase, upon which someone had scrawled "Magic Theater" and an arrow in black marker.

Feeling dubious, we descended, with my father leading the way in case we encountered anything dangerous—drunks, gypsies, rats, broken steps, hounds of hell—and after a moment emerged into a gloomy sort of room, a sort of basement vestibule to a more brightly lit room, both of which were hung with posters of the kind I associated with hippies, LSD, and nightmarish hallucinations. These were not bright-colored posters designed for black light, but were printed in muddy hues, with bulbous, droopy lettering squeezed up around distorted images of things I didn't immediately recognize but which looked as though they might pulsate if you looked away.

As our eyes grew accustomed to the gloom, we realized that there was a young woman sprawled in a beanbag chair near us. Earlier, we had become aware of a booming, cacophonous music which we now realized was emanating from the open door.

My father turned to the young woman and asked about the theater. Although it took some effort for her to understand him through the music, she roused herself to point limply to the open door and suggest that we inquire within.

My father advanced, pretending a decisiveness that he obviously didn't feel, and addressed someone inside the other room. A straggly young man appeared and they conversed, with difficulty, for a short time but apparently he had no useful information about a performance, and indeed I am sure my father was now convinced that there could be no family entertainment offered here.

And so we had sought a Magic Theater and found only a basement with disorganized-looking hippies and psychedelic posters.

SARAH

I suppose the reason I had a hard time believing Kari Zilke had ever been married was that not only did she not harp on men in conversation, but she simply seemed to be in some other world most of the time, where men's purpose wasn't to be part of A Relationship. I kind of liked this, because I would rather take that approach to men too. I haven't found that men are anything specially better or more interesting than women; I like some of them and don't like some of them, and it's horribly tedious listening to women who have nothing else on their minds, just like it's tedious listening to women who have nothing on their minds but fashion or celebrities.

I was willing to believe in passion—something incited me to secretly hope to experience it someday—but that's different. I wasn't sure, though, just what Kari's attitude was toward passion. There was definitely a passion in her, but I couldn't tell what or who it sought. As far as I could tell, her thoughts were mainly on her reading and on going out for hours and hours for walks or something. In her manuscript she wrote of going to performances in her youth, and of seeking some kind of transfigurative mythic experience in them, but not usually finding this. Well, I don't think that's exactly surprising; most people aren't looking for any such thing, so it's not readily available in theaters and concert halls. You certainly wouldn't find it at a punk rock concert. It's true that underneath, a lot of people do want to experience something transformative and uplifting, but when they admit that, they usually look for it in religion. And even then, most of them shy away from anything that might get too intense. That's understandable. It's all very well for a preacher to tell you to give up your possessions and go meditate on a mountain, but most people don't want to spend more than a weekend doing that. Besides, organized religion doesn't get much out of its few truly spiritual devotees. Churches—and I suppose synagogues and mosques—want a regular congregation. They want people who show up for the standard dose of uplift or hellfire and then put something in the collection plate. Churches want people like my aunt, who is very happy to go most Sundays and think about Jesus a bit and then go home. Once in a while I go with her, but I'm not much interested in this, which even I can see is largely a social exercise.

It's true that in my mother's day quite a few people ran after various forms of transformation and enlightenment, and some of them are still doing this. It's one of those things I feel ambivalent about. I can see where my mother and her generation figured that church wasn't really satisfying the spiritual itch, and that they decided to look elsewhere. But to go chasing after religions from other parts of the world, that came into existence to satisfy some other culture's needs, well, I really don't see much point in that. How is an American really going to get much out of pretending to be a Hindu? When you grow up being taught that there's only one god, the idea of thousands of them has to seem kind of loony. And Buddhism—well, maybe it's easier for us to become Buddhists, but I still don't see it. Yet ever since the sixties, a certain chunk of the population has been trying out every cult and alien religion they can get their hands on. My mother was big on this. She liked to claim that all religions were ultimately one, which I think is ridiculous.

So it was hard for me to imagine quite what Kari Zilke thought would be a transfigurative kind of performance. I was sure she wasn't thinking of religion, but I didn't know what she meant instead.

KARI

As I walked along that night, thinking about our long-ago attempt to find a mysterious Magic Theater, I was reminded of other theaters that I had been more successful in finding, though some of them had not been as intriguing or any more satisfactory. This led me to somewhat gloomy thoughts of old friends, people I had been more or less out of touch with for years now, who were old friends in age as well as being people I had known most of my adult life; I had just gotten word that one of them had died and that it was hoped I'd be able to attend his memorial.

I had been quite fond of Marty, an elfin character who had been a designer for one of these theaters, and I supposed I should go to his memorial despite my not really liking to go to these commemorations. Ruminating on that, I passed several noisy clubs whose entrances were marked by groups of tattered or tarty twenty-somethings who took the sidewalk as an extension of the interior where one could hear one's companions and have a smoke or two. The music spilling out of these clubs had no real appeal for me, but nonetheless I envied the twenty-somethings' easy pleasure and thought how none of them were likely to be putting off dealing with the death of an old friend and the prospect of a memorial service that might or might not bear any relation to the man himself. I quickly left the clubs behind and found my way into a café I had once frequented. It was one of those funky cafés formed out of who knew what kind of earlier establishment and furnished with cast-off furniture, with walls painted red and covered in paintings by local artists, with areas filled with near-plantations of house plants, with chalkboards of the day's offerings and a stereo system that alternated between Lou Reed and latter-day punk. I settled myself at a deserted booth, whose cracked vinyl seats had been patched with random colors, and contemplated my life under the signs 4-H Club Member Lives Here and Rainbow Road Thrift Store. Across the room, a bleached-blond, cropped-headed anorexic in black glasses and a polka-dot minidress was chatting with a flannel-shirted man with a felt hat and droopy mustache, while a Rastafarian youth with a crocheted cap over his dreads wandered back and forth as if waiting for someone to distract him from his coffee. They were all at least ten years younger than I was, but they could easily have been the café's inhabitants ten years back, reanimated to make me feel as though my thirties and my marriage had never happened.

The music turned to Malvina Reynolds singing "Little Boxes," a song that predated my own awareness of folk or protest songs, but whose tale of ticky-tacky boxes filled with businessmen whose children went to summer camp and university caused me to ruminate that while the little boxes were still there, the businessmen and their families had moved up into bigger boxes with three-car garages and a TV in every room. My landlady, at least, had one of the old-style boxes, which allowed me a certain nostalgia rather than an unsettled indigestion of conspicuous consumption. And here in my old café hangout there were still aspiring artists or writers or musicians or actors or who-knew-what, poseurs perhaps, but decidedly not businessmen, even if possibly the disenchanted children of businessmen. Or perhaps the children of former hippies who carried on some aspect of their parents' traditions. I had no idea which, nor did I really care.

After an hour or so I finished my latte and, somewhat unwillingly, but without any better idea what to do, got up and made my way back to my landlady's.

Sarah

Unlike a lot of people my age, I don't often go to clubs, cafés, or bars. I don't really see the appeal. All right—I do go to cafés now and then, but only now and then, and usually because a friend wants to go. They usually want to go to places where the counter staff have pierced noses and eyebrows, and where the bathrooms are painted in psychotic-looking patterns and overlaid with graffiti. This doesn't really do much for me, although I'm willing to sit in these places and talk.

As for bars and clubs—well, I don't drink, and I don't generally like the music played in clubs, so my friends have almost stopped asking me to go to bars and clubs. They probably find me kind of odd, but most of my friends are other musicians, or people I've known all my life, so they're used to my habits. They may tease me a bit, but they don't mind. Besides, lots of my friends are vegetarians or vegans or have other dietary restrictions, so they understand how tiresome it can be to have people persistently refuse to recognize a person's choices in this sort of thing. I don't care to be a vegetarian or vegan myself, but I understand their arguments about not wanting to slaughter sentient beings and not wanting to be at the top of the food chain when this is damaging the worldwide ecosystem, so I expect them to understand my desire to keep my mind clear at all times. With a mother who spent her adult life in a haze of dope smoke—at least during the part of it I spent with her—I had no desire to live in anything less than complete clarity. I don't respond well to situations that are too murky, to people who are too ambiguous about what they want from me or who are too extreme in their habits.

KARI

I went back and forth about whether I should go to the memorial for Marty. I knew that, from all standard perspectives, I ought to; he had been a good friend, even if not one of my closer friends, and had taken an avuncular interest in me back in my mid-twenties, when I had little to recommend me but a pleasant manner and a burning ambition to create performance art. Marty was a more traditional theater person, but this was probably the only respect in which he was more conventional than I; he was an odd and endearing character whose hair was still a natural-looking red in his late seventies, and who prided himself on having been repeatedly mistaken for an underage boy well into his middle years. Marty was known for his passionate attractions to both men and women, most of which had apparently been requited, and mutual acquaintances had informed me that not only did he delight in dressing in a style suggestive of a British schoolboy on holiday, but that he sometimes used to disconcert them by appearing in a dress. I had missed out on Marty's transvestite days, but I did once hear him read a peculiarly innocent-sounding erotic tale involving sex on a swing with multiple humans and some animals. Some of the other listeners had been shocked, and suggested that it was really not something they wanted to hear, but there was something about his childlike enthusiasm for this rather fairytale-like story that rendered it an amusingly asexual fantasy. It was, I thought, something you could imagine being illustrated by Douanier Rousseau, or in the style of the Babar stories. After all, Babar went to war and it was never gory; similarly, Marty's characters had wild sex but it was no more arousing than Babar's battles were brutal. Marty had been fond of me before reading this story, but I think he became even more enthusiastic about me after I refused to join in the outraged comments. To be sure,

I didn't tell him that the story had absolutely no erotic interest for me; we all have our different tastes and this had prompted no frisson whatsoever in me. Marty and I had therefore enjoyed many dinners in which he regaled me with stories of his youthful travels across America and the charming people he had seduced. He never made any overt effort to seduce me, perhaps recognizing that despite his still-youthful appearance, I was not likely at twenty-five to be smitten with a pixie of nearly eighty. But we had enjoyed our friendship, and through him I had met some other rather interesting people.

So, then, I supposed I ought to go to Marty's memorial, even though I was reluctant. I continued to hesitate and mull it over until the last minute, but finally set off for the Unitarian Church where it seemed as though all the memorial services for all my elderly friends were held, from Quakers to Jews. The church was a wooden building set high on a hill and had its graves scattered, unmarked, on the slope below amidst pines and cedars. It was an appealing location, and I could see why everyone wanted their ashes there, though it was not a very easy place for elderly feet to negotiate nor a good resting place for the very egotistical.

We gathered in the main hall, a cavernous, high-ceilinged space with plate-glass windows overlooking the graveyard. Marty had been a designer for more than one local theater over a period of several decades, and had also been an enthusiastic watercolor painter who exhibited frequently in some of the cafés. He had been active in various organizations that I never bothered to keep track of, and he also rented part of his large house to a succession of either attractive or decidedly odd characters who liked to hear him reminisce about Isamu Noguchi, Merce Cunningham, Ruth Asawa, and other famous people he had encountered. There were, thus, quite a few people in attendance and could have been many more had the organizers had any clear sense how to contact everyone he had known over the years. Since I knew some of the crowd and not others, and had mixed feelings about some of those I did know, I was unsure whether to plunge in or to lurk at the edges with an eye out for people I actually did like or feel in some sympathy with.

"Oh, Kari, how nice to see you," exclaimed a familiar voice in rich, nearly tearful tones, and I turned to face a handsome or even still quite beautiful woman whose elegantly styled white hair and dark eyebrows looked exactly as they had some ten or fifteen years earlier. Noreen Andrews was one of those people about whom I felt vaguely ambivalent. She was an actress of some talent, but of singularly conventional ideas, who had surely played nothing but ingénues in her youth and who in her maturer years played ingénues-grown-up plus a sprinkling of elegant career women. She was the most romantically minded person I had ever met and in addition to having accumulated at least six husbands, she was immediately moved to tears over any tale of doomed romance, provided it was sufficiently old-fashioned. I daresay she would have made a compelling Dame aux Camellias, at seventy just as at twenty, since while you could not call the Dame an ingénue, she was certainly a figure of doomed romance. Noreen and I had always been polite to each other, but we had a fundamental lack of comprehension of each other's views on life and art. Noreen could not understand why anyone would want to bother with experimental theater of any sort, or read or write anything that did not have a straightforward linear narrative or that was at all sarcastic, and she was not very successful at hiding her skepticism about anything I did, although she would not have known about any of my projects if it had not been for the fact that Marty and some of our other mutual acquaintances found them promising. She was, of course, one of those people who had had a hard time stomaching Marty's erotic story and who spoke with some degree of shocked revulsion of the days when he used to unexpectedly show up in a dress. I, for my part, found her somewhat tedious and pretentious.

"Kari, dear, why don't we ever see you anymore?" Noreen continued. "Everyone asks what's become of you."

I doubted that this was actually the case. While Noreen and I did know a certain number of people in common, she and I were not really close to the same ones.

"Oh, I've been around," I said in my vaguest manner. I could not remember whether she had known about my marriage, or for that matter how many years it was since we had last seen each other.

"Well, Kari, we have certainly missed you. And poor Marty! Had you seen him recently?"

"Not lately," I admitted, although I had at least seen him much more recently than I had Noreen, who surely had not missed me in the slightest until this very moment. Noreen was the kind of actress who would have induced my husband to produce a long-winded discourse on the lack of authentic self in actors, although I think that Noreen is less an inauthentic person than simply one for whom I have little patience.

"Oh," said Noreen with a breathless little gasp, "I feel so sad at Marty leaving us, he was such a remarkable personality. The theater around here will never be the same without him." At this, she broke down and began to weep just a little and had to bring forth a hankie, which I noticed was a pale yellow, meticulously pressed and embroidered with discreet rosebuds.

I sighed; I knew that she expected me to comfort her since there were no men immediately near us to do so. But fortunately one materialized, and with the courtly manner that Noreen brought out in men over fifty, he gently led her to sit down on a bench, where he patted her on the back and offered her an additional hankie.

My next encounter was with Marnie Gombrich, a retired costumer. Marnie was now well into her eighties and used a walker, but her mental faculties were entirely intact and we were genuinely pleased to see one another. Marnie had generally worked on the kind of plays that Noreen acted in and Marty had sometimes designed, but while her strength was in traditional theater and historically accurate costume, she liked people who did other things, and I had never known her to be disturbed by anything Marty or I did. Our conversation, however, was interrupted by various other people whom I didn't know or whose conversation was very much like Noreen's, even if their personalities did not have much in common with hers. It was oddly troubling to hear so many people who were not my close friends claim to have missed me so much, especially since some of them were doubtless entirely sincere.

Several people then eulogized Marty in a manner that played up all the dullest and most ordinary aspects of his life and character, at best praising him as a loving husband and exemplary father (which may even have been true), a designer of many memorable productions, a skilled watercolorist, a friend to famous people, and an agreeable landlord. These were things that needed to be said, and which were undeniably important, but which did not really capture the flavor of the man, who was small and seemingly quiet and unassuming and radiated a kind of innocence, but nonetheless said and did things that I doubted many people in the room had the nerve to do or to let on about if they did do them.

It gave me the irritable and unsettled feeling that if I were to drop dead and be eulogized, especially after a good long life like Marty's, I would be very disappointed to look down from the Beyond and have to listen to people platitudinizing about what a Nice Girl I was and how talented and how I gave money to Greenpeace. It would be better than listening to calumnies about how I stole from the poor and ate kittens for dessert, but it would be very tame.

Still, if none of Marty's old friends and associates were going to say a damned thing about any of his quirks or escapades, I really didn't see that it was quite my job to stir up the livelier side of his life, which would probably throw people like Noreen into new fits of weeping and perhaps annoy Marty's children, who were standing off to the side looking exceptionally bland.

After the eulogizing and ash-sprinkling and other official parts of the program, all of which failed to move me in the manner I might have liked considering it was a memorial for a person I had learned from and been fond of, people began to pour glasses of wine and of a particularly nasty-looking fruit punch. I took a glass of wine and rapidly found myself accosted by a stranger. He was a nondescript, somewhat arrogant-looking character ten or fifteen years older than I; we exchanged names and, to be polite, I asked him how he knew Marty.

"Oh, I used to rent a room from him," said he, airily. Then, before I could think of something suitable to say to this, he fixed his eye upon me and said, coldly, "Are you married?"

This was not a question I had been expecting from complete strangers, at least not as an opening gambit. It was not as though we had developed any rapport, let alone begun any kind of flirtation.

"That's a very strange question to ask," I said in my most off-putting voice. We were, after all, at a memorial service, not a singles mixer.

"I don't think it's at all strange," he replied in what I could only categorize as an insulting tone. "I like to know whether people are married."

Strangely infuriated by this arrogant asshole, and torn between the temptation to claim I had ten children and the temptation to claim I had never married and never would, I said, "I don't care what you like to know. I find your question bizarre and intrusive, and if you persist in asking me questions like that, I will kick you in the nuts with exceptional vigor."

With that, I turned sharply and walked away and out of the church, suffused with an intense rage. I walked down the hill, leaving behind me this insufferable boor, the conventionally emotional Noreen, the ashes of Marty, and the whole raft of wine-drinking alleged mourners. I walked for what might have been two or three miles, raging at this idiot and his insulting, obnoxious attitude and question.

SARAH

My mother's funeral was a peculiar event. There were not very many people there, but more than we expected; her old classmates from high school, for instance, came in surprising numbers, and so did some of her cousins and random other people, though mostly not anyone from her hippie life. My aunt, who had to organize the whole thing, was gracious but really didn't know what to do. She hadn't expected anyone but immediate family and a few people from church or something; my mother hadn't been around for a while and presumably had lost touch with nearly everyone she had grown up with, but suddenly there they were.

"Your mama really did have a lot of charm," said my aunt afterward as we sat in the kitchen and tried to figure out why twenty or thirty people had materialized out of nowhere for the funeral. "She was a sweet little girl, and she didn't stop being sweet just because she ran off and wanted to live in a commune or whatever it was. So it doesn't surprise me that lots of people liked her. But lots of kids are sweet. That doesn't mean anyone remembers them after they grow up."

"I can't see why anyone would bother to come after all this time," I said. "I wouldn't."

"Oh, Sarah," said my aunt reproachfully. "You would too."

"No I wouldn't," I said. In my defense, I should say I was about ten at the time and hated my mother passionately. I would probably go to my mother's funeral if it were occurring today. Today I think I'd be curious who would show up. But today I don't suppose quite as many people would come. I'm sure more of her high school friends have moved away or forgotten her, and that some of the other people who knew her are dead or long gone too.

"Your mama was a good person," my aunt persisted.

"Misguided and unlucky, but she had a good heart. You shouldn't forget that. Don't judge her too hard."

"She was a bad mother," I said.

As you can see, I was quite unforgiving about having started life as a hippie baby playing in the dirt. I wanted to lead a pristine life in which I looked something like the First Communion photos I had seen of my mother and my aunt; I wanted to be a solemn little white-gloved girl from the 1950s. But even my aunt didn't see any reason to dress me up in little white dresses and gloves; she thought I should put on my jeans and T-shirts and run out and play and get dirty with the other kids. For the funeral, my aunt dressed me in one of my nicer school outfits, a dark plaid jumper with a white blouse. That suited both of us; it was sober without looking like some sort of nineteenth-century mourning costume, and it was dressed-up without being fancy. My aunt, who still worked in those days, wore a suit that she normally reserved for special company functions. Normally her company didn't require anything so formal from its clerical staff, and as she didn't wear the suit very often, it no longer fit her very well. It pinched her waist slightly and it looked just vaguely out of style, though it was unlikely ever to look either terribly wrong or absolutely right. It was a very middle-of-the-road middle-class ladies' suit.

A few of my mother's old friends tried to talk to me about her, but I neither wanted to listen to them reminisce about how they used to play in the sandbox together and about the interesting things she used to say in class, nor to talk about my memories of how we had lived. I just didn't want to get involved in any of this—it just seemed like a complete waste of time talking to a bunch of yuppies who had gone to college and wore pressed clothes and clearly had next to nothing in common with my mother despite their sandbox days.

KARI

I had left my wineglass in the church, but not before draining it; as I walked and raged, I began to have the sensation that more wine was needed, perhaps considerably more, or possibly even lashings of stronger drink. I ranted to myself about the intolerableness of strangers who demanded my marital status for no discernible cause beyond idle curiosity; what would his next question have been, whether I douched or whether I flossed my teeth? All of these things were items I would have willingly divulged to other people in other circumstances; there was something about this fellow and his manner that repelled and enraged me beyond reason. There are people who have that effect upon me, but since I encounter them so seldom, most people consider me good-natured. And I did not normally encounter such infuriating characters when mourning my old friends. No, I simply could not stop running over the incident in my head and replaying its awfulness and imagining myself responding more viciously and wishing that I had carried out my threat to kick his nuts. I definitely required more drinks after this maddening encounter, so I stopped in the first bar I came to and knocked back a whiskey and soda, but I took a dislike to the bar and moved on; the thought of going back to my landlady's was intolerable, as I had mentioned I was going to the service for an old friend and she would want to know more about it and ask if I had seen old friends or been comforted or spoken up with my own recollections, and I could not possibly afflict her with the smallest detail, because I was sure she was not a person who would understand even half of the situation or my feelings about it and would only be confused and depressed to hear me talk. In fact, I could not think of anyone who was likely to understand fully, but at least a few of my friends would have heard me out and taken it calmly, or agreed that the situation was unpleasant.

So I continued wandering about, pacing the streets, muttering to myself, paying little attention to the time, feeling morosely grateful that I had not worn impractical shoes or fragile clothes, feeling that if any person on the street did approach me with antisocial intent, I would strenuously attack him before he had a chance to lay a finger on me, and he would be very, very sorry to have chosen such an irritable and dangerous mark, because I would fling myself upon him like a puma from a tree and do my best to kill him. The increasing darkness was of no concern to me. I was inflamed and filled with a restless energy and nothing settled my mind.

And where was I going in life? Yes, I had left my husband and I was glad of that, but where was I going? I couldn't live permanently with my landlady and her cello-playing niece, pretending to be quiet and well-behaved and not having lovers or playing loud rock music; my landlady's little room would work for me for a while, but as I gradually reawakened my savage and imaginative nature, no doubt it would become more and more unsuitable. My elderly old friends such as Marty were dying off, leaving the less elderly and less interesting acquaintances like Noreen, and I was out of touch with so many of the old friends of my own age who had once yearned to write or paint or whatnot; and I had no illusions about the younger generation, for why would those members of it who were not enamored of business and internet stocks and dot-coms find me of the slightest interest, a woman not involved in anything anymore and leading a relatively hermit-like existence? I was disgusted. Had I been a man, I would have spat, but even rude and uncouth women don't have the habit of spitting in disgust; even the men I've known don't spit in disgust. Had I been ten years old, I would have thrown rocks, but now as an adult I had absorbed the idea that urban stones were filthy objects covered with the soot and spit and excretions of generations, and that the mere touch of them in my hand would probably lead to

AIDS, tuberculosis, and gastrointestinal parasites (never mind that these ills don't spread via stones).

I had rejected the comforts of two or three bars, though not their liquid offerings; at last, in the dark, I stumbled into another. I had no real idea where I was; it wasn't a neighborhood I knew.

The crowd in the bar was younger than in the others I'd tried, which had tended toward hard-bitten types ten or twenty years older than I was. The place was even half café, half bar, more like European cafés where a glass of wine is as easy to order as your neighbor's coffee. There were sandwiches and brownies, although at this hour most people were drinking wine and beer. I ordered a glass of wine and contemplated the sandwiches with a vague feeling that it would behoove me to eat, although I couldn't say I wanted to and I suspected that if I ate it might simply make me sick. I took my glass of wine and flung myself onto a chair at the nearest empty table, suddenly realizing how desperately I needed to sit down.

"Are you all right?" I heard, unexpectedly, and even more unexpectedly felt an impetuous but firm hand on my forearm. I looked up to see a young man leaning over from the next table; he appeared genuinely concerned and I had no impulse whatever to attack him.

I opened my eyes wide for an instant as if to look awake, but the effort tired me and I let the lids fall all the way before I could take more of a look at him. "I'm fine," I said, employing that standard opening phrase of all who are not fine. "I feel like shit and I don't want to go home."

Two things occurred to me simultaneously: that his hand remained on my forearm, and that he was calmly, intently regarding me in a manner I was not accustomed to. It was not a worried look, or a scornful look, or a flirtatious look, or anything I could quite name. It was a calm and intent and intelligent look that had the possibility of friendliness, and it emanated from a face that was strangely and unfashionably attractive.

"You feel like shit and you don't want to go home," said

he, with a slight smile. "That's a familiar song. What's wrong at home? You don't look like you're avoiding an angry parent."

I had to laugh at that. "No, no, no. There's nothing at all wrong at home, and that's exactly why I can't go. My landlady doesn't deserve me coming home in a foul mood and spoiling her comfortable evening."

Now he laughed. "You don't want to disturb your landlady with your moodiness, so you bring it here to display to the world. That's a fine combination of thoughtfulness and disregard of humanity." He removed his hand but continued to search my face. "Drink your wine, you'll feel better. What the devil are you so tired and angry about? You look like I-don't-know-what."

I sighed. "Oh, I know it sounds stupid not to want to up-set my landlady, but a house is very different from a public place. Emotions bounce back and forth in a house and fill the atmosphere with tension, while in a bar they have to be much stronger to bother anyone. People bring their emotions to bars all the time, and most of it dissipates in the air, or only annoys the person at the next table."

"Well, maybe," he said, again with a slight smile. "Or maybe not."

Since it looked as though we might actually be starting a conversation, I began to pay more attention to the details of his looks and voice, to the nuances of his demeanor. He was young, probably even in his early twenties, but there was nothing immature in his face. He had dark, surprisingly heavy eyebrows that emphasized the delicate modeling of his face, and his hair, unusually at a time when most men his age were shaving their heads, was long and fell in abundant chestnut curls. Again unlike most men his age in that year, he was neither tall nor beefy; he had no unsightly lumps of flesh from poor diet and excessive soft drinks, but appeared to be neatly put together and compactly slim in his black T-shirt and jeans.

"Maybe I annoy the person at the next table and maybe I don't?" I said.

"I'm not annoyed," he said. "Drink your wine and spill your troubles."

"I don't have troubles, really; I'm just moody. I've been in a very, very bad mood this evening."

"And you feel bad about being in a bad mood; you're not used to being savagely pissed off."

Had I been thinking clearly, I would have been more acutely aware that young men in their early twenties are seldom so sensitive to other people's feelings, no matter how sensitive they are to their own and no matter how kind they are in general. As it was, I merely felt grateful to run into a sympathetic stranger.

"It's true I don't usually go around feeling angry and disgusted. In fact, I don't like people who go around that way all the time, but I do think everyone has a right to feel that way now and then."

"Did I suggest you don't have a right to be mondo pissed off?" said my neighbor. "That would be a little presumptuous when I don't even know what's bothering you, don't you think?" He put his hand on my forearm again, a gesture which might have annoyed me greatly from a man closer to my own age but which felt very comforting just now. "For all I know, someone's just stolen everything you care about, or told you massive lies when you trusted them, or…well, I don't know what."

"I don't know that I can categorize it as anything so serious," I said. "Sometimes I can take serious things quite calmly, and sometimes rather trivial things set me off. I'm not sure just where today falls on this spectrum, except that it feels more serious than it seems it should from any rational perspective."

"Do you think of yourself as a very rational person?" he inquired.

"Well—no, I don't at all, in fact, but I do believe it's important to be capable of rational thought and to apply it as needed."

"Like a Band-Aid?" I could see he was teasing, but I liked the concept of rational thought as a Band-Aid.

"No, no, as—as a useful tool."

"You consider yourself to be an irrational person who can hammer things home with a convenient bit of logic, or who can screw things into place with reason so that the irrational feelings can't escape?"

"You're playing with me," I said severely.

"And you're enjoying it and forgetting about being mad about your mysterious trivial aggravation."

"Well, yes, but I'm not so much an irrational person as an intuitive one, I think. Intuition works differently than reason but it's not irrational, it's just different."

"I agree," he said, "but I'm not sure why you were bringing in rational thought in the first place. It's all about how you were feeling, isn't it?"

"Well…I suppose. But all right. Here's what I'm getting at and you can tell me whether it seems stupid and trivial to you, which it very well might." And I embarked on the story of how I had gone to Marty's memorial somewhat unwillingly, and met up with Noreen and other people whom I used to know and didn't really know how to deal with under the circumstances, and had to listen to a lot of bland eulogies that seemed meaningless and dull to me, and finally had to suffer a pompous and unpleasant stranger asking me personal questions.

At the end of this rather lengthy recital, my companion laughed, but in a friendly manner. "Yes," he said, "you're right about being more an intuitive person than a rational one. You go along intuitively and then at a certain point you stop and want to analyze the situation."

"I know that perfectly well," I said impatiently. "I'm not ignorant, I do know my character by this time. But do you think I'm overreacting to trivialities?"

"Oh, now you want me to judge you so that you don't have to judge yourself," he said, tossing those remarkable chestnut curls in a most expressive gesture of derision.

"I'm not asking you to say it's objectively good or bad, I'm asking your opinion." It occurred to me that this boy had surely majored in either psychology or philosophy, with the way he was so expertly batting around all these terms and analyses without sounding in the least false or pretentious; they seemed to come forth as naturally as they might to a person my own age who was of an unusually introspective bent.

Now he was laughing. "In my opinion, you're overreacting, but naturally you wouldn't be having so strong a reaction without a reason. *Are* you married, or are you going to pulverize my balls for asking?"

"Well, legally I'm still married, but the marriage is over. And since I've actually never pulverized anyone's balls in my life, you don't have much to worry about. Only people who really rile me are in any danger of anything like that."

"I suppose your husband is in that category," he said, more seriously.

"Oh no, not at all," I said. "My husband only annoys me in stupid, boring ways that aren't very important. He doesn't infuriate me, he's just a nice person who shouldn't have married me."

My companion frowned slightly. "Are you being sarcastic about your husband or about yourself? Do you dislike him, or wish you were back together with him?"

This set of questions, while fairly perceptive, suggested that here my interlocutor was getting a little out of his depth. These were hardly mutually exclusive categories, nor did they by any means cover all the possibilities.

"If I'm being sarcastic, it's certainly as much about myself as about my husband. If I dislike him, which sometimes I do and sometimes I don't, it's not very strongly, but I really have no desire to get back together with him. On the whole I like him and on the whole I'm very glad to have left him. It's very simple and very complicated at the same time. Let's not talk about my marriage anymore just now, because I don't think it has very much to do with my reaction to that appalling asshole at Marty's memorial."

"You're so smart and so obtuse all at the same time," observed my companion.

"Well, that's probably true of you too," I protested. "You're intelligent and perceptive, but I don't see how you can possibly understand my marriage to any great degree."

"Certainly not if this is all I'm going to hear about it," he said. "But you don't want to say more about it, and damned if I'm going to be one of those slimy dudes who sit there and worm people's secrets out of them in bars."

While I didn't think my companion was even slightly slimy, he was a bit disingenuous in saying this since he had been worming out my story very skillfully from the moment I sat down. I thought, well, this is very clever and disarming but I wouldn't be telling him anything if I didn't like him.

"My marriage isn't any secret," I said. "I just don't feel like dwelling on it. It's behind me."

"Oh!" he exclaimed. "This big important piece of your life is over and behind you and not worth talking about. Are you one of those people who don't take marriage very seriously, then?" His words were more serious than his delivery, which was a little teasing again, but I had the feeling that all the same he meant it more seriously than he wanted to let on.

"I said nothing about my marriage not being worth talking about. On the contrary, I said I didn't feel like dwelling on it. So it would probably be worth talking about sometime, it just isn't what I want to talk about right now. And just because I'm done with this marriage and recognize I made a mistake to get into it doesn't mean I don't take marriage seriously or even that I think my marriage was such a bad thing. It wasn't a terrible choice, it simply wasn't the best choice."

Despite the fact that we were disputing about my marriage and its significance, and despite the fact that I was dead tired from roaming around and drinking miscellaneous glasses of wine and whiskey, I realized, with mild alarm but more plea-sure, that I was beginning to feel absurdly attracted to my companion.

I had lost all interest in sex during the course of my mar-riage, which as can be imagined was yet another good reason for giving up on that situation, but as I hadn't really met anyone new who had any reason to interest me, I hadn't been thinking much about sex or attractions other than to hope that this part of my life wasn't actually prematurely over. My present sense of alarm, then, came from the fact that my companion was clearly so much younger than I was, which would almost certainly prevent him from feeling any attraction toward me. It is true that I don't look my age; I've never looked any particular age, so in my twenties my older friends knew I was younger than they were but were never sure how much younger. But all the same I thought it very unlikely that someone who must be in his early twenties would feel an attraction to someone almost old enough to be his mother, no matter how young looking she was and no matter how much he might enjoy talking with her in a bar.

At the same time, I don't like to let my fears stop me from anything, so the probability that my attraction would be unre-ciprocated seemed no excuse for refusing to take pleasure in that small, growing spark. I looked at him with covert interest, taking in the details of his face, his hair, his expression, the way he moved. I noticed that he had a way of looking into my eyes as he spoke, engaging my gaze in a manner more typical of a lover, and I wondered whether he did that with everyone or if this was specific to our encounter.

"You want to neutralize your marriage, then," he was saying. "It wasn't so bad, it wasn't so good, it's over, you're not interest-ed in thinking about it."

"Yes," I said. "I think that's fair."

"So, instead of thinking about your marriage, you want to be upset that your friend's memorial wasn't quite what you would have liked and that at some point he'd rented a room to a guy who had the nerve to come to the memorial and say things that struck you as insulting because Mr. X is the wrong kind of weirdo."

"Mm…" I muttered noncommittally. "Look, leaving my husband is less about *him* than about recognizing that I had tak-en a wrong turn and gotten away from the things that matter to me, which have more to do with art than marriage. I mean art in the broad sense, not visual art specifically. Pursuing dreams and goals instead of getting stuck in a false domesticity and playing out somebody else's life instead of my own."

"Hmm…" he said in reply, and looked searchingly into my

eyes in that astonishingly lover-like way, or I should say that way that people often do prior to ever attempting the first kiss. I began to feel a little faint and breathless, but whether from this exchange of looks, or simply from exhaustion, I wasn't sure. I began to feel an intense desire to reach over and run my hand down his—his what? His hair? His face? His arm? His thigh? I refrained from all of these options. At length he said "So… what's your art form, exactly?"

I was almost dreading this question. It's not very comfortable to talk about neglected passions. "That's a little hard to explain," I said.

"Why?"

"Well, for one thing I've always been kind of interdisciplinary and multimedia, and then also I kind of fell out of touch with it all after I got married." Once said, this sounded truly lame to me, and I could see it sounded lame to him as well. "I was depressed," I added rather defensively.

"Sometimes you're awfully hard to follow," he observed. "I still don't know what you're trying to describe; do you do assemblage or video or performance art or what?"

"I do *what*," I said. "We can call it performance art. Theater works. Things that require too much collaboration. Things that rely too much on music and art. People were starting to get interested in my ideas and then I dropped out. I feel like I've been living in a black hole. I feel stupid trying to explain this."

"You gave up," he said flatly.

"Sort of. I temporarily gave up."

"I don't understand people giving up their art," he said. "I can't go there. If it's what you're meant to do, you don't give it up."

I used to say things like that when I was his age. I believed that it was possible to be sustained entirely by one's ambition. I believed that this was the dividing line between those of us who were genuinely driven and those who were just wannabes. That those of us who had the drive would continue to feel it unabated throughout our lives, with no interruptions, without faltering.

"That's what you think," I said.

SARAH

My cello teacher was pressing me to get more involved in chamber ensembles; she thought it wasn't enough to work on solo pieces and my orchestral parts. I had always done a certain amount of small-ensemble work, but the main type of chamber ensemble for cellists is the string quartet, and ideally the members of a string quartet stick together and become a unit rather than just collaborating on a piece or two every now and then. I hadn't had any lasting string-quartet experiences. They had all been very brief, generally in place just long enough to work up a few pieces for a concert. This hadn't bothered me, because I was perfectly happy practicing my lessons and rehearsing with the orchestra, but my teacher had decided that this was a hole in my education that I had better begin to fill. When I didn't rush out and start recruiting musicians, she concluded that I was too shy and passive, and needed to be set up with some partners.

This annoyed me a little, but I couldn't really argue; I did need to have more experience in chamber ensembles, and if I personally was too shy or placid or lazy or whatever it might be to go out and drum up my own musicians, I supposed I couldn't argue with my teacher suggesting some.

We went through lists of types of ensemble that could include cello; other than the string quartet and early-music consorts updated to modern instruments, there weren't all that many standard choices. Yes, you could find music for quite a few permutations—for cello duets, cello trios, cello quartets, and on up to about eight cellos; you could find duets for violin and cello by Bach, Beethoven, and various other composers; Haydn and Fauré had both written for violin, cello, and piano; and then there were some less common options like Haydn for two flutes and cello or Mozart writing for oboe, violin, viola, and cello. Of course, a composer could choose to stick a cello into anything, but playing in a piece for a truly nonstandard type of ensemble does pretty much rely on the composer asking you to premiere his experiment. My teacher said she would let people know I was available for that sort of thing, but I suspected most of them would be choosing cellists they already knew and who were more interested in contemporary music. In the meantime, I got together with some of her other students and began to work on those duets and trios.

KARI

I spent a while arguing with my companion about people experiencing lulls or dead spots in their careers. We had more drinks and went at the matter vigorously, as befits night barroom disputation. As I thought about it, I knew I had historical precedent on my side—countless celebrated figures have had dry spells or failures of the will to create—but unfortunately it had never occurred to me to collect their names for the purpose of debate. I had almost no hard facts to throw at my new friend. He, for his part, had to confess that he actually had heard of the phenomenon and that it wasn't only the marginally talented who gave up or spent ten years producing nothing, but he didn't see why a person should succumb to writer's block or malaise—at least not until later in life. He was resistant to the idea that any person under fifty or so who had committed him- or herself to a life in the arts would slack off for any reason short of physical collapse or acute mental illness. Neither failed love affairs nor matrimony fit his preconceptions of acceptable reasons; clearly he had not had any relationships that sapped his energy and turned him into an antisocial drudge. And maybe this doesn't happen for men, but anyone who's read *The Feminine Mystique* must know it happens to women. Even without any conscious belief that a woman's place is in the home, women waste time obsessing about the need to spend time with their mates. We imagine that just being around is going to be a good thing for both parties, whether anyone feels in the mood for all that togetherness or not. So long as you're in proximity, boring each other to death is virtuous coupledom. No, I didn't think my young companion was likely to have experienced that particular circle of hell yet. Now it's true that during my marriage I didn't absolutely stop dead and fail to come up with anything at all. I didn't stop thinking or having ideas. I just slowed down considerably and stopped working with anyone else, which in effect was like doing nothing. Had I been a painter or novelist or even a composer, I could have carried on to some extent; I would have slowed, but since painting and novel-writing and even composition tend to be rather solitary pursuits, the effects would have been less extreme. I had made the mistake of going into a collaborative genre, where although I could sketch out designs or come up with simple ideas for music, there was no way of seeing whether any of it worked without other people. Unlike some people, I'm not a one-woman show.

After a time we did get on to the topic of what exactly I did have up my sleeve; you can only argue for so long about whether people can abandon their art. I told him about a few of my ideas, and they seemed to interest him, or he made a good pretense of interest. Eventually, though, it got to be closing time, and we saw that it was raining outside.

"Oh—rats!" I exclaimed. "It's raining, it's after midnight, etc etc etc. My poor landlady."

I knew I ought to get a cab and never mind whether my landlady woke up at the sound of the door, but I didn't want to go home.

"Your poor landlady," mocked my companion. "Why are you so obsessed with her feelings?"

"I like her," I said, "so of course I don't want to bother her." This was only partly true, or partly my excuse.

"You're awfully silly," he said. "I'm sure you know how to creep into the house quietly when you really want to."

"Well, I told you right off the bat that I didn't want to go home. If I'd wanted to go home, I'd have gone hours ago, instead of putting it off by wandering into bars in strange neighborhoods."

"This isn't a strange neighborhood, this is my neighborhood," he said. "In fact, I happen to like my neighborhood. I'm surprised you don't know about it."

"I can't know about every neighborhood," I said. "If it's so nice, you can acquaint me with it sometime."

"I don't know how I can do that if I don't even know your

name," he said. "You'll just wander off and vanish into your landlady's like a hermit crab into its shell, and I'll just say 'Well, that nameless person I met in the bar went off and was never seen again.'"

"Now you're being silly," I said, restraining myself from leaning up against his lithe and enticing form as we stood under the bar awning pretending to look out into the rain. "I'm Kari and I don't always disappear forever. Here, I'll give you my card." I had had some cards made for business purposes, but in truth I almost never used them, because I never met anyone who needed one. It felt silly to give someone like him my card—ridiculously formal—but if I wasn't going to give my card to people I wanted to know, then there certainly wasn't any point in having a card in the first place.

"Ah," he said, scrutinizing the thing in the gleam of the streetlights. "Ms. Kari Zilke who edits books when not out doing other things. You didn't mention you had a trade."

"You wouldn't want to read the books I edit. You don't need self-help books or economics texts."

"Vileness," said he. "Well, you don't want to go home, and I live around the corner, so I suppose you can come home with me. I do have a couch."

I proffered the suitable hesitations—I could go home if he preferred—only if it was really all right—all that—but it was a done deal.

Sarah

I didn't always pay a great deal of attention to the other music students around me. If I knew them from our orchestra practices or from different ensembles, or had seen them perform, that was one thing. I often had lunch with those I knew, or went out for coffee or snacks. We had a nice, quiet, mostly professional sort of acquaintance. Kari Zilke went to one of the concerts with me once, because she had mentioned liking baroque music, but we didn't really talk to anyone beyond my saying hello to a few people. And actually I really only knew people who played orchestral instruments. I didn't know many vocalists or saxophonists or guitarists. The ones I knew were those I had studied theory with or something like that, or who were friends of my friends. I don't go out looking for new acquaintances, because I already know enough people to satisfy my need for conversation. While I wouldn't describe myself as exactly introverted, my social needs are modest.

In the course of adding on more ensemble work, however, I did begin to get to know a few more people. And one day another cellist mentioned that she knew a guy who played classical guitar and wanted to explore the repertoire for cello and guitar.

"The what?" I said. I had never heard that there was a duet repertoire for this particular pairing, or at least not a repertoire large enough to "explore."

"He says it's mostly nineteenth- and twentieth-century music," she said, "not a very well-known area. It sounds like it could be fun, but I'm really booked up for the next few months."

I was intrigued. I could easily imagine classical guitar as a good partner to cello, provided the cello didn't drown it out. "I might be interested," I said. "Who is this guy? Where would I get in touch with him?"

"His name's Joey Caro. I see him most days; I'll tell him to talk to you."

"What's he like?"

She shrugged. "He's nice. You'll like him. And he's really good."

"Okay," I said. "Tell him to get hold of me one of these days."

KARI

It was raining fairly hard; puddles were forming in the street and the streetlights picked up gleams from the oil slicks left by passing cars. I like rainy nights, but I don't like getting drenched. And, since neither of us had brought an umbrella, we were pretty wet by the time my companion unlocked the front door of his building. We trailed a certain amount of water behind us as we went up the stairs.

"Oof, I'm wet as a dog," I said. "I hope I don't leave your floor all wet."

"You can leave your shoes on the mat," he said, switching on the light.

I was curious to see what sort of place my companion lived in, so I glanced about a bit as I pulled off my shoes and jacket. It was a studio apartment, and not a very big one, but more appealing than most places I had seen inhabited by men under thirty. There were some art prints on the walls and he had tacked a length of India-print fabric to the ceiling to billow over his bed like some sort of luxurious tent hanging while another length of the same fabric hung on the wall. There was a music stand in the middle of the floor and a collection of instrument cases and amps along one of the walls; the couch had probably once belonged to his parents, but was draped with another length of the India print, which hid any imperfections nicely. There was a smallish bookcase mostly full of books, a little table with two chairs and a lamp, and that was about it. Well—a stereo, of course, and at the far end a kitchenette and a door to what I assumed was the bathroom, but not a great deal more. Some candles, a plant here and there. There was only so much I could take in right away.

"Would you like a cup of tea, or something stronger?" he

inquired. "You can hang up your jacket here," he added, gesturing to some hooks by the door.

"What are you having? Something hot is always nice after coming in out of the rain."

"I was thinking of brandy and hot water," said he, heading toward the stove and the teakettle.

"Well, then that's what I'll have too."

Once the water was on, he stopped at the stereo and deliberated over some CDs. "Do you know the work of Terry Riley?"

"I've heard the name, but that's all," I said.

"I think you might like this," he said. "It's called *Salome Dances for Peace*. He wrote it for the Kronos Quartet. It's pretty long but we could listen to the first CD, anyway." He passed me the insert to look at.

It's always hard to read these things carefully when someone is standing there wondering what you'll think, but I skimmed it and gathered that the piece was intended as a ballet in which the biblical Salome, that naughty girl, was reincarnated as a dancing shaman and summoned by the Great Spirit to redeem herself by winning back peace from the forces of evil. Evidently the ballet aspect eventually fell away and the piece remained purely instrumental, combining Minimalism with aspects of blues, raga, and Mongolian music.

It sounded like the kind of thing I like when it works and that I find disappointing and pretentious when it doesn't. But the initial measures at least sounded like something suitable to listen to late at night over brandy and hot water: provocative but relatively meditative, and not too noisy.

The teakettle whistled and my companion went off to pour our drinks while I took the opportunity to examine his bookshelves. In addition to music texts, he had some Dostoevsky, some Hesse, some Rumi, some Philip K. Dick, Edwin Abbott's *Flatland*, Alain-Fournier's *Le Grand Meaulnes*, and Jostein Gaarder's *Sophie's World*. It was a respectable little collection, with a mildly philosophical bent.

"Your brandy, madame," said a voice beside me.

"Oh, yes—thank you," I said, taking the mug. I was glad

he hadn't called me ma'am or madam, which always make me feel like a stout matron in a comic strip. We clinked glasses and went and sat on the couch. We weren't sitting right next to each other, more like at an indefinite sort of distance. I wasn't sure what this meant, because after all I had no experience whatsoever dealing with men his age. That is, from the vantage point of my present age. I knew how to deal with men my own age and men somewhat older; yes, everyone is different, but overall, with them it really comes down to whether or not they're attracted. If they aren't, that usually becomes clear fairly soon, and if they are, well, that too usually becomes clear. It's been my experience that men over thirty-five either know how to make a move (whether a gross and offensive one or a subtle but clear one) or they've pretty much given up hope of learning. The latter are outside my romantic and sexual experience, but I'm well aware of their existence. Men under thirty, however—well, they're very unpredictable. It was my recollection that they were learning what to do, and since when I was under thirty the same was true of me, the results were best described as uneven. Someone was always misreading someone else's cues, even if sooner or later we got to the physical part, which mostly we were better able to manage. So—what should I be expecting and how should I be reading this one's cues?

"What do you think of *Salome Dances for Peace?*" he asked.

"Well, so far I like it," I said. "It doesn't sound like she's begun dancing yet, though."

"Maybe she hasn't," he said. "I don't think she gets going until later in the piece. And I don't know the piece all that well. Where're the liner notes I gave you?"

"Over there," I said, pointing. He leaped up and retrieved them and looked to see which track was playing.

"Well, she hasn't hit the main dance-for-peace stuff yet. That seems to be on the second CD." He bounced back to the couch and planted himself against the far end, but facing me and with his foot in my vicinity. He looked relaxed but alert. Had he been anywhere near my own age, I would have immediately interpreted this as a move. As it was, I wasn't sure. He might just be into the music. It would be very embarrassing if I made a move and then discovered it was a big mistake. He might even be gay, although I really didn't think so.

"It's interesting music," I said. "I wouldn't say I really find I follow the story without the program notes, but I like listening to it." While I have some musical background, I am not particularly good at discussing what I hear beyond being able to say things like that the strings are flat or that I like the orchestration or that I disapprove of the conductor's interpretation. I hoped my companion was not going to expect me to produce discourse on a high musicological level, because if he did, he would be sorely disappointed. To put this fear out of my mind, I concentrated my attention on his nearly recumbent form, which continued to strike me as surprisingly alluring. We were still in mostly wet clothes, I realized, despite having shed our shoes and jackets. There were wet streaks down the front of his T-shirt where water had evidently dripped down from the collar of his jacket. His jeans were harder hit.

"You're a bit wet still," I remarked. "That was a vigorous rain."

"You're wet too," he observed, prodding my damp thigh with his bare foot.

"It would be hard not to be," I said, "under the circumstances."

"You're an odd character, Kari Zilke," he said, testing my thigh further with his foot. "Do you often go home with guys without asking their names?"

Ow! How had I failed to ask his name? My discomfiture at this faux pas quite negated my enjoyment of the rest of the situation. I sat up straight and grasped his foot, although admittedly in the interests of keeping it in my domain. "I've never, *ever* gone home with someone before without knowing his name," I said vehemently. "I'm really astounded. I can't believe I didn't notice I didn't know your name. Well, we've got to remedy that. What's your name?"

He rolled his eyes and started laughing. "Kari Zilke, you are a most ridiculous person. You talk to me all evening, revealing all sorts of things about yourself and telling me your troubles and your dearest aspirations, and you don't think to tell me your name until we're nearly in my apartment and even then you don't think to ask me *my* name. You are completely absurd. And I think that your punishment for this bit of stupidity—no, don't let go of my foot now, your hands are nice and warm—your punishment is not to learn my name tonight."

"What?" I said, rather stupidly indeed.

"You'll have to spend the whole night wondering."

"You're bad," I said. "How can you possibly not tell me your name?"

"Just as easily as I would have told you if you'd asked me an hour or two ago. You can find out some other time."

"I'll bite you," I warned, lifting his foot to my mouth.

"Go right ahead," he said, so I did. Not hard, of course.

Sarah

When I began looking through the papers Kari Zilke left behind, I really never dreamed that there would be graphic details of the more sordid aspects of her sex life. I never thought, actually, that there would be anything at *all* about her sex life. I was very dismayed and uncomfortable to discover that she even had one, although this was not very reasonable of me. I suppose most people have a sex life of some sort, sooner or later.

KARI

Had I been thinking clearly, I would have realized that it would be pretty easy to find out his name. It was probably on his mailbox downstairs, maybe on his doorbell, and most likely written in some of his books and definitely on the mail and bills. But I was tired and discombobulated and for that matter I have pretty reliable judgment about people. They may prove to be hard to deal with or irresponsible about money, but no one I've ever liked has ever turned out to be bad at heart. I wasn't worried about this boy mistreating me.

"You're tickling me!" he exclaimed, wrestling with my hands, but there was no question he was enjoying it, so I bit him again.

"I can't believe you won't tell me your name," I said.

"Some other time, I told you. Not tonight. You lost your chance to find out tonight. Tonight I'm one of those magic beings whose name is a secret."

Our faces were very close; we were gazing fiercely into each other's eyes.

"Well, at least you're better looking than Rumpelstiltskin," I said.

"I certainly am! Eeeeyuck, there are more interesting magic beings than Rumpelstiltskin. Think of your Welsh mythology or something with a little more style to it."

I was surprised to hear him throwing in Welsh mythology, but then I remembered that things that were pretty esoteric when I was his age have become common knowledge. He was probably reading the *Mabinogi* at fifteen or something.

"And if I grab hold of you, will you turn into a wild horse or a boar?"

"You'll have to find out for yourself, questing female."

I took a handful of his hair, which was rich and springy against my fingers, and we kissed. It was a good long breathless kiss, but it didn't lead to anything further because when we finally paused for air, he stood up and announced that it was time to put the sheets on the couch for me.

"I'm sleeping on the couch?" I said in disbelief.

"That's what I offered you a while back."

"Yes, but…"

"Well, since you didn't find out my name when you had a chance, I think you can suffer a little bit. I like you, but you'll just have to sleep on the couch tonight. If you come marauding into my bed, no doubt I'll enjoy whatever you do to me, but I'll pretend to be asleep the whole time. Things might be different some other time, but that's what you get tonight." He grinned at me and I felt very sulky about it. "Now get off the couch so I can lay these sheets down properly."

I stood up and watched him. I hadn't desired anyone so intensely in years, and he was being annoying about it. It was very difficult not to spring upon him and peel away his clothes. I don't know why men always insist on so many delays and restrictions. They like to claim that women tease, but I've always found that it's the other way around. It's always the man who pulls away and claims this isn't a good time or that he's too emotionally confused about someone else or some such thing. Well, perhaps not quite always, but usually. We need not go into the times I've taken that stance. It hasn't been often.

He made up the couch quite nicely, with green-and-white-striped sheets, and then handed me an old T-shirt. "The bathroom is in there."

Wasn't he ever unsure about anything? I couldn't think of anyone I had known in my early twenties who was so assured. I had known arrogant people, but you could tell it was bluff. Their false confidence was merely repellent.

I took the T-shirt and slunk into the bathroom to change. It was a black T-shirt with the name of a local bookstore across the front, so I supposed things could have been worse. The bathroom itself was small and relatively Spartan. The only very interesting thing about it was that on top of the toilet tank he had arranged a small plant, two candles, and a collection of smooth stones in a stoneware dish. I stood looking at the arrangement for a moment, then glanced in the mirror. My face was a little drawn and gaunt, making me look older than usual, but not really worse. My hair was all askew, so I took the liberty of borrowing his comb.

When I emerged, he was shutting off the stereo.

"All right, you can have a goodnight kiss," he said. I went over to him and we exchanged another long, intense kiss, our bodies almost entirely separate. Then he looked at me fondly, mischievously, and ran his hand lightly across my breasts before going over to turn off the light. *The rat.* "Go to bed," he said. "On your couch."

I hesitated, then climbed in. It was too dark to see just how much clothing he was removing. Since his clothes were damp, I preferred to imagine that he had disposed of all of them. I imagined him as a perfect, naked body under the sheets.

I contemplated whether to pursue his half-suggestion that I go over and do things to him, but decided that this would just be an exercise in frustration. He would enjoy it thoroughly, he would pretend to be asleep the entire goddamn time, and it would just madden me. If he was going to punish me for not asking his name, I could punish him in return. But it was difficult. I lay on the couch for a very long time, awake and all too aware of him lying in his bed across the room.

SARAH

When I say I did not expect Kari Zilke to have a sex life, I mean I hadn't expected her to have one while she was living at my aunt's house.

There was no reason for her not to have one while living with us; I'm sure some of our renters carried on an active love life. We didn't even tell them not to bring anyone home with them. It's true we would have objected had any of them made a regular practice of it, because after all it is my aunt's house and she does have a right to some privacy and peace at home, as do I, and we wouldn't have wanted to listen to a regular program of sex noises coming from people we didn't know all that well or want to get to know that well either, but my aunt didn't actually mind if a renter occasionally brought someone home and they behaved quietly. She takes the view that everyone needs human affection and that it is not our place to judge where they find it so long as they are not inconsiderate about imposing it on other people, namely herself and me. I personally preferred them not to bring anyone home at all, but I deferred to my aunt's flexible standards on this. We did agree that if our renters acquired serious lovers who required regular attention, it was time for the renters to find a nice apartment on their own or to move in with their lovers. Our renters did not, however, mostly find serious partners. Most of them were in that category who were somewhat embittered about the opposite sex and while usually anxious to find a mate, were convinced that all the good men were taken or that most women were as deep as Dixie cups. Even our gay and lesbian renters were not all that successful in finding mates, having something of a similar attitude about the scarcity of suitable partners. From this, you may gather that most of our renters were people going through transitions in life, who did not stay terribly long with us despite the low rent and my aunt's friendly personality, and in fact I cannot really think of any one of them for whom this was not true. My aunt's house is a waystation for slightly lost souls. We don't want them to be very far lost, but they always seem to be at least a little down on their luck or uncertain where to go next. This suppresses their sexuality to a considerable degree, or at least in most cases it seems to. As Kari Zilke gave the impression of not needing men in her life, I made the mistake of imagining that this meant there wouldn't be any.

KARI

When I finally, finally drifted off to sleep, it was with deep exhaustion. But it was not a deep sleep, I think. I wandered into a dream in which I came upon Girodet's Endymion asleep in the glade, but by himself, not accompanied by dog or Eros. And I must have been Selene, because I looked upon him with pleasure and advanced, prepared to run my fingers over his somnolent body and to kiss his unresponsive lips.

In the morning, as I was waking, I thought I felt a caress run down my back, and lips touching my earlobe, but when I dared open my eyes to look, all I saw was my nameless companion sitting on his bed in his shorts, looking at me.

He looked good, just as good as the previous night, only with the advantage of more skin. He looked considerably like Girodet's Endymion, only better, with a more intriguing face and a less androgynous figure.

"You're Endymion!" I exclaimed.

"Clever," he remarked, and began pulling on his pants.

"I dreamt of Endymion, as he looks in the Girodet painting. Do you know the painting?"

"No, only that Endymion received eternal sleep in exchange for nightly visitations."

"Well, in the painting he lies sleeping in a glade, caressed by moonlight and attended by Eros and a sleeping dog. He looks quite a bit like you; the same hair, anyway. There are some differences otherwise. Girodet's version is a little lacking in body hair."

"In your dream or in the painting?"

"In the painting. He probably had a normal amount in my dream. Did you dream of being Endymion?"

"I don't need to dream of being Endymion when I take on the role by choice."

I examined his torso while I had the chance. Unlike the Girodet painting, he possessed chest hair, as a kind of accent. He was not an especially hairy person, but the figure in the painting is epicene. Its only body hair consists of a very minimal degree of pubic hair around its classically tiny genitalia. But I suppose we can hardly expect eighteenth-century beauties to match our own preferences in every detail.

"Did you wish I had marauded into your bed, Endymion?"

"I was a little disappointed," he admitted. "But I don't have any condoms and I didn't think you were likely to have taken any to your friend's memorial."

His generation, I have heard, is more scrupulous about these things than mine. My generation remembers what life was like before AIDS. My generation is perhaps more inclined to associate risk with specific behaviors and populations. We educated his generation to be risk-averse. That is, the part of his generation that received an education in such things.

"You're so well prepared, mentally," I said.

"Just not practically."

"Well, a person can't prepare for every eventuality."

I was hoping he would offer to make some breakfast, but instead he said, "I'm sorry, but we're going to have to get out of here. I have an appointment at ten."

I looked at my watch. "Oh!" It was after nine, closer to nine-thirty. "I had no idea." I jumped up and ran into the bathroom where my clothes were still waiting from the night before. There was no time to wash; I just threw them on.

"All right," I said, emerging. "We can go. But will I see you again? I apologize for not asking your name."

He had selected a guitar case and was putting some sheet music into a backpack. "Sure, I'm not hard to find."

"What do you mean, I've never found you before."

"But now you know where to find me."

"Yes, but do you *want* me to find you?"

"You're so difficult," he said. "Meet me in the same place next Tuesday at seven and we'll get some dinner. You can think about Endymion in the meantime and tell me all about it, and then we can go dancing. Is that detailed enough to suit you?"

"That's very elaborate," I said. "What would you like me to wear?"

"Clothing is always suitable, last I heard. You can use your imagination."

We had reached the front door. "What made you notice me in the bar last night?" I asked.

"Oh, I don't often see women come in there looking like maenads who've just torn someone apart, or like Kali stomping on corpses."

"And this somehow appealed to you?"

"No, but it intrigued me. Now come on, we've got to hurry to catch the bus."

SARAH

Joey Caro and I met, inevitably, in one of those cafés that my friends like and that do nothing much for me. As far as I was concerned, we could have met in a practice room, but I suppose it is a little more civilized to have business meetings—even musical ones—over food and drink. He had his guitar with him, but since we obviously weren't going to do any sight-reading in a café, I had left my cello in a more convenient location. Admittedly, the guitar made it easy to guess who he was, since no one else happened to be toting one at the time.

"You must be Joey," I said.

"Right," said the guitarist. "You must be Sarah."

"Yes," I said. "Nice to meet you. I'm sitting over there." I had arrived several minutes early and he was slightly late, so I had already gotten my coffee. He wasn't late enough for me to think he was really unpunctual, but he was late enough that I noticed.

Joey brought over a café au lait and a huge muffin. He did offer me some of the muffin, but I was glad I refused, because he devoured the whole thing almost before we said a word.

"So," I said. "Wanda tells me you're thinking about doing some guitar and cello duets. Tell me more."

He stuffed the last bit of muffin into his mouth and washed it down. "Sorry, I was famished." He looked distracted as well as famished to me. This did not impress me. Still, many musicians can be a little spacey when not actually playing, and a person has to give them time to come back to earth. In this case, when Joey Caro got back to earth, he began explaining that he had run across some music for guitar and cello, and that this had prompted him to look around for more, because he liked the possibilities in the timbres of the two instruments, and because most of the works for this combination seemed to be by relatively obscure nineteenth- and twentieth-century composers.

Resurrecting obscure composers has never really been one of my interests—I tend to think they must be obscure for a reason—but Joey made this sound like an exciting project. He said most music for guitar was composed by guitarists, some of the composers had died young, many were Spanish and therefore a little out of the mainstream because of that, and, finally, that just because certain instrumental combinations became well established as the nineteenth century progressed, it didn't mean the combinations that didn't become so well established weren't worthwhile.

"Think about woodwind quartets and quintets," he said. "There's a decent repertoire, and people do perform them, but they're not all that mainstream."

"A lot more mainstream than guitar and cello duets," I said. "I agree the combination could be pleasing, but is the music all that good?"

"I found a recording of several pieces; they had a certain appeal. I want to explore this material some and maybe find some works that haven't yet been recorded. Wanda said you're pretty proficient and that you're looking to branch out into some different types of ensembles. Does this sound like a project that would interest you, or not?"

I was unquestionably intrigued, and it sounded like a good opportunity, so I tried to keep the skepticism and hesitation out of my voice.

"Yes, I am interested," I said, "but I'd like to hear the recording you found and try out a few pieces before making a decision."

"All right, let's do that then," he said.

So we went over to the music library and listened.

KARI

I thought I would go home quietly enough and escape notice, but as it happened I met my landlady on the stairs. Normally I don't see all that much of her, despite my spending quite a bit of time working in my room, because she likes to go out and visit friends in the neighborhood for coffee, and join them on little walks with their dogs, and from time to time she goes to matinees.

This time, she took one look at me and said, "Well, Kari, who did you meet at your memorial service? An old friend or someone new?" She sounded much amused.

"Oh, I saw quite a few people there, but unfortunately most of them weren't anyone I wanted to talk to."

"Have you had any breakfast? Can I make you some coffee or tea?" she inquired.

I very seldom ate with my landlady or her niece, but I did want breakfast and I did feel comforted by her calm and friendly manner. I had gone through such varied emotions in the past twenty-four hours that a simple cup of morning coffee with my landlady had its appeal. We went into the kitchen and she started a new pot, saying that what was already there had gone cold, and offered me a piece of coffee cake, which she said had just come out of the oven ten minutes earlier.

The coffee cake was so much like the kind my mother used to make that I suspected the two both used the same recipe— perhaps one from the old red Betty Crocker cookbook. I hadn't tasted coffee cake in years, and the spices temporarily returned me to my childhood, which was comforting.

"So, what was this memorial like?" she asked. "Had you known this friend a long time?"

"I met him in my mid-twenties," I said. "He was one of those people who always encouraged me and supported my ideas. A generous person, with many friends. He used to do stage design at some of the local theaters."

"You must feel a great loss, then," said my landlady.

"Well—a loss, certainly. I don't know yet whether a great loss. We hadn't seen each other much in recent years. And he was very elderly, so I wasn't surprised to hear he had died."

She asked me a few more questions about the memorial—where it had been held, whether there had been many flowers, and that sort of thing—and I ended up telling her about the man who asked if I was married.

"I don't know why it made me so angry, but it did. I felt that it was absolutely none of his business—we weren't friends, we weren't colleagues, he didn't even put it in a friendly tone—it was just weird. What do you think, was I being unreasonable?" I thought that if anyone was going to tell me I was unreasonable, it would probably be my landlady, who probably wanted to ask me the same question, but she surprised me.

"I think it's very natural you were annoyed," she said. "I suppose most people wouldn't have walked out after a question like that, but I'm sure you were also feeling upset at losing your old friend. When people die, we feel a sense of loss, even if we don't realize it, because it reminds us that our time is short too." She paused to think. "It was thoughtless and rude of this man to ask a stranger a question like that at a time of mourning. And it's not nice to be asked that kind of question by strangers, anyway. I'm sure you know it's no longer legal for employers to ask job applicants their marital status, and that's a very good thing. Back when I first went to work, I hated being asked that. I always felt that since I wasn't married, they thought I couldn't find a husband, and that if I did find one, I'd up and leave. People always used to make little jokes about how secretaries were only working in order to find husbands."

"Yes," I said. This was one of the longer speeches I had ever heard my landlady bring forth, and I gathered that my experience had brought back some unpleasant memories.

"And then, when you left the memorial, what did you do?"

she asked with a smile. "There's a beautiful garden near the Unitarian Church—did you go look?"

"No," I said, "I didn't even think of that. I might have enjoyed walking in a garden. But I just walked around town for a long time until finally I went into a café and ended up in a conversation with a nice musician."

It felt mildly dishonest to refer to my companion of the night before as "a nice musician," but it wasn't untrue and it seemed like a description that my landlady would understand, given that her niece plays cello. I explained that we had talked for a long time about music and other things and that eventually I had spent the night on his couch. It was all true, but it left out everything that made the encounter compelling to me. So often it seems necessary to edit out the heart of things when describing them to others; the facts and trappings are often all they can understand. Perhaps I was misjudging my landlady in not telling her more about my evening's encounter, but I had had so many experiences, even with close friends, where whatever I was describing shocked or disgusted them in some way that completely mystified me. I don't, after all, lead a particularly abandoned life. I was quite accurate when I said I had never before gone home with anyone whose name I didn't know, and for that matter I have almost never gone home with anyone I have just met. I don't think I do anything unusually strange, but all the same, people do sometimes misinterpret my descriptions of people I meet and conversations I've had and, of course, any sort of vaguely or explicitly romantic encounter. And, of course, while no one in the world ever will fully understand any other person, there are people to whom I reveal myself more freely than others. My landlady, I suspected, might be better able to understand me than I supposed, but my rapport with the young man of the night before had been almost immediate. He might not always understand me, but he was on the same kind of wavelength. Something was going to come of that encounter. I didn't know what, but I was sure that something, somehow, would.

Sarah

These Von Call works probably won't interest you that much," said Joey. "I'd put them under the heading of very minor classical stuff. Cute but lacking in substance—let's just say Frederick the Great wrote better, and he only wrote music in his spare time, when not reviewing his troops. But the Dotzauer and Matiegka definitely have something going on for the cello. Less for the guitar part, but at least the guitar is moving away from being purely continuo."

"I've heard of Dotzauer," I said. "He was a cellist and wrote mainly for cello, I think. At least, he wrote loads of exercises and things for solo cello. Who was this Matiegka person?"

"My understanding is that he was a Bohemian contemporary of Dotzauer who composed quite a bit for guitar. Schubert and Count Esterházy apparently thought well of his work."

"All right," I said. "Let's give them a listen. We can listen to the Von Call, too, just in case I like him better than you do."

Kari

Now that I had arranged to meet with Endymion (whatever his real name might be) on Tuesday, I could think of nothing else. I don't fall in love at first sight, nor did I expect to end up falling in love at all, but I was enthralled. My life in recent years has been almost devoid of fascinating new people of either sex; I had almost forgotten what it was like to run into them. Leading a nearly hermit-like married life will have that effect on a person.

I had the feeling that this encounter was terribly important, that something exciting would come of it and change my life in some wonderful way. I knew better than to imagine that Endymion himself would magically transform my life, but I could see he was intelligent and quick-witted, and it appeared he had interests somewhat akin to mine. I did not yet know much about his musical background or goals, but he seemed knowledgeable and to have a genuine curiosity about life. I felt a peculiar certainty that he would thus prove a spur to my own development, whatever direction that might happen to go. I don't know why I felt this, exactly, but I felt it strongly: this person will be important to me and I must know him. Yes, I also found him attractive, but that was not the main thing; rather, it was convenient in that it had helped keep me awake and attentive.

When I say this, I do not mean to suggest that the attraction itself was trivial, insignificant, or to be taken lightly. It was a surprisingly strong attraction given that I usually take some time to develop a physical attraction to a person, and indeed, I wasn't about to ignore it. The fact that Endymion seemed to feel some corresponding attraction to me reinforced my intention to see where this attraction led. But all the same this sexual interest was more of a support for the feeling that in some fashion he would help precipitate my next stage of development.

What, I wondered, would our next meeting be like? Dinner—well, I didn't devote any energy to imagining the food and drink. But he'd said we would go dancing. What sort of dancing did he have in mind? Where would we dance? To what kind of music? How athletic would it be? I hadn't really danced in years, although I used to be an enthusiastic dancer.

And then, swirling around the deeper reaches of my mind, there was the idea of the mythic Endymion. My present-day Endymion had told me to think about Endymion and tell him about it. What would arise to be told?

The story we read in mythology books is that Selene, or Diana, or Artemis (take your pick of her name, but I always prefer Selene as the version who is never specified as a goddess of chastity) looked down upon the earth and caught sight of the lovely Endymion tending his sheep. Or sleeping in the midst of his sheep, as you wish. The goddess was smitten, and—perhaps to maintain Endymion's youthful beauty, or at least to keep him from turning into a grasshopper like the mortal loved by her sister Eos—Zeus granted him eternal sleep.

But as Bulfinch suggests, Endymion had no further adventures worthy of mention, unless one might happen to choose him as a subject for erotic fiction, in which case I supposed one might invent a fine collection of his dreams. I imagine, at any rate, that Selene as either moonbeam or physical incarnation would be a more felicitous lover than Zeus as an eagle or swan. I would not mind the feathers especially, but surely one would be more likely to respond to a fellow mammal.

So—that's all I knew from mythology about Endymion. I presumed it was also all that *my* Endymion knew on the subject. But this did not mean that there was nothing more to be divined, or nothing more to be imagined. I began to let my mind run loose on the subject, returning from time to time to the thought of "my" Endymion in his bed, naked or nearly so, as I lay sleepless on his couch refraining from creeping across the floor and caressing his purportedly sleeping form. And as I let these thoughts circulate over the next few days, I began to have some ideas.

Sarah

I'm not entirely sure how I ended up a classical musician, but when I think about it, it seems completely natural to my personality and approach to life. Whether I would have liked classical music if my mother hadn't subjected me to all kinds of other music is another question. I don't think of myself as even slightly rebellious, but I suppose that technically my response to her life and habits is one of rebellion and reaction.

Most children like to learn and repeat nursery songs like "Row, Row, Row Your Boat" and "She'll Be Coming Round the Mountain," and I was no exception there; my mother did sing me these songs and I enjoyed them. She and her friends did play ordinary games with me like "This Little Piggy Went to Market" and they let me ride horseback on their knees; I suppose that adults worldwide in every culture throughout history have done such things to entertain children, and that only the most limited and troubled parents do not. My mother, though seriously lacking in so many ways, was fond enough of me and had a normal maternal desire to play with me. She thought that babies were "cool."

But she did not mostly play music that I would really consider suitable for children. These days expectant parents play Mozart for their unborn, and immerse their babies in even more Mozart, and I'm sure that does the kids much more good than the Jimi Hendrix and other things I mostly heard. After a few years of the music my mother and her friends liked, my aunt's sappy oldies were an improvement—at least they were jolly or melancholy and could be fun to sing along with. My aunt also has an old upright piano that she taught me to play "Chopsticks" and other simple tunes on, and she taught me how to read music at a basic level—and after watching a certain amount of Boston Pops on TV, I got very excited about joining the school orchestra when the time came. We had a good orchestra teacher, who rehearsed us twice a week and miraculously taught all the instruments so that with astonishing speed we all made some sort of acceptable sounds.

But, as usually happens, most of my classmates soon gave up their instruments for other pursuits, and only a few of us continued, getting scholarships to summer music camps and auditioning for the city youth orchestra. We took to the classical repertoire as if it were an arcane science practiced by a secret society, which maybe it was since none of our other friends or classmates had any liking for it at all. Different ones of us developed different passions; Emily became obsessed with baroque music and Justin wanted to know why we never got to play any Shostakovich or Khachaturian. My tastes were more conservative; I liked most of the big names from Vivaldi and Bach up to Debussy, Ravel, and Prokofiev. I don't care for atonal, twelve-tone, or very dissonant music, although when necessary I play it; and medieval and Renaissance music, though all right, does not charm me to the degree it does many of my friends. I am not terribly fond of Wagner either, or of other excessive late-nineteenth-century composers. My cello teacher regards my present tastes as a limitation, but thinks I will grow out of them, which is another reason that she wanted me to get involved in more chamber ensemble work and have new experiences. I am not opposed to this, because I realize that tastes do develop and change, but all the same I would have been perfectly content working on pieces by Bach, Beethoven, Mozart, Schubert, and so forth.

The duets that Joey Caro played for me did pique my interest. They were not great works, but they were enjoyable, and I liked the sound of the guitar with the cello. He had dug up a couple of scores, so after listening to sections on the CD, we went to a practice room and did some sight-reading. It was fun, and Wanda was right about his being a good musician. I'm not a good judge of guitarists, but he had a deft touch on the strings, made few mistakes, and had a sense of tempo and phrasing. I agreed to work up some of the duets with him.

KARI

I never truly doubted that Endymion would be awaiting me at seven o'clock on Tuesday, perhaps even sitting in the same chair at the same table, but this did not prevent me from nervous anxieties and suspense as the time grew nearer. It was exciting to find myself in this kind of state of anticipation once again, a state I had not experienced in years. It was slightly frightening, but not in a bad way, given that I was so out of practice in feeling excitements and anticipations. No; it was a little like starting to go fast downhill on a bike—scary but exhilarating. You pick up speed, you feel the wind rushing past, you hope not to hit a pothole or to discover a dangerous cross street, but you glory in the sensation.

I had hesitated and fretted over what to wear, since I wanted to confirm that I was an interesting person as well as arrive in something appropriate for dancing. For the memorial, I had been wearing a long slim skirt of brown linen with a darker top; it had been relatively sober but not strictly funereal, and my necklace, made of pieces of small conch shells, had added an element of undefinable barbaric splendor to an otherwise subdued ensemble. Something more cheerful, or at least less formal, as well as more flexible, ought to be brought out for this dance adventure. It had been so long since I had done any dancing to speak of that I was slightly at a loss; essentially, pants or a mid-length skirt would let me move, but whatever I wore had to be something that could absorb sweat. It always seems as though clothes that would look pretty on a dance floor are completely impractical, and in truth I no longer had all that many clothes to choose from. But I dug around and came up with a full-skirted, handkerchief-hemmed purple dress. It was a wonder I still had this, because I never had anywhere to wear it anymore, but I had always been fond of it, and it reminded me of livelier days, so there it was. With a necklace and some sort of comfortable shoes (did I have anything suitable for dancing?), it would do nicely at anything short of a fancy-dress ball. Thus, eventually, I readied myself and went off to Endymion's haunt.

There he sat, in the same place as before, in essentially the same clothes as before: a black T-shirt and jeans, although this was not the same black T-shirt since it had the remains of red and white lettering. It was not a very new T-shirt, but it fit him well. Of people who wear black professionally, he looked most like a stagehand, rather than like (for example) a violinist or a bunraku puppeteer.

I was not quite sure how to greet him, so I said, "Endymion!"

He stood up with an amused look and said, "Nice dress."

Each of us looked over the other with an admittedly sexual interest before sitting down, although even as we did so, I was aware that we were able to do this precisely because it was not our fundamental reason for interest in one another. We drank a glass or two of wine and I tried to make up for my previous stupidities by asking him things like whether the Terry Riley quartet was a particular favorite of his and if he preferred contemporary music to that of earlier periods.

He said that while he had a considerable interest in contemporary music, he didn't know as much about it as about earlier music because, for the most part, a person has to seek it out, whereas anyone who studies music learns about the baroque or classical or romantic periods.

Since, once upon a time, I did play a certain amount of music myself, I found that entirely comprehensible. Things had obviously not changed since my childhood, when one learned to play things like Offenbach's "Barcarolle" and selections from Anna Magdalena Bach's notebook, but composers like Kabalevsky were considered terribly modern because they were (horrors!) still alive.

"Actually, my interests are all over the map," said Endymion. "I like early music, I like romanticism, I like a lot of twentieth-century music, I like a lot of non-western music. It's all a process of exploration."

"Excellent!" I exclaimed. "Well—that's my approach, so naturally I like it in other people. I'm not an expert, but I like to discover different things. I used to just go to the used record stores and comb through their bins."

Somewhere in the midst of all this, we got sandwiches and bowls of soup, which were nothing remarkable, but nonetheless quite acceptable.

"And so, Kari Zilke," said my companion after a time, "have you done as I suggested and contemplated Endymion?"

I put down my spoon and examined him. "Yes," I said, "I have indeed. I'm not done with this contemplation, but I've begun."

"That's very…hmmm…gratifying," he said. "And what comes to mind after all this contemplation?"

"Well," I said, "it has occurred to me that the myth could make an interesting theater piece."

"Indeed," said he. "Tell me more."

We leaned forward over the table and our dishes and I said "I am sure, from what I know of you, that you are familiar with the outlines of the story."

"I am, obviously," he said. "You are not going to tell me the basic, unadorned story, I assume."

"No, but I am not going to go into wild elaboration, either," I said. "This is a relatively undeveloped idea, and you might have suggestions. In any case, as you might know, the story of Endymion is sometimes attached to the goddess Artemis or Diana, and sometimes to the more specific moon-goddess Selene. Personally, I prefer Selene, a pre-Olympian goddess of Titan parentage; she's an archaic figure of whom we know somewhat less than we do of Artemis/Diana, with whom she became conflated. I prefer her in part because the legend was originally hers, and because she is not a goddess of chastity or the hunt, but of the moon. As you may or may not know, she and Endymion produced no fewer than fifty daughters, the Menae, who presided over the lunar months."

"That's terribly productive of them," my companion observed. "I wonder why so many figures from Greek myths produced fifty daughters. Or fifty sons. Niobe, for instance, all tears. But pray continue."

"I'm not really thinking of incorporating fifty daughters into a theater piece," I said, "but it is certainly not something one associates with a goddess of chastity."

"Hardly," he agreed.

"I looked into the story a bit," I said, "and it's murkier than what we've read before, although again there might not be any reason to add these details to a theater piece. For instance, there seem to be several Endymions, but over time they've evidently been confused. I've always thought of Endymion as a handsome shepherd, but there's some disagreement on that. He might even have been a king, but I think we should throw that out—there are enough other kings without making Endymion one."

"Quite," said my companion. "We could make him a Marxist instead."

"Well—I don't know about that, but perhaps. Are you a Marxist?"

"Not especially. The thought just came bubbling up out of nowhere. I think I'll be an anarcho-communist instead."

"I have no idea what that is."

"It's very early twentieth century. I could be the only one left."

"Well, we can leave Endymion's political sympathies to the side for the moment. I object to his being a king, that's all. But Pliny the Elder claims that Endymion was the first human to observe the movements of the moon, which suggests that unlike the Endymion who founded Elis, he must have been born a very long time ago indeed."

"I should think so. The *first* human to observe the movements of the moon? He must have been prehistoric."

"He was prehistoric no matter what. The Greek myths predated writing. Even Mycenae is considered prehistoric." As I said this, I felt I was being a bit pedantic, but how often does one have the chance to throw around references to Mycenae?

"I was being colloquial," said my companion, "and putting him back in the Ice Age with the woolly mammoths or something. Have you considered making Endymion a Neanderthal?"

"No," I said, "that really doesn't fit with my vision. Endymion has to be fabulously beautiful, and no one thinks the Neanderthals were beautiful. Besides, I don't want to drag in woolly mammoths and sabertooths and all that sort of thing. They would just clutter up the scenery, which I envision as being fairly simple in design and mostly involving lighting effects."

"Ah," said my companion. "And what do you envision including in this piece? Will we just have Endymion lying around the stage napping while a spectacular light show occurs? You could put on an aurora borealis overhead and he'd sleep right through it."

"You jest," I said.

"I do," he agreed. "I am cluttering up your idea with my own rude silliness. Tell me what you have in mind."

"I am having thoughts of a divided-stage production in which on one side we have a modern-day tale and on the other we have the mythic Endymion as a sort of counterpoint. I don't think we would have him visibly sleeping the whole time, but maybe we could. I think we use projections, partly of Girodet's *Endymion*—"

"Which I've now looked up—"

"Excellent. And miscellaneous other projections as deemed suitable, so perhaps Selene would be a projection, and then lots of dappled light from gobos for moonlight in the forest. I was looking over parts of a long poem by Keats on the subject, and while it's horribly full of references to every imaginable god, goddess, hero, and piece of vegetation, there are some bits that would set the scene well on that side of the stage. Of course, Keats would have to be credited in the program, but his work is in the public domain so we can plunder it without paying royalties to his publisher."

"You are remarkably thorough," said my companion. "What are you thinking of for the present-day side?"

"Well, I'm not entirely sure yet. The idea is still forming. I'm sure you could contribute to its development."

"That's quite possible," said he. "And does this piece have any music?"

"Not yet, but it would, of course."

"Endymion's sheep could be suggested with the use of those lamb-baa toys. You know the ones? You turn them over and they *baa*. Or *moo*. Or impersonate whatever animal they are."

"Do you think it really needs sheep?" I inquired.

"Who knows? A little lamb-baa might be just the right touch."

"I'm dubious about that, but we can leave the possibility open."

"Well, it could certainly have regular music as well as sound effects. It could start off with Stephen Foster's 'Beautiful Dreamer,' with a few minor adjustments to the lyrics."

"My god, you're full of bizarre ideas tonight," I said.

"Bizarre ideas, you say? Well, maybe, maybe not. You don't want to get too serious with this thing or it won't seem serious enough in the real sense. I like this outline, I think it has considerable potential, but it's not a tragedy, is it?"

"Presumably not," I said, "although a person can't help wondering what goes through Endymion's mind as he lies there sleeping year after year. I think part of the thing needs to involve his dreams. There can be a voice-over of him recounting his dreams."

"Splendid. Very sexy."

"Not *too* sexy, it's theater."

"You can be pretty sexy in avant-garde theater," he said.

"Well...true."

"So—his dreams remain to be invented."

"On the whole, yes. But they would make a nice contrast to selections of Keats and scenes of the modern-day story."

"Which also remains to be invented."

"Yes."

"Well, I think this is very promising, and unless you have more brilliant ideas about Endymion to tell me, I think it is time to go dancing."

During the course of our dinner and conversation, I had almost forgotten the plan to go dancing. Now I became mildly nervous. We hadn't discussed the dancing at all. It had been several years since I had danced and I was suddenly afraid that we would go to some kind of rap club where I didn't like the music and had no idea how to dance to it.

"Where did you have in mind?" I asked. "What kind of dancing are we talking about?"

"Oh, I don't know—a little swing, a little waltz, the Charleston—kind of depends on what the band plays, doesn't it?"

I was distinctly alarmed. "I don't know how to do any of those dances," I said.

"Aw, sure you do," he said.

"No I don't," I said. "I've never learned any of those dances that involve knowing steps." This was quite true, since even when we did square dancing and folk dance in grade school, I was completely baffled, and we certainly didn't learn other types of dance.

Endymion looked at me with a kind of pained disbelief, as if I could not possibly be serious. "Well, what kind of dancing do you do?"

"Normal ordinary make-it-up-as-you-go-along kind of dancing," I said. That was what everyone my age did, and had always done. That was the baby-boomer contribution, what the older brothers and sisters and cousins had pioneered in the sixties and what my cohort had accepted as natural. Some people did learn the Hustle during the brief days of disco, but not all that many of us. A few people later got into ballroom dance or folk dance or historical dance, but those were very niche preferences that inspired envy more than emulation. They seemed very esoteric to most of us; where were you likely, if you learned that sort of thing, to find anyone else who could do it? I knew some folk-dance enthusiasts through my theater contacts, but they were all experts; they put on shows and charged admission. And while I was aware that there was a bit of a resurgence of swing, I didn't know much about it because my husband hated to dance and didn't like it when I danced with anyone else. Besides, I had assumed that the revival of swing was entirely the province of people under twenty-five. Which was, of course, why Endymion knew all about it.

And Endymion looked almost comically dismayed. "What, you just sort of shamble along to the Grateful Dead?"

"I have never in my life 'shambled along' to the Grateful Dead," I said. "People usually like the way I dance. I try to make it interesting. Don't you ever make up what you're doing?"

"Of course. Dancers need to be able to improvise. But I like doing what you call 'dances with steps.' They include improvisation." He gestured expansively. "Well, you can learn some dances tonight. You have the easy part—following is intuitive. If you pay attention and have a good lead, you'll grasp what to do even if you don't know all the steps."

"I'm not so sure," I said. "It always looks very difficult."

"Don't set up ridiculous barriers for yourself," he said. "I'm sure you'll pick it up fast if you don't think too hard about it. It's not about mental thinking. It's like walking: you don't normally think about how to put one foot in front of the other, you just pay attention to where you need to go and shift your balance as needed."

"Well, maybe, but I did have to learn to walk once upon a time. I'm sure it wasn't easy at the time."

"Oh, it wasn't that hard. When babies are developmentally ready to walk, they want to walk and most of them are on their feet in a hurry. They wobble a bit for a while, but next thing you know they're running. You must not have any nieces or nephews. Humans are designed to walk, run, and dance. Get up and we'll go prove it."

I sighed and let him pull me out of my chair. I did want to learn, I was just afraid of stepping on both our feet and looking stiff and stupid.

SARAH

My aunt did not usually pay much attention to Kari Zilke's comings and goings, but she confided, with a mischievous look, that Kari had spent the night out.

"So?" I said. I was more intrigued by Kari than I liked to admit, but I did not think it was appropriate to start watching her movements like we were some kind of nosy old busybodies.

"An old friend of hers died, so she went to the memorial service, but afterwards she got talking with someone," said my aunt with some satisfaction.

I threw my hands in the air. "And why is that important? I'm sure she must know at least a few people here and there."

My aunt looked at me as though I were an immature person who understood very little about life. Which may have been correct, but it was annoying. "Kari has been a sad and lonely person, but I think now she'll start coming out of it," she said mildly. "She lost a friend who meant something to her, but she's found someone who interests her."

I sometimes felt that my aunt's interest in the renters' personal lives, even though it was polite and restrained, was simply a little much. Here she was, imagining a whole scenario about our renter and her feelings, and on what basis?

"How can you invent all this stuff?" I exclaimed. "Okay, so one of her friends died. I'm sure she's sad, but where do you get all the rest of it? You imagine whole lives for these people, out of nothing."

My aunt sighed. "Sarah, you pay so little attention to others sometimes. You have a kind heart, but you don't listen to it. You refuse to notice other people's feelings, even when they're obvious. And even when you notice, you want to forget it right away. You didn't want me to rent to Kari because you thought she'd be a problem. You saw that she was unhappy. But now that she hasn't been a problem, you don't want to remember that you saw she was unhappy. Sarah, you'll have a very hard time in life if you don't notice other people's feelings. Oh, my dear, you try so hard to do the right thing and treat people nicely, but if it doesn't come from within, it will just keep you apart from them."

Well, really. My aunt rarely lectured me, because as she said I do try to do the right thing and treat others well, but it was very irritating and uncomfortable to be told I behave like some kind of heartless bitch who ignores other people's feelings, just because I thought she was making up a big story about Kari Zilke.

"It's none of our business if Kari goes to funerals and stays out carousing at the wake with her friends, or whatever she was doing. Actually, if she didn't come home all night, I'm surprised you weren't worrying that she'd met up with a serial killer. But that's beside the point, evidently she came home in one piece." I changed tack, thinking we'd beaten this topic into the ground. "You didn't ask what I did today," I said. "I'm going to work on a new set of pieces, with a guitarist this time."

"A guitarist!" said my aunt, falling in with my change of subject. "That's unusual, isn't it?"

"Yes," I said. "It's even more unusual than I thought. People have written for guitar and different combinations of strings, but guitar and cello is uncommon and not much of the music has been recorded."

"That sounds very exciting," said my aunt. "Who's the guitarist? Is it another student?"

"I suppose he is," I said. "Another cellist put us in touch. He seems pretty knowledgeable, and he plays well. I think it will be fun."

"That's lovely," said my aunt. "You'll have to tell me more when you get further into the project. Is he nice?"

"I suppose," I said. Was Joey Caro nice? Well, I had no reason to believe he wasn't. "He seems nice enough. I'm sure I can work with him. He's a serious musician."

My aunt smiled. "You should get to know him, then. It won't hurt you to get to know a few nice young men."

Oh, I was glad my aunt didn't usually turn things in this direction. I could tolerate it once in a while, which was how often she tried it, but I was very glad that she wasn't one of those people who harp on the need to find a mate. Since she had never married, I assumed she had some understanding of how tiresome the topic could be, but I knew she thought I would be better off if I found a boyfriend. My aunt had had a boyfriend once herself, but he had died in Vietnam. If she had had any subsequent boyfriends, I hadn't heard about them. She claimed she was particular, and I suppose this was true. You don't often hear about women whose only boyfriends died in Vietnam. Carrying the torch for someone dead for thirty years isn't common these days, and I wasn't even that sure that my aunt still pined for the guy. Bob. What a funny, old-fashioned name. Only old guys are named Bob. Or Dick, a worse name. But my aunt had loved her Bob while he lasted, and she thought I should find a Robert or Justin or Nathan. I wasn't in any hurry, though.

KARI

Endymion took me to an establishment not far away that apparently hosted much dancing of various kinds; its flooring was all hardwood, one wall was mirrored, the other walls were marked by piles of jackets and street shoes, and a band was playing in one corner. There were many dancers, and while most were young, some were at least as old as I was and a few were much older. They were not all doing the same thing at all, but they all looked very competent and full of energy. It was simultaneously daunting and enticing. I wanted very much to be able to do what they were doing, but it seemed unlikely that I could possibly learn this without years of practice.

"I feel quite unsure of myself," I confided, I hoped not loudly enough for anyone but Endymion to hear me. "They're all so good."

"Oh, stop worrying about it," he said. "You can do this. We won't start with anything complex. You're a theater person, you've done some kind of movement exercises at some point. Well, we'll just start off to the side and get used to moving together."

So we went to an unoccupied corner and began mirroring each other to the rhythm of the music, an exercise which does indeed force a couple to learn to move together and which is very difficult with some partners and strangely magical with others. With Endymion, our tendency to lock eyes made the movements paradoxically easier; focused on each other's gaze, only our peripheral vision tracked our movements. As we were, to some extent, dancing, we didn't fully mirror one another as in the standard theater exercise, but mirrored our hand movements and to some extent our heads and torsos. Rather than letting my eyes race around trying to keep track of whatever he did, I concentrated on our steady, intent gaze, and everything else followed remarkably well.

We did this for what seemed a very long time—fortunately the band was going straight from one piece to the next—and then Endymion stepped forward, took my hand, and moved us into a basic sort of dance position, all in time with the music. Since he was not much taller than I was, it was not too difficult to keep a similar kind of focus, although we were no longer locked in an unbroken gaze. And to my surprise, I found I had little trouble continuing to follow his movements, even though I had no idea what kind of dance we were doing.

At first we simply circled around, very plainly, but that went well, so he began to lead me into doing turns. I didn't always spin around exactly on cue or always return to him with complete grace, but on the whole these attempts were successful, so we did more and more of them. I began to feel very pleased with myself, and much in awe of my teacher. How had he learned so many things and gained so many skills already? It is true that when I was his age, I too knew quite a few things and had a respectable number of skills, but I was always terribly aware of all the things I didn't know and couldn't do, and most of the people who understood more than one or two of the things I knew or could do were older people like Marty and his friends, which was one reason I had ended up with such a collection of elderly comrades. Endymion did not seem to suffer from any sense of insufficiency about whatever it was he didn't know (had I ever seemed that confident?), nor did he seem at all hesitant about spending an evening publicly dancing with a woman on the verge of turning forty.

"Well," said Endymion when the band finally stopped for a break, "I think you'll agree I was right. You can dance perfectly well."

"Not *perfectly*," I said. "Better than I expected."

"Perfectly in the sense of satisfactorily. You know how to move, you're learning how to follow. Learning the details will come. Since we're being so educational, I think that after the break you should dance with some other people, because you need to learn to follow other people's cues too."

That didn't please me. I didn't want to dance with strangers when I already had a good partner to learn with. "I'd rather just dance with you tonight," I said.

"No, that's not how it's done," said Endymion. "It's time to share. We can dance together some more later in the evening."

"But I don't know anyone else here," I said.

"That doesn't matter at all. People have seen you dancing with me, so they've seen you in action and they'll ask you pretty quickly. Or you can ask them, it doesn't matter. It's not like some kind of old-fashioned high school dance where all the girls stand around like idiots watching all the boys standing around *being* idiots."

"Well…" I said doubtfully. I really didn't want to test my skills with anyone else yet, but as soon as the band started up again, Endymion wandered off and got someone else out on the dance floor. The two of them did much more complicated things, and I was feeling grumpy and sorry for myself when someone came up and invited me to dance too. I agreed with a warning that I wasn't very experienced at this, and we went on out and gave it a try. It was true I didn't dance as well with my new partner as with Endymion, but I didn't step on his feet too frequently, and on the whole the experiment was a success. My new partner was kind enough to dance with me for ten minutes or so and helped me practice some turns, so it wasn't an overwhelming surprise when I got additional partners subsequently. Some of them were much easier to dance with than others, but enough of them were all right and undemanding enough of me that I developed some degree of confidence, even though I could see Endymion practicing all kinds of elaborate maneuvers with his other partners, some of whom it appeared he already knew very well. By the time he returned to me, I was very sweaty and well exercised, but ready for more.

"You seem to be doing very well," he observed. "I didn't see you standing around much."

"Well, I do like to dance," I said, "I just haven't done this kind of dancing before. I was glad people came up and asked me, because I don't really like asking strangers to dance."

"Yes, you put all the burden on your partners there," he said.

"No," I said, "I believe both men and women should do the asking, but I'm only used to asking people I know. I'm well aware of the unfairness of expecting men to do all the asking. But they're much too quick to say no, too."

"Well, it doesn't look like anyone has been saying no on either side tonight. Are you going to ask me to dance or are you waiting for me to ask you?"

"I will ask you, I think," I said, "since you hint that you would like to be asked."

"I always like to be asked," he said. So I took his hand and we returned to the dance floor.

Now that it was getting toward the end of the evening, and we were both well warmed up, our dancing took a different direction. Endymion was now less focused on teaching me via easy steps, and expected me to follow him with less direction. At the same time, our dancing became more sensual. My attention was, again, fully attuned to his movements, in a way that I realized it had not been to those of my other partners. I was purely and completely focused, unaware of anything external. We were dancing more closely, responding to slight but firm hand pressures on each other's backs. It was glorious, somewhat like good sex but different, of course. And like good sex, I wanted it to go on and on.

But the evening was coming to an end, or the dance portion anyhow, and the band played its last encore. Everyone milled around talking and collecting jackets, but we didn't linger; we walked out into the cool evening, where this time there was no rain in the street.

"That was fun," I said. "I'm glad we went."

"See? You should pay attention to what I say."

"I do," I said, aware that I would detest hearing this from anyone my own age unless he was very obviously joking, "but why do you say that? You should pay attention to what I say too."

"As you know I do," he said. "But you have to pay attention to what I say because that's what you *need* to do."

"You must be crazy," I said. "What're you talking about?"

"That's where you are right now, or that's the impression I get. You need to pay attention to *me* so that other people will pay attention to *you.*"

"Aw, bullshit," I said.

"You're not paying attention," he said.

"Okay, but what are you saying?"

"When we were dancing, you were paying attention. We were both paying attention. And it worked, no?"

"Yes."

"Well, there you go. Pay attention to people who matter to you."

We walked on for a moment. "I don't know why you matter to me, but you do," I admitted.

"You know why," he said. "You just aren't putting it into words."

"I'm not in love with you," I said hastily. Not to generalize, but men hate to be fallen in love with.

"Don't be trite," he said. "That's not what it is."

"Well, if I were Selene and you were Endymion…"

"That's desire. Since when does Selene pay attention to anything but Endymion's beauty?"

"It's still a powerful myth."

"Yes, but you want more from me than sex."

"How do you know that?" I said, dangerously. Sometimes I say things that are beyond unwise. But sometimes I have to push things to their limits.

Endymion fixed a look of utmost skepticism upon me, from the corner of his eye. "Because I am not stupid," he said. "You know in your heart, and I know in mine, that something in you matches something in me. Maybe we'll fall in love, and we'll probably have sex, but it's something else. We're going to collaborate, right?"

"Yes," I said, relieved, "you're right. I did know that." I turned to him, in the street, and we looked at one another seriously, for a long time. "Maybe I do love you!"

He tried not to laugh. "Aw, you wanna jump my bones."

Then we both laughed.

SARAH

My aunt had had, briefly, her Bob; my mother had had, presumably, Tom, Dick, and Harry. I met a couple of her high school beaux at her funeral, but since I was ten years old at the time, I wasn't receptive to stories about the high school dances they had attended or about how they used to make out at football games. I suppose these were nice enough boys, or at least my aunt seemed glad to see them at the funeral, but their memories of my mother had nothing in common with mine and didn't seem like much I wanted to hear about. I remember hearing them say, like my aunt, that she was sweet and pretty and fun to be around. And I didn't care if she was sweet or pretty or fun, because she was my bad mother.

I don't think I saw Eli the poet after I was old enough to talk. Or at least old enough to remember talking. I'd gathered that he was around for a while, and then was gone. Whether there was a fight, or whether one or the other party just up and left, I didn't know. What I remember is that my mother called various bearded characters "my old man" and that I called them names like Sam, Rick, Dave, and Donny. I suppose they weren't bad in their way; they didn't mistreat me, at least not intentionally, and they were usually friendly. But they were pretty nebulous. I didn't know them well then and I wouldn't recognize them now. My mother and her friends saw me, I think, as a special type of pet. It didn't cross their minds that I understood much of anything they said, and of course a lot of what they did say was completely baffling to me, but all the same I did understand a lot of the words, just not what they meant by them. They thought I was cute and fun to watch, but nobody liked to change my diaper and nobody bothered to take me to play with other kids. I suppose all this didn't bug me much when I was a toddler, but I wasn't happy about it once I began to realize that my life was peculiar, and once I had to go to kindergarten, where it became glaringly obvious that the other kids had a completely different way of life.

It's possible that my kindergarten teacher would have intervened and told Child Protective Services that I was neglected, but before anything like that could happen, my mother completely lost her marbles and the people she lived with recognized that this was a situation beyond their capacities, and so my aunt, who had already spent a couple of years taking my grandparents to chemo and radiation treatments that hadn't done them any good, stepped in and became my guardian and arranged to have my mother committed.

I overheard someone say once that somebody had given my mother a PCP-laced joint and that that was what screwed her up, but I don't know if that's true. My aunt says she doesn't remember anyone saying that. It could be that my mother was just destined to end up locked up.

KARI

When I left my husband, I really had no plan for anything but starting afresh. I had no plan to return to theater, and certainly no plan to pick up younger lovers. I simply wanted to put myself in a neutral state that would enable me to find which way to turn. I could look back on my twenties and see who I was then—a person I mostly thought well of but didn't want to be quite like again—and I could look back on my thirties and see a different self that, despite its many good qualities, definitely had to be left behind. I hadn't intentionally left behind the self of my twenties, but I was very intentionally abandoning the self of my thirties in favor of whoever or whatever might come next. It was a leap in the dark, but one I had to make before I lost my nerve.

And here I was, walking down the street with Endymion, so much younger than I was yet appearing so much more sure of himself—was it the confidence of youth, or something else?

"Are you a magical being?" I teased him.

"Naturally," he said. "I told you that before. I'm a magical being whose name is a secret."

I ran my fingers down his backbone as he unlocked the door to his building. "I am in your power, but you're also in my power," I said.

"Exactly," he said. "Collaboration works that way."

"Does that ever make you nervous?"

"No. Global warming, people with guns, and thoughts of nuclear war make me nervous. Collaboration doesn't."

"It doesn't make you nervous to entrust your ideas to other people's skills and interpretations?"

"Not particularly. If something doesn't work with one person, or one group, I can try it with someone else. But I haven't done anything big. I haven't done anything quite like this theater piece you're talking about. That's exciting. And it could get scary. It would be a one-shot chance to make it work."

"Are we really going to do it?" I said, like someone asking if she was really going steady or really going to rob a bank.

"Damn, Kari, you're loony! Why wouldn't we?"

"Just checking," I said.

"Listen," he said, taking my hand. "You have interesting ideas. I have friends who know some of your friends. People wondered where you went. You made a big impression on them and then really dropped out."

I said nothing. I knew there were people who liked me and who liked my ideas, but surely he exaggerated.

"Well," he said, "I want to see what we come up with. I have ideas, too, and I like to have someone to bounce them off of, especially someone who knows what I'm talking about and whose ideas give me new ideas."

I still said nothing. We were standing in front of the door to his apartment, and he hadn't unlocked it because he was still holding my hand.

"You're not saying anything," he said. "Talk to me. What do you want?"

I looked at him standing there beside me. His hair curled down over his shoulders, and his clothes, while not wet this time, were slightly damp with sweat and fitted him closely. I knew he wanted me to say something intellectual and creative; brilliant, even. But I didn't feel brilliant just then. I felt a great tenderness toward him, conceivably even a precursor to falling in love.

"The moon is full. I want to fuck your brains out, Endymi-on."

SARAH

Joey Caro was not exactly my type, no matter what my aunt might hope. His hair was too long and his looks in general were too scruffy. He was also shorter than I am, although that's trivial and I've always disliked hearing other tall women refuse to consider men who were under six foot. But when you consider that most younger white and Black men these days are tall, maybe it's not too much to ask.

But, of course, I wasn't rehearsing with him with intentions of any non-musical type of attachment. And other than his occasionally being a few minutes late—no more than anyone else I knew—he was a reliable and generally satisfactory partner. He was clearly very intelligent and hardworking, and now and then we got into conversation after our practice sessions. We sometimes sat in the café where we'd first met, having a snack and talking about music.

Joey liked the same kinds of music I did, but it was clear that for him this was only a starting point. He spent quite a bit of time in the music library, where he worked part-time, investigating the CD and LP collections. He also liked to go to stores that had a good selection of used CDs and flip through the bins looking for things he'd never heard of, which he could buy cheap and sometimes sell back later. The things he listened to made Kari Zilke's box of LPs look limited, but to some extent they liked the same kinds of things: a little of almost anything. Most of the other musicians I knew, or at least most of those I had visited, had more cohesive collections: usually a big classical section, sometimes with a jazz section or a batch of whatever bands they had liked in high school, and maybe some other quirky things like show tunes or film scores or African music. Joey had some of all of that, and more, from the sound of it. Now and then he even lent me something to listen to on the bus, but most of what he lent me was a little too offbeat for my taste. I wasn't sure whether he wanted to convert me to his kind of musical tastes, or whether he just thought everyone he knew would be equally excited when he found a CD of Central Asian throat singing or of Scott Joplin's opera *Treemonisha*. It was all interesting enough, just not music I was likely to want to hear over and over.

KARI

"You want to do *what?*" said Endymion, evidently surprised by my phrasing.

SARAH

Mostly, though, I only saw Joey when we met to rehearse, because our duets were only one of what were apparently many things occupying his time. He took lessons; he gave lessons; he worked in the music library; he dug up scores and recordings; he carried around a copy of the *Ramayana* to read on the bus; he mentioned films he had seen; I'm sure that all that was only the tip of the iceberg. I couldn't imagine how anyone could fit all the things he seemed to do into one life. For me, music, some reading, a part-time job at a copy shop, and an occasional movie filled up the time pretty thoroughly. A person does have to sleep, after all.

KARI

I traced the outline of his face with one finger and said, "I want to do everything. I feel tired and happy and full of energy all at the same time. I want to do this play with you, I want to know what your ideas are, I want to experience everything. I want it all. I want your mind *and* your body. Open the door, Endymion, that I might love thee."

He was not, I think, quite expecting any of this. He had gotten just slightly used to telling me what to do in my moments of uncertainty, and I for that matter was not really in the habit of throwing my weight around with men since experience shows that most of them don't like it, but I had the strong and almost mystical sense that we were equals, and more than that, we were bound to each other like Picasso and Braque in 1907, which was when they invented cubism together as an inseparable team. Endymion and I were bound to one another now, and for the first time since I had met him, I saw a glimmer of alarm pass over his face as he grasped the power of the goddess flowing through me and realized that I too was a magical being. It was only a brief glimmer, though, because he is strong and had willingly chosen to throw in his lot with me.

"Beloved, your light is bright," said he, "almost as bright as day. Allow me to undo the lock."

We went through the door and kicked off our shoes and stood in the moonlight that streamed in through his window, gazing intently at one another.

"You are mine," I said—not something I had ever said to anyone ever before, no matter how much in love I was with them or they with me.

"I am yours," he said, "but you are also mine."

"Yes," I said. We leaned toward each other and kissed for the third time. This time we pressed our bodies close. I had felt his body close to mine when we danced, but this was intensified. Embraces differ, even with the same person, and this one added up the anticipation, the close synchrony of our dancing, and the excitement of our collaborative energies, with perhaps the radiant lunar erotic energy of the goddess Selene and her dazzling consort. It made me simultaneously hyper-aware and on the verge of fainting.

"Do," said Endymion, "what you will with me. Make me yours."

SARAH

Sometimes I got tired of Joey Caro's enthusiasms, which were so numerous and went so far beyond my own. He would ask me if I'd heard of something, or considered doing something, and nearly always my answer was no. I may have misled him a little because once or twice he saw me carrying books Kari Zilke had lent me, books that were not really my type of thing. Still, I didn't pretend to be anything other than what I was. I don't fake being more intellectual or more cosmopolitan or more of a glittering conversationalist than I really am. I'm just a young musician starting my career, not any kind of brilliant prodigy. But I did find Joey interesting. He was likable; you couldn't really not like him, because he was smart and enthusiastic, and because he was generous in his enthusiasms. He made a person curious what he'd come up with next. And he was nice to me; he included me in bits of his world without having unrealistic expectations about me or taking it amiss when I was ignorant or not very interested. He offered up his enthusiasms for me to share, but he didn't nag me to join in or get dismissive of me when I didn't. He didn't tease me, or at least not very much. So I began to tell myself that probably I would like at least a few of the things he told me about. It was just a question of which ones. After all, I liked our duets.

KARI

I kissed him again. We melted into each other. His body had a different feel than I had known in recent years: the firm, springy feel of healthy youth. I suppose that I must have embraced bodies like that in my own healthy youth, but each person is so different: skinny and stringy, round and plump, hard and muscular, bouncy, squishy, soft-skinned, rough-skinned, fine-grained, coarse-pored, smooth, hairy, and on and on. It wasn't that I had so many people in my past or wanted to make comparisons, as that I simply found myself rejoicing in his particular feel, which at that moment seemed uniquely perfect to me, even through his clothes. No wonder he qualified as Endymion. I began to pull up his T-shirt in order to feel his skin directly: his warm, firm back against my palms and fingers. My dress became a disadvantage, with no detachable top to pull up in order to press skin to skin, but we could take our time.

I kissed his throat and the top of his shoulder; I moved slowly down his torso, discovering the various textures of his skin along the front of his body. The smoothness of the skin itself, alternating with patterns of hair that invited my hand to explore, followed by my lips and tongue…ah, splendid. After a moment I stood again and we moved slowly, like tango dancers in a trance, toward his bed.

"Endymion," I said, "you are indeed lovely in the moonlight."

Sarah

"You know, Sarah," said Joey one day after our practice session, "you're a good musician, but what on earth do you do with yourself when you're not practicing?"

"What do you mean?" I said. I was a little insulted, because he sounded like he thought I didn't do anything at all, or had no other interests whatsoever. Like I curled myself into a ball and slept in a little cave whenever I was out of his sight.

"You talk only about music, and the things you say about music do keep to the surface, as if you were always at a lesson figuring out your fingering and phrasing. It's a little peculiar, that's all."

"What do you expect me to talk about?" I said. "We're musicians, and besides, we don't know each other all that well."

He looked at me as if this were a bizarre answer that confirmed I hibernated in a cave most of the time. "Well," he said, "we'll probably never know each other very well, then."

"I didn't say we *never* would," I protested; *never* seemed excessive. I had been kind of enjoying the process of getting acquainted with him, and it hadn't occurred to me that there was anything wrong with the way we talked. It had been perfectly fine with *me*.

"Oh," he said. "Well, I suppose you baffle me a little. Usually when I work one-on-one with someone, we develop a certain degree of closeness."

"Closeness!" I said. "What *kind* of closeness?" If he was trying to proposition me, he could give up right there.

"What kind of closeness do you think?"

"Look, I'm here to practice, not to fool around."

"You're awfully defensive. Why are you afraid of being as close to me as—oh, I don't know, as my friend Julio who jams with me every week? Or as close as anyone else I spend this much time with? I mean, okay, I was a little disappointed that Wanda didn't have time to do the duets, because I was, well, kind of attracted to her, but that's beside the point. That was about her, not about whether you'd be good to work with."

It hadn't even crossed my mind that he might have been attracted to Wanda. Now I began to wonder if he had come up with the whole duet idea in the hopes of pursuing her, and then gotten stuck with me. I wasn't going to ask about that. He could still run after Wanda in his free time. "That's none of my business," I said severely.

Now he was really looking at me as though I had dropped from another planet. "I'm only saying that I usually get to be friends with people I work closely with. Being kind of attracted to Wanda doesn't have much to do with whether I can work well with you."

"That's exactly what I'm saying."

"Well, not exactly, no, but I'll take it as agreement. This is what I'm getting at, though. This conversation we're having right now, which I find a fairly weird exchange, is probably the most intimate conversation we've ever had."

"I'm not trying to be intimate with you," I said. "I'm not trying to be intimate with anyone, thank you."

"Evidently not," he said. "And I'm not used to talking to people who define closeness and intimacy purely in terms of sex, which it sounds like you do."

"This conversation is beginning to bother me," I said, because there are times when you really have to set limits with people.

"It's certainly beginning to bother *me*," he said. "Why are you twisting around everything I say to make it sound like I'm some kind of creep who invades your privacy and has an advanced degree in sexual harassment? We don't have to be friends if you don't want. We don't even have to keep practicing the duets."

"I don't understand why we're having this conversation," I said. "I was enjoying working with you and we were getting to know each other in a perfectly normal ordinary way, but something about that doesn't satisfy you. Well, I'm not stopping you from seeing Wanda." As I said this, I had a sudden vision of Wanda herself. Wanda has long straight hair and the sort of curvy figure that most women could only achieve with a corset and some padding. I supposed she was often subject to men wanting to follow her around. She was pretty by almost any standard I could think of.

Joey didn't seem any more content than before. "I was a little hesitant about you when we first met, but there was something intriguing about you too. You seemed a little uptight but I had the feeling you were worth getting to know anyway. Are you?"

"That's a strange question to ask. Why wouldn't I be?" Immediately, though, I began to wonder whether people looked at me and concluded I was boring. "What are you getting at?"

"Well, right now I feel like I'm meeting all your most messed-up aspects. I'd rather meet your best side, whatever that is. There must be more to it than just being able to play music and hold relatively mundane conversations about why you like Mendelssohn. I assume there's something deeper going on in you."

"I am not messed up," I said. "Maybe you are."

He looked perturbed. "I'd rather understand what I like about you than get into a dumb pissing match about which of us is messed up."

Well, I just didn't know what to say to that, and to my great horror, I began to cry.

KARI

I cried out in pleasure, in joy, as we moved together; our voices came together; our rhythms were well matched—"Endymion!" I said. "Do you fuck this well in your sleep?"

"Only you can know," he said, laughing. "Right now I'm awake. I'm sure the experience is very different. I wouldn't participate in quite the same way. I wouldn't be likely to do… *this*…or *this*. Keep that in mind before you have me cast into eternal sleep."

I considered his activities, with vast, intense pleasure. "Mmm, I don't think I want to let you sleep. I like the way you do all these things. Pray continue."

SARAH

Joey looked at me, more gently I think, although it was hard to tell with tears in my eyes. I hate to cry—I'm sure everyone does, but most people manage not to—and I thought I had learned to be pretty good at avoiding situations where I might cry in front of other people. I get so incoherent and miserable, dripping tear after tear and snuffling and making horrible noises, that I'm just not fit to be seen. I completely lose any ability to carry on a conversation. I panic and feel like a baby. It's disgusting.

Joey continued to look at me for a while, as if he was trying to decide what to do, which he probably was, and I just stared at him through my tears, feeling trapped and awful. At last he said, "I'm sorry. Do you want a hankie?"

I couldn't say anything, I was too stuck in my tears, so I put out my hand even though I suspected his hankie of having spent a long time in his pocket collecting dust and lint and germs and possibly even grosser things than that. The hankie he put in my hand was colorful, with a pattern I couldn't even recognize as paisley until I'd used it to wipe my eyes, so I couldn't tell whether it was clean or dirty. Wiping my eyes didn't stop my tears, unfortunately.

"I'm sorry you're upset," Joey elaborated. He kept looking at me, intently, as though he expected to learn something about me, and that was intolerable so I put my head between my knees where I couldn't see him. After a moment he reached out and petted my hair as though I were a nervous animal. I didn't want him to do that, but I was too incapacitated to stop him. It wasn't so bad, I just didn't want anyone doing that. Other than my aunt, that is. She brought me up, so she can comfort me. But there I sat in the practice room with Joey slowly stroking my hair.

"I hate this," I finally managed to say.

"So I can see," he said. "Should I lead you to the bathroom to wash your face?"

"No!" I said. That would be awful. Everyone in the hallway would see me in this horrible state and wonder what had happened to me that I had to be led to the bathroom.

So we just sat there for a long time until I cried away whatever it was and could sit up again.

"I'm sorry you feel so bad," he said. "Listen, I'll walk you to the bathroom and you can pretend you got something in your eye and can't see."

I gave in and we went. I hoped he wouldn't be waiting outside the bathroom door when I came out, but he was.

"You look like you need a cup of tea or a hot chocolate or something," he said. "Let's get our stuff and go to the café."

Really, I just wanted to go home and go to bed, but I had other things to do that day, so I followed him and drank some chamomile tea, which did make me feel a little better. He stopped trying to get me to say anything and instead just kept an eye on me, asking if I wanted more tea, or anything to eat, and that sort of thing. After a while he said he had to meet his friend Julio. "You can come along if you want," he said.

"Why?" I said. I still couldn't say much for fear it would set me off again.

"Why not?" he said. "You might like him."

I didn't think that was very likely just then, no matter what Julio was like, because I didn't feel very well disposed toward anyone at that moment.

"I think you'd like him," said Joey. "Maybe not right away, but when you got to know him."

I didn't have to be anywhere for another couple of hours, so I gave in yet again and followed him.

KARI

Endymion and I began to plan out our play, or performance art, or theater piece, or whatever it was, in earnest. We decided to steep ourselves in anything and everything that might possibly relate, or be made to relate, or could inspire us; and at the same time, to leave ourselves open to whatever might strike us as useful, no matter how odd.

I began, for instance, to hunt up artists' depictions of the myth, which I carefully photographed out of art books. That is, I photocopied the first few for reference, and then realized that what I wanted was slides so that we could project these pictures as part of the set and lighting design. This meant I had to get hold of an old friend who had a camera stand and special lights, so that the results would be good and not have to be redone. My friend, who showed some signs of hoping to renew a long-dead affair between us, regarded my project with a mild curiosity but did not ask terribly many questions about it, which was exactly what I wanted at this stage of things, when the project was still relatively inchoate and difficult to discuss with anyone but Endymion.

Initially, as I looked at these pictures, it seemed obvious that the Girodet Endymion, even if lacking some details that might add to his perfection for the present-day viewer, was decidedly the most appealing of the artistic renditions. Compare it, for instance, to the baroque ceiling fresco by Orelli, which although charming enough in its rendering, shows a fully clothed and nearly awake Endymion curling himself around some boulders in a manner unlike any sleeping male I have ever seen. And Ricci's baroque painting removes most of the clothing but makes it seem that Endymion has collapsed in a heap at Selene's feet, with grotesquely contorted limbs that attempt to give the impression of languor but which merely look as though someone (perhaps a disciple of Pontormo) has bent him out of shape. Furthermore, I do not find that the addition of putti at all adds to the eroticism. The one hovering above in the Ricci painting looks poised to drop a seagull-like splodge on Endymion's head. Ugh.

As if these were not disappointing enough, there was Godward's unspeakable confection of 1893, which turns Endymion into a girl sleeping on a pile of skins on a palace floor. This travesty, while not *utterly* devoid of sex appeal, has no hint of masculinity and at most suggests a transgender torch singer sleeping it off after a show. But then, Godward's numerous Greek women all have faces like twelve-year-old boys, so what can I say. Their androgyny is sexier than that of the feminized Endymion.

The seventeenth-century gravure by Chauveau, on the other hand, has considerable emblematic appeal with its dramatic figure of Selene flinging up her hands in amazement, but Endymion himself is nothing special. Still, I thought Chauveau's image might work well on the program cover. But in my early researches, the only picture that came close to Girodet's was that by the obscure romantic painter Jérôme-Martin Langlois, which portrays Eros (or a random putto) displaying the sleeping beauty to a hovering Diana. Like Girodet's version, this nude Endymion reclines, stretching seductively, but alas, while the painter provides him with a pleasingly lifelike fuzz of golden fur on his legs and underarm, his brassy curls look patently fake with his dark eyebrows. Oh well. He is not bad otherwise.

It was not long before my collaborator and I came up with the beginnings of a scenario. At the outset, we decided, we'd show a projection of the Girodet painting onto a scrim at the back. The mythic Endymion would enter to the sound of—yes—a slightly revised version of Stephen Foster's "Beautiful Dreamer," followed by a bit of scene-setting lyricism from Keats. We'd use gobos to illuminate him with dappled pools of soft light; he'd lie down upstage to the sound of—yes, these too—some mechanical lamb-baas.

We'd then divide the stage, with a black-garbed stagehand

pulling the divider into place, and the present-day part of the play would begin.

My collaborator, despite having plenty of other responsibilities, spent time thinking about our music: when to have quiet guitar pieces, when to knock coconuts or rattle a thunder sheet a little, whether we might want panpipes or some other exotic instrument. It became clear to me that he was not only a skilled musician, but he had some theater experience and a knack for sound design. His ideas sometimes initially struck me as peculiar, like the lamb-baa and "Beautiful Dreamer," but it rarely took long before I realized how they would contribute to the final effect. We met every few days to go over what we had come up with, and afterwards we usually went dancing, which meant not only that my dancing improved considerably, but that I began to feel much more alert and cheerful the rest of the time, no longer wondering lugubriously what on earth was supposed to become of me during the rest of my life and whether I had bypassed and neglected every chance I'd had to do interesting things and lead a life worth living.

At the same time, I began to learn more about my companion. We did not go into the usual routine of telling one another everything about our selves and our histories as new couples generally do, perhaps because we didn't regard ourselves as a couple. What were we? The right term is elusive. We were lovers, true, but that wasn't the heart of it, so we didn't use that term, at least not to other people. In an earlier day we could have called ourselves partners, but that term was becoming standard for unmarried but seriously involved couples, and it prompted thoughts of phrases like "My partner and I just bought a house" and "My partner works in biotech," so we couldn't possibly call ourselves partners. We were collaborators, but the word was excessively long for frequent use and without a context it sounded as though we ought to be executed for helping the Nazis. So—we said we were friends, which was true, just a little generic. Friends working on a project together.

And as friends, naturally we did learn a lot about each other over time, just not in that headlong sharing of selves that characterizes new couples. There were many things we didn't learn, and we didn't keep close track of each other. We had our separate lives, which we pursued a good percentage of the time. I did not particularly want to bring anyone home to my rented room, so at most I took Endymion there once or twice, briefly, whereas his apartment was entirely his own and he liked to have me visit, whether for a few minutes or for hours and nights, and whether to talk or listen to music or see how long we could make love without getting tired or hungry. The latter, we said, was not just some form of tantric sex magic, although we thought it might be that too, but was fodder for Endymion's dreams, which we had to construct in a manner that would be compelling and sexy as theater but would not actually go so far that our play would run the risk of being shut down by the police.

We supposed that Endymion's dream narration could be relatively explicit, at least at times, so long as it was not accompanied by actions or images that were equally so. Thus, for instance, Endymion could dream that Selene wafted down naked from the clouds and licked every inch of his body like a mother cat washing a kitten, but such a dream could hardly be represented visually by some sort of still from a porn movie, while perhaps we could juxtapose photos of nudes and cats, flashing quickly out of the darkness at the moment of the simile. Or Endymion could dream, more startlingly, that divine beings other than Selene visited him and commented on his attractions. They could be represented by images of eagles (Zeus) or Botticelli's Venus, or the like.

In my search for suitable imagery for these dreams, I happened upon the work of an artist named Joan Semmel, who had done large paintings of lovers during the 1970s, in which the viewer sees the couples' bodies from the perspective of the woman as she looks out over her own and her lover's body. Some of the paintings were in relatively natural-looking flesh tones and others in bright colors, and while the paintings had been groundbreaking in the seventies, I did not think they would upset our end-of-the-century audiences. So we appropriated the Semmel paintings, or the idea of them—we weren't sure whether to use photos of the paintings themselves, which would involve contacting the artist, or to find someone else to create something similar and more dream-like. For the time being, we thought we would wait and see how many color reproductions we could actually find, and how suitable they proved to be.

In the meantime, we began to meet some of one another's friends and associates. Endymion played in a local band that performed, at rather sporadic gigs, experimental works by its members. In theory you could say it had the usual lineup of two electric guitars, bass, keyboards, and drums, but in practice the members played various instruments at various times and you could never be sure who would be playing what next. The other members—Rory, Evan, Ahmed, and Adam—were intelligent and thoughtful people whose spiritual kinship to Endymion was obvious and who immediately seemed to accept me as a part of their circle. When they first heard me call their comrade 'Endymion,' they laughed and immediately began to call him that too. It appeared that he had already told them about our project, but whether they knew more about our relationship than that was unclear to me. I assumed that they probably divined everything, but in case they did not, I avoided making anything too obvious. After all, I was never sure quite how people would react to my being an Older Woman even though I knew it was difficult for anyone to guess my age. I didn't want people taking Endymion aside and giving him lectures about how he ought to get out from under the influence of that cradle-robbing old broad. Mostly, though, he introduced me to people in regard to our project. We were both working on finding a venue to put on this piece of ours, and we both knew people who might have ideas, but his contacts were much more up to date than mine.

SARAH

Joey's friend Julio was an older Hispanic guy, short and sturdy, with gray-streaked hair pulled back in a ponytail. He was wearing a Hawaiian shirt, though not a particularly loud one, with jeans and huaraches. He didn't look like he cared whether he met me or not, although he said he was pleased to meet me. I was okay with that, because I didn't care whether I met him either, and just wanted to have a chance to settle myself down and forget about whatever strange internal meltdown had hit me earlier. I was afraid that if Julio wanted to talk to me too much, I might have another episode, one that would have even less relation to anything anyone said. At least with Joey, I knew that the direction of the conversation had begun to bother me. But maybe they would do most of the talking and I could just sit back and daydream, do some mental practice. People say that brain research shows mental practice benefits musicians almost as much as actual physical practice. This is good, because it's hard to carry the cello around everywhere, and also because pianists, for instance, can eventually get carpal tunnel from too much practicing.

Joey and Julio started talking about people they knew, none of whom were anybody I knew—what this one or that one was doing, who they'd seen lately, what films were playing at the different art houses. This all seemed like stuff I could ignore; I didn't know their friends, didn't know their projects, hadn't seen most of the films. They didn't exclude me from the conversation so much as that I didn't do much to join it. Instead, I sat on Julio's couch, which was draped with a Mexican blanket and some woven fabrics that I supposed were also Mexican, or possibly from somewhere else in Central America, and looked around. He had an interesting place, I had to admit. There were lots of photos and real paintings on the walls, and lots of plants and rugs. It was a comfortable place to sit, and even though there was a lot more red and orange in the color scheme than I usually like, somehow the result was relaxing.

After a while, Joey and Julio got out their guitars. They tuned for a minute, and Joey remarked that he didn't usually use this guitar when he played with Julio, because this was the one he liked to use for a more classical repertoire and it would need retuning. Then Julio settled his guitar on his knee and played a few chords.

"Something like that, eh, Joey?" he said.

"Sure," said Joey, repeating the chords.

"Okay, then," said Julio. He began to play, some sort of jazz that I really couldn't identify, and after a minute Joey joined in.

I'm not that fond of jazz. But I realize there are many varieties, and some I like better than others. My aunt likes some kinds of what I think of as lounge jazz, stuff that bores me silly. Anything with a marimba is practically a cue for me to tune out. And I don't like some of the flashier jazz; I don't usually like music that involves a lot of showing off—not even the cadenzas in classical pieces, where the composer intended the soloist to improvise but everyone now plays sections written by later arrangers. But there's jazz I don't mind, and now and then I hear jazz I even kind of like. While I couldn't classify Joey and Julio's jazz by type, I kind of liked it. It was meditative at one moment, lively at another. It used a lot of seven-chords, both major and minor, but beyond that it wasn't especially dissonant.

They played for quite a while without stopping, and I found myself listening more closely than I had expected. Finally they drew to a close, watching each other intently for the last minute or so, coming to their end together and then both bursting out laughing.

"Man, you're not so bad!" exclaimed Julio.

"Hey, I try!" said Joey. "You were seeing if you could throw me there, weren't you?"

"Nah, I wouldn't do that, would I?" said Julio. "Whaddaya think, Sarah? I wouldn't try to throw off my pal here in the middle of things." He grinned at me.

I shrugged. How would I know?

"You like to test me," said Joey. "Man, you like to test me."

"We don't play no rinky-dink stuff here," said Julio. "Whadd-aya think, Sarah? Was that any good?"

"It sounded fine to me," I said. "What's it supposed to sound like? I don't know the piece."

"What's it supposed to sound like? Like what you just heard, I guess. You don't know the piece 'cause we just made it up."

"Oh," I said. I felt like Julio was teasing me on this and that it wasn't completely fair, but it seemed to be friendly teasing. "I don't do much improvising. If you just made it up, that was pretty impressive."

"Shit, we do that all the time," said Julio. "Don't we, Joey?"

"Yep," said Joey. "We do. But Julio's the master," he said to me. "He keeps me from getting too wrapped up in sheet music."

"You got your band too," said Julio.

"Yeah, but that's different," said Joey. "Different music, different energy. We write the songs before we mess with 'em. We sit at home and write them out in Finale before rehearsal."

"Well," said Julio, "to each his own. Or her own. You don't like to improvise, Ms. Sarah?"

"I don't know," I said. "I don't think cellists improvise much."

"Aaah, cellists, I'm not talkin' about cellists, I'm talkin' about *you*. I don't care about the average cellist. You're not the average cellist, are you?"

"Well, I don't know," I said. "Maybe I am."

"She's not the average cellist, is she, Joey?"

"I hope not," said Joey. "Maybe that's something she has to figure out."

"I'm not the average guitarist, and neither is Joey here," said Julio. "We may not be the world's finest, but we have our little plan to take over the world."

I didn't know exactly what to say to that. What do you say to people who make that kind of joke?

"Dang, girl," Julio went on after a minute, "you're kind of the silent type, aren't you?"

"Don't bug her too much," said Joey. "I told her she'd like you, not that you'd give her a hard time. She plays classical music. She's pretty good."

"I ain't giving her a hard time," said Julio. He seemed to think that if he grinned at me from time to time, I wouldn't mind what he said.

"Yeah, you are," said Joey. "I already gave her a hard time today. She's had enough of that. Let's play some more. You liked that last one, didn't you, Sarah?"

"Yeah," I admitted. "It was good."

"So, we'll play another and maybe you'll like that one too. You could play with us if you want."

"No, I think I'll just listen. You were playing complicated stuff. I don't think I could keep up."

"We could do something easier," said Joey.

"Nah," said Julio. "She should listen first. She can play later if she feels like it."

"You're the boss," said Joey.

"So," said Julio, playing a few bars, "something like this?"

"Sounds good," said Joey. And they were off again.

I sat there feeling a little stupid, but not exactly bad. I didn't like Julio prodding me and teasing me, but some part of me liked him anyway. He was a good musician, no question about it. He knew things I didn't know and didn't understand. He was good in a tradition I wasn't very familiar with, and evidently he was teaching Joey how to operate in this other tradition. It even sounded like he was willing to teach me something about it, if I listened first and decided I was interested. I couldn't really imagine what jazz would be like with a cello, but I knew that was just my limited thinking because jazz violinists aren't unheard of and of course lots of jazz groups feature a string bass player plunking away. I've never really understood the appeal of string bass for the performer, but you can't deny that the instrument adds plenty of flavor.

I tried to listen attentively, and I did find myself liking this piece as well, but I found I had trouble concentrating. I realized that I was tired, so I let my mind stop trying to keep track of what they were doing and stopped analyzing the patterns and structures, especially after they started fooling around with shifting time signatures and going back and forth between triple and quintuple time. The shifting rhythms started messing with my ability to think straight, although I couldn't see why they should, and I started obsessively staring at the leaves of an aloe vera plant on an end table next to the couch, staring at the slight variations in color on the leaf surface and trying not to think how pointy and fierce the leaves were (if you could even call them leaves, since leaves should be fragile and aloe vera plants are thick and spiky). It occurred to me that this was probably the kind of experience my mother used to have on drugs, only for her the aloe vera plant would probably have moved and pulsated and turned different colors. I was glad the aloe vera wasn't doing anything like that, because it was too much for me even without moving and turning psychedelic colors. At last I forced myself to turn my gaze onto a nearby plant instead, a small, bulbous thing that I supposed was an unfamiliar type of succulent.

Eventually the piece came to an end and I realized Joey and Julio were giving each other some kind of high five and joking again about how Julio had been trying to lose Joey along the way.

"Oh, man, Julio, you are wicked," said Joey.

"No way, no way, you're no babe in the woods, I can't leave you anywhere, you just run right after me. You don't get lost, man, you try your own tricks on me. Don't give me no bull about getting lost."

"You are wicked, man," repeated Joey, laughing. They both seemed intensely pleased with themselves.

"We can jam, Sarah," said Julio, "for like two hours straight. We're sparing you. This is nothing."

"Oh my god," I said, "that must wear out your fingers, two hours without resting."

"Two hours? Nah. You practice more than that in a day."

"Not without breaks. I don't play two hours straight."

"Well, I'll tell you a secret," said Julio. "It's a big secret. You can't tell people." He lowered his voice. "We're *gods*."

I flopped back on the couch. "Gods. Oh my god."

Joey slapped Julio's arm. "You can't tell her these big secrets. She doesn't want to know that we're gods. Tell her to forget it right away. We're not divine beings, we're traveling magicians."

"Bull*shit*, we are gods," said Julio.

"Do we look like gods?" said Joey.

"Not in the least," I said from the depths of the couch.

"Well, we are gods," said Julio. "Don't listen to him, he's bullshitting you. We have the divine ichor in our veins. We drink ambrosia. That's why we play so good."

"Okay," I said. "You're gods."

"You don't believe for a minute that we're gods," said Joey.

"No," I said. "I'm just saying that to humor you guys."

"She's crafty," observed Julio.

"No," said Joey, "she's yawning. I think it's time to go. You had some other things to do today, right, Sarah?"

"Yeah, I do," I said.

"Well, we should go, then." He started putting away his guitar. "I'll see you again at the usual time, right, Julio?"

"Sure thing. Same bat-time, same bat-channel."

"I've got a project to discuss with you, but it can wait."

"Sure, whenever you want."

We went out and headed for the bus stop.

"Well," said Joey, "I don't know whether you liked him or not, but that's Julio."

"He's all right," I said. "He's a good musician. That's what counts."

"No," said Joey, "that's not what counts."

"No?"

"He's my friend. And besides, he *is* a god."

KARI

In my twenties I used to travel. Not very much, because I couldn't afford it, but as much as I could manage. I took car trips, went to Europe a couple of times. I would have traveled more if I'd had more money; I assumed I'd travel more once I did get more money, which of course I wanted to earn in my own way rather than by chaining myself to a day job. I've known people who traveled to Peru or Nepal; I always wanted to do it too, but after I got married, that idea evaporated. Not only was there no money, but my husband had no interest at all in travel. He used to tell me about his friends traveling to amazing places, and then say, "Isn't it nice not to have to do that?" I didn't know what to say to that.

Now, the thought of travel began to resurface: I wanted to go somewhere and see new things, feed my eyes and smell different scents. I still didn't have any money, but even a little travel was tempting, so when I happened to lament about this to Endymion and he proposed that we borrow a car and spend a night or two camping in the woods, I agreed instantly.

"I'd love that!" I said. "It's been ages since I did anything like that. When can we go?"

"Well, I might have to rearrange my schedule a little, but maybe this weekend. I'll let you know."

I was overjoyed. I began to imagine every possible kind of forest—primeval forests, oak forests, coniferous forests, redwood forests, birch forests, lodgepole pine forests, fall color forests, rain forests, forests full of sphagnum moss and lichen, petrified forests, kelp forests full of fish—there was no end to it. I envisioned birds, wild animals—squirrels, chipmunks, raccoons, deer, wolves, bears, wild boars—of course, I did not imagine wolves or wild boar would invade our campsite, but if I was going to imagine forests, I might as well imagine wolves and wild boars as well as squirrels and chipmunks. And perhaps a primeval darkness, or else a little clearing from which we could see the moon and stars…

"It's heavenly!" I exclaimed when we arrived, taking deep breaths of warm pine sap. "Can I ravish you immediately, Endymion, O handsome shepherd?"

He flung his head back and laughed. "You are not to be denied. But isn't the stillness splendid? Doesn't it bring to mind something like 'The Lark Ascending'? Just a flutter of movement high above the stillness?"

"I wish I could remember it. I know I like it, but I don't have your memory for specific works."

"Well, it might be more appropriate to an English meadow than to an American wood, but still, it's music for a sunny afternoon outdoors."

"I never heard a Vaughan Williams piece I didn't like. I wish it was coming back to me the way it does for you." I wrapped myself around him. "The scent of the woods intoxicates me. Everything intoxicates me. I'm ecstatic."

"There's no stopping an ecstatic goddess," he said, lifting my hair from my neck and making it seem to float in the air. "I am but a powerless mortal."

"But an awakened one."

"Decidedly."

It was a good thing no one else seemed to be anywhere nearby in the campground just then. It was a small campground, with just a few spaces. None of the tents were near ours, and no one seemed to be in any of them. I suppose all the other campers were hiking. Later on, after we too had gone hiking, the campground acquired voices and campfires. It had the evening charm of happy campgrounds, which we enjoyed as we roasted our dinner, but the convivial charm of a campground bore no relation to the myth of Endymion visited by Selene as he tended his sheep, so after a while we wandered off again, up a trail to a clearing where we could see the moon. We spread out a small blanket and laid ourselves in the moonlight; it was just warm enough that we could do this, just beginning to be balmy enough that we could pull off each other's clothes and not shiver as we lay awaiting or giving kisses on all the desirous parts, lifting each other into different positions, rocking back and forth together. Then, eventually, sated and sticky with each other's juices, we dressed and returned to our tent, where we slept curled neatly together.

Sarah

I wasn't sure what to think of my strange day with Joey and Julio. I couldn't understand what was going on with me that I let a few remarks upset me to the point of tears. Nor could I see why Joey pressed me about lack of depth in my conversation; what did he want from me? What did he think was so much deeper about his exchanges with Julio?

Musically, yes, I supposed he and Julio had a deeper connection. Not only had they known each other longer, but they had to have a more profound connection in order to invent whole new pieces together on the spur of the moment. They weren't just interpreting someone else's score, which takes enough skill and thought in itself. But I didn't hear anything notable in their conversation other than that they knew each other well. It wasn't a remarkable conversation, it was just two guys yakking and periodically teasing me a little. I didn't see what I was supposed to learn from that. I couldn't magically become an old friend, or another guy, or a teacher, or a better musician. I thought it was unfair of Joey to expect that he and I would have a working relationship similar to what he had with Julio. It was silly of him to call Julio a god, but it would have been a lot sillier if he'd begun calling *me* one.

Still, I felt a little discontented. Was Joey unreasonable or was I somehow not putting quite enough into our rehearsals? Was there some way that I should be connecting with him and wasn't? None of the other musicians I had worked with had complained, but it was true that I didn't have anyone special with whom I regularly worked; people worked with me on specific projects, but I had no ongoing long-term musical partners. No one suggested I join them in any lasting small ensemble. Did that mean that there was some lack in my contribution? I had to wonder.

KARI

I think we have a venue!" said Endymion. "I talked to a friend of mine who knows a friend of yours, and there's a new theater starting up, primarily to produce new works and especially experimental pieces. We could get ours into the lineup pretty quickly if we want."

"That's great!" I said. The script had been moving along well, as had other aspects of the piece, and I felt confident that everything would really begin to fall into place once we had a few actors to work with, some additional crew, and a specific space to work in and design for. "Do we know anything about the space?"

"I said we could come and meet with their people sometime this week and take a look and talk about the specifics. They have a small collective, which does have to agree on new projects, but it sounds like ours is likely to get approval. We could either direct it ourselves, have one of their members direct, or bring in an outside director, and the same is pretty much true for design."

"I think what I'd like is to have someone work with us on blocking and movement," I said, "especially on the present-day part of the script. We have a fairly good idea of a lot of the direction, but that's not really my strength. I'm open to suggestions."

"That sounds reasonable," said Endymion. "I'll set up the meeting since my schedule's trickier than yours."

A few days later we were looking around an old-fashioned proscenium theater, renovated to have a bit of an apron over the former orchestra pit.

"It's a removable apron," said one of the collective members, "in case anyone actually wants to use the pit. And it's got a trapdoor."

"That's pretty neat," said Endymion. "Flexible."

Carol, Steven, Matt, Gordon, Rhiannon, and Susan consti-tuted the collective. Rhiannon, the youngest, was Endymion's friend, and I knew Steven slightly from long ago. The group had been together for a year or so, but had only recently gotten a theater of their own, which would allow them to expand their activities.

"We had some successful productions right at the start, very low-budget stuff," Steven said, "so that helped us get some grant money. And now that we have the theater, we can slot in more productions, especially pieces that don't require much in the way of set and props, because of course those have to be found or built and then they take up space."

"We don't anticipate that this production would be unusu-ally heavy on set and props," I said. "Of course, it could end up with more than we think, but presently we're thinking of a relatively minimal set, probably mostly easy to store, since we'd rely heavily on lighting and projections. We want some kind of a hillock upstage for the Endymion character to recline upon, and a divider that could be rolled out or pulled out by one stagehand—something fairly light, maybe just a framework so that it would define the space without impairing visibility for audience members on the far right or left. As for props, I'm guessing most of them could fit in a box."

"Yeah," said Endymion. "Props will be things like a lineup of sheep that Endymion pulls behind him as he comes onstage—you know, like a pull-toy—and a similar lineup of archaic Greek maidens that will issue forth from an image of Selene when she gives birth to their fifty daughters. And about five of those lamb-baa toys that baa when you turn them upside-down. A chair or two for the modern characters. Well—that's set rather than props. Anyway, a table and a bed, or facsimiles thereof. They could have their bed down on the apron and it could consist of a down comforter or a quilt. It wouldn't have to be a bed-bed."

"Yeah, I like bedding them on the apron on something cushy," I said. "They can be stylized in their movements."

"You could represent them via shadows on the scrim," suggested Susan. "The actors could do stylized movements downstage on the apron in very low light and be echoed by much bigger, more visible shadows if we backlight another pair of actors behind the scrim. Like live shadow puppets."

"I like that," I said.

"We couldn't have as much depth to the stage that way since part of our depth would be lost to behind-scrim lights and all, but I think there might be enough to spare, given that the apron extends the downstage area."

We went on in this way for quite a while, throwing around ideas and jotting them down. It was clear the production was a go and that the collective was excited about it.

Sarah

"Is there something lacking in my playing," I asked my teacher, "that I should know about? I mean, something I should have at this stage but don't?"

My teacher looked at me with some surprise and pointed out that everyone progresses at a different pace. Did I have something particular in mind? What did I feel I was lacking?

"Well, that's the trouble. I don't know," I said. "I wondered what you thought."

Clearly, she hadn't been expecting me to start questioning her in this way. "What makes you ask?" she said after a moment.

"I'm not sure," I said, trying to decide just what to say. After all, Joey hadn't said there was anything wrong with my playing; it was my conversation that didn't satisfy him. And you could hardly make a rational case that there was something wrong with my playing if all you had to go on was my unsatisfactory conversation. But I felt like it bore some relation to my playing. "What do you think about the duets and ensembles I've been doing and how I work with others?"

"Well, I won't really be able to assess what you're doing until I hear you perform with the others. It all depends on how you work as a team, after all."

"Yes. Well, I do try to work well with others and pay attention to what they're doing, but I'm not sure they always think I am." That was it. That was the disconnect I was trying to get at. "For instance—well—the guitarist I'm working with—well—I was watching him improvise with another guitarist the other day, inventing whole pieces together, and in order to do that— well—um—they need to be really—um—really together in a lot of ways. I know it's a different kind of music, but…" I felt as though I was getting unusually incapable of saying anything clearly. Still, it's true I don't usually talk about anything very complex. I think about complex-enough things, I suppose, but I don't have much reason to talk about them. Maybe that was part of Joey's complaint, but while Joey is articulate, I didn't think his exchanges with Julio were any shining example of conversational brilliance.

"Improvising in that way is a real talent," said my teacher. "Still, it's also a skill that people develop with practice. We don't emphasize it in classical training, but even so, many classical musicians also devote time to improvisational genres. It's good to branch out and try different things. If you learn to improvise together with another person or in a group, that would have to have a positive effect on your ensemble work in general."

"I suppose," I said. It certainly made sense that this would be the case. Whether it would have any effect on my conversational skills was another question. I didn't want to think there was anything wrong with them, but maybe there was. I didn't plan to start spilling my guts to every musician I worked with, but I didn't like the idea of people thinking I was boring either. I'm not a big talker, and I dislike small talk when it goes beyond its purpose of priming the conversational pump, but I supposed I could say a little more and stick to things that sounded worthwhile, not babble a lot of trivialities.

"It sounds to me like you should do a little improvising," said my teacher. "You can always improvise in your practice at home, but if you want it to have an effect on your ensemble work, you'd better get experience in group improvisation. Maybe you can get your guitarist to help you."

"Well, maybe," I said. This made me nervous. I didn't want to have any more crying fits. I felt hesitant about the whole thing. But I do, also, think it's important to improve oneself.

KARI

The camping trip made clear to me, in the most physical and sensory way, that spring was upon us: that the vernal outdoors beckoned and blossomed. Thus I noticed, which I might otherwise not have, that my landlady was a gardener. Not a showy or exceptionally fine gardener, but one who was happy to get outside with her peonies and petunias, who planted masses of impatiens in the shade and marigolds in the sun, who along with these traditional favorites was trendy enough to add dazzling blue lobelias and purplish coneflowers next to the marigolds, and who had some foxgloves in rows by the fence and some tomatoes ready to train up the side of the house.

I missed gardening, so from time to time now I joined her in the yard and helped put in new plants or yank weeds or deadhead the roses. This pleased her; she said her tenants didn't often take an interest in the garden other than, maybe, to compliment it or say it must be a lot of work. It meant we got to know each other somewhat better, but we still kept a certain level of distance as far as what we revealed to one another. I knew that she was proud of her niece's talent and hard work, for instance, but she said very little about how her niece had come to live with her except that her niece's mother was long dead and no one knew what had become of the father. My landlady did also express occasional concern that her niece might be too single-minded in her pursuit of music; my landlady recognized that a serious musician has to practice a lot, but she thought her niece was strangely lacking in other interests.

"She reads," I said, not that I thought the niece read all that much, but enough to be curious about my own books.

"Oh, well…" said my landlady. "She reads the way she watches movies. She has some favorites, but she's not very interested in finding anything new. It wouldn't be surprising in an old lady, but I don't understand why anyone her age would be so stuck on the same old things. It seems to me she'd want to read all the new books and see all the latest movies and get a boyfriend or two and get into a little mischief. I'm glad she's grown up to be a serious person with a goal in life, but enough is enough. She's always been serious, and too much seriousness can't be a good thing any more than too little."

I agreed with her in principle, but I thought her niece was probably just getting into mischief that we didn't know about. Girls are good at getting into mischief, especially grown-up girls who lead fairly independent lives. Just because Sarah seemed like such a paragon of rectitude at home didn't mean she wasn't out there earning pocket money as a drug dealer or an exotic dancer. Well—I didn't think either of these were actually *likely*, and I didn't suggest that Sarah might be up to anything truly reprehensible or socially unacceptable, but I did think she probably got into more ordinary middle-class kinds of mischief. After all, don't most people in their youth? Or was Sarah waiting until she was in a position to move out of her aunt's house before she began drinking herself blind or participating in nameless orgies or going to raves or whatever struck her as the most liberating passage to an adulthood where she could settle back down to being a Terribly Serious Musician? It occurred to me that my landlady's niece must be nearly as old as Endymion, but she gave an altogether different impression. She gave the impression that she was mature because she was staid and intelligent, not because she was wise, I thought. Whereas Endymion looked young but otherwise gave no particular signal of his age, because he sought wisdom in his own inimitable, enthusiastic way. But I decided you could hardly compare the two. Endymion, I thought, was brilliant and sparkling. My landlady's niece was merely repressed, and who knew what lay under the surface?

"Well," said my landlady, "I'm sure she's happy enough. I just worry about her a little."

Sarah

I decided I should put aside my hesitations and swallow my pride, and tell Joey that if he and Julio were willing to let me join them now and then, I'd like to learn what it was like to improvise with them. I felt nervous and depressed thinking this out and making the decision, because it felt like an admission of my inferiority and wrongness, and I didn't believe I was either inferior or wrong, but I said to myself that clearly improvisation was something that would make me a better musician, so even if I didn't like it, I should at least give it a little try. And I had no reason to believe I wouldn't like it, I just didn't expect to be any good at it. Being bad at things is humiliating, but being a beginner is nothing to be ashamed of, and I had to keep telling myself that I would just be a beginner and couldn't expect to learn very quickly, because it was new to me.

When I finally told Joey that I would like to learn to improvise, he showed no special enthusiasm.

"I'll have to talk to Julio," he said. "I took you over there the other day because I thought it would do you some good, in that state you were in, but I don't really know how many people he wants dragged in. It's generous of him to spend so much time with me already, but he's a busy guy. Like I said, he's a god."

"I don't know why you keep saying he's a god," I said. "You guys can have your joke about being gods, but really, I just thought over how you had asked me if I wanted to play, and I thought maybe I should do it after all."

"Sometimes you only get one chance to do a thing," said Joey. "Maybe you screwed up when you refused. But it's not up to me. I'll ask him."

"He said I should listen first and play later if I wanted," I said, starting to get mad but trying not to show it.

"Yeah, he did, and I'll ask him. Just don't expect anything.

You don't understand how capricious gods can be. You want things from them, you have to catch their interest."

More of that nonsense about gods. I was already tired of it. "You're giving me all that crazy talk. What do you mean, catch their interest?"

"Make yourself interesting. Offer them something." He paused and looked straight at me, intently. "Open yourself. It's dangerous. You should do it more often."

"I don't do anything dangerous, thank you."

"And that's just what's wrong with you."

"You're trying to get me upset again," I said. "I don't understand you."

"I don't try to get anybody upset, Sarah. I gave you a suggestion. If you want to work with people like Julio, you have to make it worth their while in some way. Your talent is one draw, but lots of people are talented."

This was getting complicated. "I wasn't saying I wanted to take lessons or work on some kind of serious thing with you guys. I just said maybe I could come along now and then and get a little experience improvising."

"Which you don't seem to think is a serious thing," said Joey. He looked severe as he said that, but then he laughed. "We think it's a very serious thing, and that's why we take it so playfully. Do you know how to be that playful?"

"You don't know..." I stopped. Not only did he have no way of knowing whether I could be playful, but maybe I didn't know either.

"I don't know what?"

"You don't know *me*," I concluded.

"No, which is what I was complaining about last time I saw you. We play music together but I don't know you, because you don't think I need to. Who are you, anyway, Sarah?"

"What am I supposed to say?" I said. "What do you want to know about me, anyway? It's not like there's that much to know."

"How can you imagine that there's so little to know about yourself? That's a horrible thing to say."

"You don't want to know where I live or what I eat for breakfast. That's boring."

"Um… yes. Especially if you make it boring. Do you think every aspect of your life outside of music is boring?"

"No."

"No, and no details. Are you like an oyster, Sarah?"

"What on earth are you talking about? How could I be like an oyster?"

"You're hard to pry open, and no one knows whether you have a pearl or just the makings of oyster stew."

"That's disgusting, Joey!"

"No it's not. I'm sure every oyster opens nicely when she wants to and doesn't feel threatened. But why do you take everything as a threat?"

"I don't, but if you keep comparing me to an oyster, I will. I don't like oysters and I think they should be left in peace."

Joey suddenly began to laugh, which annoyed me even more. "What are you laughing about?"

"I just thought of that old line, 'The world is my oyster.' I don't know where it came from, but I first heard it on TV when I was a little kid watching reruns of *The Addams Family*. I think Uncle Fester was the one who announced that the world was his oyster. I thought that was the weirdest, silliest, funniest thing I had ever heard. I had no idea anyone had ever said it before Uncle Fester. I rolled around the floor laughing at the idea of the world being Uncle Fester's oyster. Did you ever see that episode?"

"I don't think so," I said. It didn't sound familiar. I didn't really care for programs like *The Addams Family*.

"Tell me, Sarah, was there anything that ever, ever, ever made you roll on the floor laughing when you were little?"

Now there was a good question. I knew there had to have been. But what? "How little?" I said, stalling.

He shrugged. "Any kind of little. Something that completely delighted you. That you thought was absolutely hilarious."

I knew there had been something. There had to have been more than one something.

"Some joke somebody made. Something you read. Something on TV. You must remember *something*."

I was beginning to remember, vaguely, one of my mother's boyfriends tickling me and calling me a pumpkin. The tickling had made me laugh, but I also thought it was awfully funny to be called a pumpkin, since I knew I didn't look at all like a pumpkin.

"I remember," I said slowly, "laughing because somebody called me a pumpkin. I guess I was about three. I knew I didn't look anything like a pumpkin. I thought he was really silly, to call me a pumpkin. So I laughed really hard."

"You definitely don't look like a pumpkin now," said Joey. "Maybe a crookneck squash or a zucchini, but not a pumpkin."

Despite myself, I giggled.

"Who was this character who likened you to a pumpkin? I'll bet you had fat little round cheeks and grinned like a jolly jack-o-lantern."

"Well, I don't know about that. Maybe fat cheeks, all kids have those, but I don't think I ever looked like a jack-o-lantern. It was some boyfriend of my mother's, I don't really remember which one. I just remember he was tickling me and calling me a pumpkin, and I thought it was funny."

"Not just the tickling, but the pumpkin."

"Yes. I think the tickling was incidental. I guess it added. I thought it was awfully funny to be a pumpkin when I knew I was a girl. I think people may have called me different animals sometimes, like kitten or giraffe—" I didn't know where inside me this information was coming from, because it seemed new to me—"but I guess being called a pumpkin seemed like being called a lightbulb or a saltshaker. Just bizarre."

"You're a little lightbulb," said Joey experimentally. "Yeah, that's kind of odd. Better to be a lightning bug. But people do call little kids pumpkins. I don't know why. Did your mother have a lot of boyfriends?"

"I don't know. It seemed like it to me at the time. Maybe it wasn't all that many. Maybe it was a normal number. Maybe they weren't even all her boyfriends. I really don't know. We lived in some kind of commune."

As I said this, it hit me that I had confessed I had once lived in a commune. I was a bit mortified. While it's not a secret, I prefer not to tell people about it.

"I guess you reacted against that, then," he said. "Me, I just lived in an ordinary house with my parents and brothers and sisters."

"I didn't like it," I admitted. "I was glad when I got to live in an ordinary house."

"But..." said Joey slowly, "it sounds like you do have some good memories from the commune. If you liked laughing about being a pumpkin, that is."

"I suppose I liked it. Why would I laugh, if I didn't like it?"

"Well," said Joey, "you were being tickled at the same time. You might not have been able to help laughing. But I hope you laughed because you were happy."

I thought about it. I wasn't entirely sure, but after all I did think it was funny to be called a pumpkin. "I might have been happy," I said. "I don't really know."

KARI

How do you know when you're happy?" inquired Endymion one night; it may have been the night we'd lain on the blanket on the hill and looked up at the sky and listened to the sound of night insects and rustling leaves.

"How?" I said. "I just know. I'm happy right now, incidentally."

"Yes, that was my impression."

"Are *you* happy?"

"Indubitably. I lie with the goddess in the moonlight."

I laughed. "Who has not yet cast you into eternal sleep."

"Is it easy to make you happy, do you think?"

"Pretty easy," I said. "Even when I'm miserable and depressed and half-suicidal, I know that eventually it will pass. That's why I'm still alive. I know I have a good capacity for happiness. I always find it eventually, sooner or later."

"Do you think there are people who are unable to recognize happiness? Their own, I mean."

I considered this. "Yes. Probably. People who have little experience of it, maybe. Maybe it's so foreign to them that when it hits them they assume it's something else. Maybe it scares them and messes with their self-image as unhappy victims. I don't know. I'm just guessing."

"Some people do seem to think it's ignoble to be happy. A character flaw or a lack of intelligence. That no sensitive person could be happy when people are starving or cruel. What do you think about that?"

"You know what I think about that, Endymion," I said. "You don't even have to ask. I believe enlightened happiness brings compassion. I'm not very enlightened, of course, so my compassion has its limits, but at least I know where I need to improve."

"You are, in other words, Selene rather than Kuan Yin."

"Well, I like to think I am more than just Selene, but it would be very inaccurate to call me Kuan Yin. How many acts of compassion have you seen me perform?"

"I think you're compassionate," said Endymion. "You're not Kuan Yin, though."

"I'm compassionate when it suits me," I said, "which is not very impressive. And you? I think you are compassionate."

"I'd like to be. I'm not sure I am. Maybe I just stir up trouble."

"Hah," I said. I was not used to hearing Endymion express any self-doubt. Since I didn't find him arrogant, I assumed he experienced as many doubts as the next person, but they did not tend to come up in conversation. "What kind of trouble? Am I trouble?"

"Stirring up trouble with you always seems to turn out well," he said. "Stirring up trouble with other people—I'm not so sure. Maybe it's dangerous to stir up trouble with people who are fundamentally unhappy."

"I suppose it depends on the kind of trouble. You aren't inciting a peasant revolution, are you?"

"I'm only thinking about unhappy individuals. The masses have been placated with consumer goods, at least in North America. But I don't know whether I sometimes prod people too much. Maybe it's unwise to awaken them."

"What are you awakening in them?"

"That's the problem. I'm not sure. What if I wanted to awaken good things and only succeeded in awakening anxiety, distrust, and pain?"

I felt a rush of love for this strange character, this paramour who had befriended me in one of my own trickier moments. "You should be brave and persevere, I think," I said.

Sarah

I was driving: driving up a vertical highway steeper than the ramps they build to stop runaway trucks. I was tense and on edge, afraid the car would lose its grip and slide back down; I had to concentrate in order to keep going up. But what was up there and why was I going there? I had no idea; I knew only that I had to keep driving. Though I rarely drive, I had a grim sense of déjà vu about climbing this impossible road. It wasn't a sense of déjà vu that assured me I'd safely make it to the top, only an awful feeling that I'd struggled with similar vertical roads before. Meanwhile, I didn't even have any idea what kind of scenery might be going by; my attention was fixed on the road directly ahead and on the fear of falling.

Later, somehow, I was lying down. Where was I lying down? I wasn't sure. It was a place without much identity. I suppose I was in a room, but whether I was on a bed or a bench, there was no telling. It was here that things began to get really weird and uncomfortable, because Joey Caro came in and first told me that my aunt was about to die, and then, as if my aunt's impending death meant he could do anything whatsoever, he reached toward me and began to kiss me, transferring some kind of hallucinogens from his mouth to mine. I tried to resist but found myself strangely weak, and, writhing uselessly, I began to fall into a coma as he continued to kiss me.

This was what I dreamt the night before Joey took me back to Julio's to join them in some improvisation. I recognized the dream of the vertical highway as one I had had before, despite the fact that I almost never drive, but the dream of Joey apparently murdering first my aunt and then me with hallucinogenic kisses was new and so dreadful that I woke up kicking and struggling as I descended into the dream-coma. I lay in my bed for a long time then, very still, feeling the darkness of the room through my closed eyes, wondering in a half-awake kind of way what horrors awaited me at rehearsal and why Joey wanted to destroy me with his terrible, tainted kisses. My mind, which was not exactly clear, fixated on how I had to be sure never to let him kiss any part of me, because if he kissed even my hand, let alone some more private part of my body, I would go mad and spend the rest of my life in a mental hospital, probably with snakes crawling down my legs and the attendants laughing at me for letting Joey kiss me. When it got light out, of course, I began to realize that this was all an overreaction; why on earth would Joey do anything genuinely dangerous to me? He might say things that bothered me, but he was, after all, a good person. Still, it made me nervous. I had trouble shaking the sense of anxiety and doom that oppressed me after waking. It was still bothering me after lunch and into the late afternoon when I met up with Joey and we went over to Julio's.

"So, you're back, Ms. Sarah," said Julio as he opened the door and led us in. "Joey says you wanna learn to jam with us."

"Yeah, I'd like to give it a try," I said. "I hope you don't mind."

"Mind? Why should I mind? A friend of Joey's is a friend of mine."

I didn't say anything; I wasn't going to say that Joey didn't seem to think that. Besides, did Joey think of me as his friend? I wasn't sure.

We sat down in the living room, and again Joey and Julio talked about people I didn't know and things I wasn't all that familiar with. I didn't listen all that closely, although I supposed perhaps I ought to. If they were having this conversation in front of me, it wasn't private, yet at the same time it didn't seem to concern me, so my impulse was to tune it out. I was focusing my attention on one of Julio's paintings, which was big and showed a woman standing in an impossibly red and yellow desert—the colors were almost primary hues, not natural, with a brilliant yellow sun blazing in a paler yellow sky—and then I realized that Julio had lit up a joint and passed it to Joey.

Now, in addition to having seen this routine countless times as a child, I had certainly been in situations as a teenager and as an adult where people lit up doobies; I disliked it, but there wasn't always that much I could do about it. My long-time friends knew not to do it around me, but other people usually thought I was some sort of Nancy Reagan spoilsport if I complained, although that didn't necessarily stop me from asking them to stop.

I wasn't sure, however, what to do or say in this situation. I had made the decision to jam with Joey and Julio, and if I complained, Julio might decide not to include me. I didn't think Joey would care one way or the other whether I took a toke, but it didn't seem to be up to Joey whether I played with them. I looked at them a little uncertainly, trying to decide whether to say something or just put up with it.

Joey began to hand the joint back to Julio.

"No man, pass it to Sarah," said Julio.

"No, no, I don't want any," I said hastily, so Joey continued to offer it to Julio.

Julio took it from Joey and held it out to me, very confidently.

"She doesn't want any," said Joey. "Don't bug her."

It was a strange moment. Joey was standing up for me, probably not at all surprised by my refusal, and Julio was ignoring both of us and continuing to offer it to me, but not in an offensive way. I almost repeated my refusal, and then, surprising myself enormously, I reached out and took the joint.

A part of me was ready to stamp it out on the floor and stomp out of the room, or to perform some similar vehement action, but I did nothing of the kind. Instead, I repeated the motions I had seen so many times as a small child and occasionally in my more recent life, and took a cautious toke, careful not to inhale too deeply. Joey watched in disbelief and perhaps some alarm, while Julio paid no special attention; after all, he barely knew me, so presumably he had next to no idea what to expect from me.

Afterwards we took out our instruments and tuned up. As before, Julio played a short section for Joey's approval, and indeed for mine, although I had no idea what I should be approving since I had no idea what I might be playing to go along with this embryonic piece.

"You know how to play continuo, right?" Joey asked before we began.

"I've never really done it," I said. "I don't do much early music."

"Well, you might want to think in terms of continuo to start with," he said. "Give us some tonic. Give us some underlying tones, you know, following the chords. That'll give you a start if you don't have any other ideas at first. And if you make a mistake and play something that sounds bad, turn it into something intentional."

"You talk too much, man," said Julio. "Let her figure it out."

"She hasn't done this before."

"She can figure it out," repeated Julio. "She's got ears."

He started up, and then Joey joined in. It sounded complex, but was less so than the experiments I'd heard on my first visit. I listened a minute, then tried Joey's advice to find and maintain some straightforward notes as a bass line. I was, after all, taking the role of the bass. The difficulty was not so much in finding my notes as in sensing when to shift. Their chord changes and modulations were unpredictable and not the kind of thing I was accustomed to, so I had to make frequent use of the suggestion to make my mistakes sound intentional. Even as a classical musician, I have some skill in that, because no matter how good you get, from time to time you do hit a wrong note and have to brazen your way out of it. It was tough here, though, because the style wasn't one I was at home in. I kept to the slowest, simplest changes I could get away with. Still, as we went on, I began to do things here and there with my bowing to accentuate rhythms that I heard the others creating. It seemed to work.

This was a tiring endeavor, though. It was hard mental and physical work. It was hard mentally because I had to pay such close attention in order to keep up with and occasionally anticipate what they were doing, and it was hard physically because the mental strain made my body more tense. Playing a relatively complicated piece from written music would have been easier for me in many ways, because I know how to follow written music pretty well both in sight-reading and after practicing a piece. I can always improve my skill at performing written music, but it's something I'm used to doing every day. This was exercising different parts of my brain, and it made me weary. I wondered whether the joint was having any detrimental effect, but that didn't seem likely—I hadn't had much and I didn't feel any different than before. I was pretty sure I wasn't stoned. And while I avoid dope smoking, I know perfectly well that in moderation it's no big deal. I don't fear it the way I had feared the mysterious hallucinogens in my dream.

We played a couple of pieces, both of them fairly long. After a while my tension and anxiety about playing began to give way to a state more like what I would associate with a trance, in which I had less need to consciously think out what to do next and often moved almost automatically to an appropriate pitch. While I supposed this might have some relation to the dope, I thought it might equally well be my getting accustomed to what we were doing. I wasn't wild about feeling like an automaton, but I was glad to feel that I was catching on.

When we finally came to a stop, Julio looked at me. "So."

"It was hard, but I'm starting to get the idea," I said.

"First you listen, then you get the feeling," he said.

"I guess so," I said. I felt worn out, mentally exhausted.

"Joey, your band's playing tonight?" said Julio.

"Yeah, at Tarrasco."

"You taking Sarah?"

"Not that I know of. Why?"

"Take her."

"She might not want to go."

"Sure she does."

Throughout this exchange, I sat in a state of mild bemusement. Why were they having this conversation? Why did Julio think I should go listen to some band? "What are you talking about?" I finally said.

"My band's got a gig tonight and Julio thinks you should go," said Joey, as if this was any more informative than what I'd already heard.

"Yeah, but what kind of band? Why should I go?" As soon as the latter question was out of my mouth, I realized it sounded rude; you don't ask a musician why you should go to his performance as if it were a financial seminar that you suspect of wanting your money. "Sorry—I mean, I didn't know you had a show tonight." I didn't really want to go, but a person can always claim a prior engagement. I didn't need to sound like I thought it was crap when it was probably just not my kind of music.

"It's progressive rock, sort of," said Joey. "You don't have to go if you don't want to."

"Joey, Joey, how you gonna build up your audience if you don't get your friends to go?"

"I tell some of them. The ones I think might like the music."

"Shit, man, don't be so particular. Tell 'em all. How do you know what they're gonna like?"

"Well, I try to pay attention to their tastes. Not everyone likes our kind of thing. It's not like anything they hear on the radio."

"Is it all original compositions?" I asked, figuring I had better get back into the conversation.

"So far," said Joey. "At first we pulled everything out of group improvisation. These days we're more inclined to write things out in advance. Not in detail, but one person will compose a basic piece and notate it, and then together we fill it out and add to it. Each of us has a different approach to composition, but once we start to work on a piece together, it becomes more of a blend of ideas. Some of us are more meditative, one or two are more inclined to throw in some heavy metal to shake things up. Me, I usually start with improvisation and then I try to structure it a little more carefully as I write down the ideas."

"I could never do that," I said, impressed.

"You haven't tried, you mean," said Joey. "I guess your teachers don't make you write any music."

"Well, I'm not a composition student," I said.

Julio laid down his guitar. "Composition student, bullshit. You go hear Joey's band tonight, okay?"

It didn't look like there was any way to get out of this politely, at least not while we were at Julio's. "Okay," I said.

KARI

Now that we had a performance space lined up, Endymion and I threw ourselves into our preparations. The newness of the theater, which called itself The Dolphin, and the fact that the piece was relatively far along in the writing and planning, meant we weren't far down in the lineup. The fact that I had done a couple of similar pieces before, and that both of us were known to members of the collective, meant that our work could be taken partly on trust, especially once we had shown what we had already planned out and what still needed to be developed.

I was to be the director, but Susan would help me choreograph some of the staging and Steven would coach me on other aspects. Endymion was in charge of music and sound design, but he offered suggestions in other areas from time to time as well. Rhiannon was our main designer, and Matt was our set and props fabricator. We had to collect some actors, however. We needed so few that auditions seemed a little pointless. After some consultation, we came up with dancers Bryce Benton and Meryl White to play Endymion and Selene, since these were not really speaking roles, and actors Siobhan Garry and Nick Novato to play the modern characters. None of them were people I had worked with previously, but my collaborators assured me that they were skilled and reliable.

There was, meanwhile, a great deal of work to do before we went into rehearsals, and most of it was up to me. I had to finish the script, such as it was; the actors would be contributing in rehearsal, but I had to have my draft finished. The production would not be so long as to require an intermission, but it would be longer than a standard one-act. An audience can sit through a ninety-minute film without an intermission, but ninety minutes is probably about all an audience will sit still for without a break, so I was trying for a running time of between an hour and an hour and a half. We hoped that with the alternation between the mythic and the modern, and shifts in tempo and rhythm between modern diction, bits of Keats and the Elizabethan playwright John Lyly, and segments of pantomime and dream, the audience would not begin to feel that everything was too much the same kind of thing and that they needed to stand up and analyze the show for ten minutes midway.

The modern part of the piece, which in some ways I found more challenging than the mythic part, was not so much difficult to write as simply a little scary, because I was using aspects of my own relationship with Endymion, even things we had said to one another. It was not a story about us personally, so much as about a pair of modern people connecting to a myth and pushing the mythic aspect—but still. Endymion was well aware what I was writing; this was a collaboration in which to some extent we enacted our roles in real life to test them for the play, but we did this consciously, as a game. At specific moments we were strictly, or almost strictly, our modern-day, recognizable, not explicitly mythic selves, and at other specific moments we moved into our mythic roles and enacted those. Since very few people knew that we actually did this, even if they did know or guess that we slept together, we worked under the assumption that to put this into a performance piece would not be to reveal too much about our true selves. Still, it could hardly help but have some amount of personal resonance, because this game was, of course, an important element of our partnership and how we had developed our collaboration. Many people do explicitly play roles in their sexual relationships; it's quite common, possibly even ordinary, for them to set up entire scenarios with characters and rules which are then enacted according to plan. This was not, however, something either of us had ever done before or had any particular expectation of doing again. Well—we might perhaps do it again, but it was not part of our pasts and we saw it as something *present*, something that amused us and fed our collaboration, not as a kinky activity that we had developed a taste for and expected to repeat. In any case, we supposed that we could get away with using this small part of ourselves, just as writers always end up using large or small pieces of their experiences, whether openly or in camouflage.

The script for this modern portion was relatively straightforward, then, in terms of writing technique; it was merely a little tricky emotionally because I wanted to use aspects of what we did and said, but not to duplicate our own lives onstage. And then there was the interweaving of it with the mythic side. The modern side was more talky but less poetic; the mythic side was more visual, more musical, and more often expressed by the poetic speech we were borrowing from Keats and Lyly. In a sense, perhaps, the modern side was a more analytical mindset in contrast with a more intuitive one. But only to a degree. After all, you could hardly call Keats and Lyly purely intuitive.

I had found Keats's epic "Endymion" almost immediately. The poem, which was inordinately long, had prompted such strong critical reactions in its day that Shelley had even blamed the critics for Keats's early death, although this was probably going a little far considering that the poet died of consumption. My own reaction, as a late-twentieth-century reader with no habit of reading lengthy narrative poems, was that the critics had been right in regarding the work as flawed. It has many wonderful passages, some of which I was borrowing, but as I had told my collaborator when first we discussed doing a play, Keats threw in far too many random mythological figures and clogged up the works with excessive descriptions of vegetation. Perhaps this is the modern philistine in me speaking and I am unable to appreciate the niceties of Romantic poetry, but as a person with a reasonable knowledge of mythology and a fondness for the natural world, I thought we could assume that my tolerance for random gods and nymphs and for lush descriptions of nature was probably greater than that of most people who would be in our audience. Furthermore, Keats had set up his narrative so that Endymion was a ruler who dreamt of a goddess named Cynthia and then told his sister all about this disorienting experience. I did not want to drag in temple rites, royal duties, extra names for Selene, and a sisterly confidante, so my use of Keats was very selective.

As for John Lyly, I encountered him somewhat later in my digging. Lyly, an Elizabethan playwright, had written quite a different work on the Endymion theme, a comedy that many commentators believe deals with the relationship of one or another male courtier to the Virgin Queen. Lyly's style, much like that of Shakespeare and Marlowe, impressed me as both poetic and engaging. Most of his story line, however, which involved Endymion's jealous cast-off love persuading a witch to put him to sleep, was useless to me and made clear, in its general thinness, why Lyly is not known to today's theatergoers. The play was an enjoyable read, however, and I thought that at least some of the dialogue could be appropriated for our evocation of the mythic Endymion.

SARAH

Joey did not seem too enthusiastic about the idea of my going to hear his band. I wasn't sure whether he simply didn't think I'd like the music or if he felt that he was already spending more time with me than he wanted. Maybe it was both.

"You don't *have* to go," he assured me after we left Julio's. "I don't know why he thinks you should. Being exposed to Julio is one thing, he's brilliant. Being exposed to my band is different. We're good, but we're not *that* good. We're a work in progress."

"I can go," I said. "I'd like to see what it's like." After all, it's important to support what other musicians are doing, even if it's only now and then. I've sat through plenty of concerts that didn't appeal to me all that much; I take it as part of my education.

"Well, you don't have to stick around if you don't like it. No one will notice; we usually get a pretty good crowd."

"That must mean people like what you play," I said.

"Yeah, we try to get rid of them, but they keep coming back. And we keep trying to break up, but we can't keep from showing up to rehearse. It's a very sad situation. I guess we'll have to start taking drastic measures. Puke on people at the concerts or throw things into the audience. Maybe we should throw Molotov cocktails, that might keep them away."

I concluded he had to be joking. Even punk bands don't throw Molotov cocktails at their audiences.

"You know," he said, "you don't have to like *every* kind of music. It really won't hurt my feelings if you don't go or if you don't like my band."

"Are you trying to keep me from going?" I asked. "I really don't mind. It might be interesting."

He wouldn't admit to not wanting me to go, and I was pretty much locked into a position where I had to go and make the best of it, so ultimately I got the address out of him and we separated to get some things done in the meantime.

KARI

With a traditional play, the script is paramount. The director can take liberties with it—Shakespearean plays are often, even typically, performed with cuts—but as a rule the script is pre-existing and guides the director, even if he or she chooses to set the action in a completely different century or culture, as has become popular with Shakespeare productions. Plays by living authors are usually done with the words intact, however.

I point this out not because I am opposed to respecting the text as written—as a rule I'm a strong proponent of sticking to the playwright's words and intentions, because most playwrights are not Shakespeare and thus don't have the luxury of countless productions of a single play—but because people often forget that there are other ways of creating a play. While most productions come about because a playwright has written a script and a director has chosen to put together a production of that script, sometimes the script has a smaller role; sometimes the script is improvised during performance to follow a basic story line (I've often had dreams, slightly unnerving ones, where I've got to present a play created entirely by improvising the dialogue on the night of performance); and more often people like me come up with a hybrid species that's written and designed and blocked pretty much simultaneously and requires considerable input from several people in a manner rather different from that of a traditional director getting designs from costume, set, and lighting specialists.

I was glad, therefore, that the people I was working with on the Endymion project were not stuck in traditional modes of thinking about theater. Theater people sometimes, after all, admire experimental theater but have no concept how differently it may need to be formed—some people work using only the techniques they have already learned. And while it's good to know traditional techniques, it's important to be able to use them in new ways or to combine them in unexpected ways or even to be ready to abandon them. In this, Endymion and I found we had bold collaborators from the collective. The two of us were already forming our production in a manner akin to a shared dream; our new collaborators, fortunately, seemed able to climb aboard this dream-ship and share our vision as we worked out the details. I knew from past experience how rare this was, so I was intensely grateful to be spared conflicts of will, disjunctures of vision, and incompatible personalities. When a production is in harmony, it is a beautiful, living, sublime entity; more often, however, it succeeds despite tension and disagreements, or it fails to gel as either a collaboration or a work of art.

SARAH

Joey's band performed in one of those little spaces typical of emerging bands. I was relieved to find it was a small art gallery rather than a bar; the performance was part of a neighborhood gallery crawl and there was neither smoking nor drinking. The stage was minimal and the group's performance followed one by an Indian tabla player. There were some big drippy-looking paintings on the walls, but the lights were dimmed so I couldn't see those very well, not that I was probably missing much there. Audience members, who came and went to some extent, either sat on the floor or stood; most of us stood since there wasn't much room and, as Joey had predicted, there was something of a crowd. Whether most people were there mainly because of the band or mainly as part of the gallery crawl, I wasn't sure, but I recognized a few musicians who must have been friends of Joey's. Much of the crowd looked young, but not like most of the younger musicians I knew; this was a more insistently multi-ethnic, neo-hippie group, with lots of people in dreadlocks and clothes that looked straight out of the Goodwill store or the Save Tibet store. I supposed this was more Joey's natural milieu even though he is a fine classical guitarist; he was wearing jeans with ripped knees, which I personally wouldn't even wear at home, let alone perform in. As for the rest of the band, they seemed like a standard-looking group of young male rockers; I didn't recognize any of them. One of them had dreads and another was wearing cutoffs with striped socks and black high-top sneakers, but other than that there was nothing very notable about their appearance.

The other classical musicians in the crowd were too far away for me to join without stepping on some people, but Julio caught sight of me and somehow made his way over to where I was standing.

"Hey, Sarah! That's good you're here, you should really hear Joey's band."

"Well, I try to go to things when I know one of the performers," I said, for lack of any better response.

"Yeah, I kept telling Joey he should tell more people," said Julio. "That's how you get a crowd, it's natural your friends want to support you."

Someone, possibly the gallery owner, gave a few introductory remarks, claiming that the group was well known to local audiences and destined for great things. The usual. People clapped. The group members glanced at each other and then plunged in.

The first piece was instrumental. It was, I thought, cacophonous in a different way than most rock bands I had heard, although admittedly I've always avoided these things, especially live concerts where I might have to worry about protecting my hearing. This wasn't as loud as some, so I thought I might not have to put in the earplugs I had brought.

The audience quickly began to get into the music. Maybe more of them were familiar with the band than I had realized, or maybe Joey's group simply appealed to audiences of gallery-crawlers. It was hard for me to know, since I don't hang out in galleries much. Julio was as enthusiastic as the rest, although I would have thought that as a jazz musician, he might have had reservations about this. Still, Joey was his protégé, and he had instructed me to go, so I supposed I shouldn't be surprised that he liked it.

There was very little space on the gallery floor, but a few people somehow found room to dance without trampling any of the others. It always amazes me that people can do this, but it always seems to happen at these things. I don't suppose anyone at the royal courts of Europe used to jump up and break into a minuet when Haydn or Mozart premiered a new work; I'm sure that that would have been quite the breach of protocol. Random dancing seems more appropriate at street fairs or parties.

I couldn't help thinking it was odd that an accomplished

classical guitarist like Joey would want to play in this kind of group, but unquestionably Joey was a very different kind of musician than I. As far as I could tell, he was enthusiastic about every kind of music he encountered. I couldn't think of anything he had ever mentioned not liking, no matter how peculiar or noisy. He even thought composers like John Cage and Milton Babbitt were interesting, and while I knew they were important, I didn't like anything I had heard of theirs, so I didn't listen to them any more than I had to.

"They're good, huh?" said Julio.

I made a vague gesture. I didn't think they were awful, they just weren't my kind of thing. What was I supposed to do? I was there to support Joey, and because Julio had maneuvered me into going.

The group moved on to the next piece. Much of what they played was relatively slow and long; they seemed to prefer wandering sorts of pieces that I would have thought were more suitable for going into a trance than dancing, especially since the time signatures changed frequently and seemed liable to confuse most dancers. I wondered which ones Joey had written, but since nothing was said about authorship, there was no real way of telling. At times the pieces seemed minimalist, but in a discordant way; I found it hard to classify what the performers were really doing other than that it was, as Joey had indicated, some form of progressive rock. I supposed you could call it that, if you defined "progressive rock" simply as rock that goes outside the boundaries of short, relatively simple, top-40ish songs. Even I, with next to no interest in rock, know that progressive rock was big in the seventies and that groups like Jethro Tull, Genesis, and Pink Floyd were among the major names in the genre. But this band was nothing like any of those. It seemed to do solely instrumental pieces, which entirely removed its work from those bands' tendency toward story-telling. Its basic instrumentation was that of a standard rock band, but the performers often changed places or put down their usual instruments in order to pick up unexpected things like a saxophone or flute. At times they stripped things down to medieval-like progressions of parallel fourths. At other times, Joey treated his guitar like a mandolin and plucked the same note repeatedly as though the string had no staying power. Now and then the keyboardist set his instrument to sound eerily like a cello and played a plaintive-sounding bass line. Was this what progressive rock was like in 1999, or were they doing something truly new? I didn't actually know.

I wasn't crazy about it, but I had to admit it wasn't dull.

KARI

It was Open Studio week and Endymion's band was to perform at a small gallery. I had heard them rehearse a couple of times, sitting at the edge of the room, listening while I made some preliminary sketches for our set design. There's an art, I think, to attending a rehearsal: it's important to pay attention to what's going on, but it's also important not to look too intent, because that can distract the performers and remind them what an incomplete and imperfect thing the guest is getting. The likes of directors, dramaturges, producers, and so on are not guests; the friends and lovers of the performers are always guests.

So I sat, as inconspicuously as possible, and sketched and listened. The group was pretty good, I thought. It was not, perhaps, music that I would choose to listen to every day, but it was intelligent and thought provoking. Nobody sang, other than maybe occasionally humming along; these pieces were long explorations without words. The group had a good energy: their connection to one another was strong. They could parlay teasing insults back and forth between pieces, but I never saw them petulant or rancorous or even in much disagreement. They had been playing together, said Endymion, for several years now and while the band was no one's primary focus or project, everyone in the group clearly valued it. They did not very actively seek out gigs, and had no particular ambition to land a recording contract, but they had developed enough of a following that from time to time people invited them to play at a bar or a gallery or a festival, where they sometimes sold copies of a self-produced CD. It was an interesting way of proceeding, unlike that of any other band I had encountered over the years, as those were all busily trying to get gigs and dreaming of making it big or at least of becoming a popular party band. It sounded as though Endymion's band, which called itself Ophion after a primordial Greek deity, had bypassed all the usual huckstering and become, in its small way, a local cult group.

I was, therefore, greatly looking forward to hearing them in performance, where the synergy of musicians and audience makes changes in the music, adding that electrical charge of excitement to works that can be quiet or even unmemorable in the studio.

But on the afternoon of the show, I offered to take all my landlady's glass recycling down the street to the truck that sat in the parking lot of the local grocery store, ready to pay back deposits and take everything away. We had amassed something of a collection, between juice bottles and mineral water bottles, and my landlady and I agreed that it was time to do something about them. We both believed firmly in the importance of recycling, but the city was only slowly improving its recycling programs and had not done much to help the average house-holder contribute.

So we loaded up a cardboard box and I headed out the door—when the bottom fell out of the box and the whole load went tumbling down onto my feet, which were imperfectly pro-tected by a pair of black cotton Chinese shoes.

It was quite the crashing disaster, of the small household variety. The various bottles made a great din on the front steps and some of them broke, and my feet immediately hurt like hell so I let out a howl before bending over and planting myself on a glass-free bit of step where I could rock back and forth in pain. I was going to gather up the pieces once I could bear to stand up, but my landlady heard the racket and came rushing out, so after adding a few exclamations to the racket, she was the one who actually picked up the pieces and put them in a sack while making countless futile apologies for having let me get hurt taking away her darn-fool recycling.

After a few minutes, it became clear to us that my feet were too beaten up for me to do much more than stagger or pref-erably crawl back into the house, so my landlady suggested I situate myself on the couch where she could ice my feet. Since we both thought I should elevate the feet as well as icing them, we ended up icing them with sacks of frozen peas, a remedy I can recommend to anyone who hasn't been keeping one of those medicinal ice packs on hand.

"We can make some kind of a pea recipe for supper," said my landlady in her practical way. "Sarah won't be home for supper, so if you don't mind eating a lot of peas, none of these will go to waste."

"I like peas just fine," I said. "I can eat a big dish of buttered peas, never mind a recipe."

What was striking me as I lay on the couch, shifting the bags of peas and watching the tops of my feet turn all manner of disagreeable colors, was that my chances of going to hear Endymion's band that night were pretty much nil. I was unhappy about that, because I knew he was expecting me and I wasn't sure he'd be home to get any messages. Still, I supposed he might take it into his head to call home and check for messages, so after an hour or so I dragged myself over to my landlady's princess phone and left the message that I had managed to disable myself in a most ignominious and presumably short-term fashion.

After a while, he called back, and my landlady kindly brought me the phone on what proved to be an extremely long cord, which I gathered she had gotten for just such moments, only hers had involved a bout of sciatica.

"You wouldn't believe the pain," she said as she brought over the phone. "I don't know if it's worse than being hit with a load of bottles, but sciatica just *lasts*."

I didn't really want to hear about sciatica or any other painful thing just then, but she was being so nice to me that I was not about to complain.

"You've damaged yourself!" exclaimed Endymion.

"Yes, it's nasty," I said. "It's a very stupid accident and I'm lying on the couch icing my feet with packages of frozen peas. I don't think I can go anywhere until at least tomorrow."

"That's distressing. Have you got anything to do?"

"Not downstairs. I suppose I've got things in my room. I'm sure I can cope."

"Was that your landlady on the phone a minute ago?"

"Of course. She's being very kind."

"Your sainted landlady is repaying you for never waking her up coming home in the middle of the night."

"Don't be silly, she's always nice to me. I wouldn't live somewhere where the natives were mean to me. I have a very fine landlady."

"So you've indicated. Listen, can I get you anything?"

"Not that I know of. Not unless you've got amazing painkillers or a giant bottle of that renowned early American anesthetic, straight whiskey. But you don't have time to come over here anyway." I wanted to see him, but I didn't really want him to come over. My landlady and I had the situation under control, insofar as that was possible.

"Time? I might or might not have time. We don't go on until nine."

"I don't think you have time. You've got supper and schlepping and setup. You've only got one car for all the gear."

"Don't underestimate me," said he. "If I turn out to have time, you'll see me live and in person in your living room."

"Only if you have plenty of time," I said. It was clear there was no point in arguing the matter; he would only be more likely to show up.

My landlady thought we should leave the phone near the couch in case I needed to make or take any more calls. I saw no reason to think I would, but I was happy to leave it where it was. At suppertime, she boiled up the mostly melted peas and we ate them together in the living room, which I thought was a surprising breach of protocol for a woman with such separate realms of the house as kitchen and dining room. My mother certainly didn't let anyone eat in the living room, except for nuts and Christmas candy on Christmas Eve. As a good Norwegian American, she has always been very protective of her carpet and her off-white couch. To be sure, we didn't really use our living room for anything other than Christmas celebrations and entertaining company. Well—that's not quite accurate. We listened to records in the living room because that was where the stereo sat, and I played the piano and the flute there. I didn't play the flute there much because it tended to make me hyperventilate, but I did play the piano a good deal, racing through exciting, passionate pieces like "Für Elise" and "Liebestraum." My landlady had a piano, too, but I hadn't tested it; I thought it was probably enough to have one musician in the household, especially since I don't really qualify as a musician. But I thought about these things as I lay on the couch eating buttered peas with my landlady and chatting about the garden and her niece's recent moodiness.

"I wonder whether she's in love," said my landlady.

"Has she been in love before?" I asked. I couldn't really imagine her niece in love with anything but a particularly fine cello, although I thought this was surely a failure of imagination on my part.

"Not that I know of," said my landlady. "She's gone a lot these days, but she claims it's all rehearsals."

I realized I hadn't seen or heard as much of her niece as usual; apart from the sound of the cello, we had a very quiet household.

"Well," I said, "she's certainly very serious about her music." I didn't feel as though I should make too many other assumptions about her niece, who was pleasant enough but struck me as unusually determined to keep her thoughts to herself except when letting out the occasional remark about music or literature or, god forbid, hippies, a topic that seemed to bring forth remarkable venom. I was a bit baffled why a person her age, who hadn't even been alive during most of the hippie era, would have such strong feelings about hippies when her aunt, my landlady, seemed to have no particular animosity toward them.

"I don't know," said my landlady. "I don't quite understand her. Sometimes I feel like she's a pressure cooker, but I really don't know why she'd be under any pressure. She never gets into any *trouble*, so I don't feel I have to put any pressure on her to *behave*. She's not much like her mother; her mother was a sweet kid who just had to try everything. Lee Ann was open to everything and Sarah's not."

I muttered something or other in reply. I was reasonably interested, but I had the feeling that neither of us had much idea what was going on with her niece, other than the necessary singlemindedness of an aspiring classical musician. It's been my impression that most aspiring classical performers gradually put themselves more and more into a world obsessed with lessons and practicing and concerts; they have to do this in order to succeed in their profession. Those who find that too limiting tend to give up and become some other kind of musician, or become musicologists, or go into some other line of work entirely.

After supper, my landlady took the dishes into the kitchen and disappeared into her room with the instruction that I was to call if I needed anything. She had recently taken up quilting and wanted to commune with her sewing machine, which sounded like a fine thing to me. I was curious to see what she would come up with, whether it would be beautiful, match the cabbage roses in the living room, or look like a pitiful mess. My landlady is fairly conventional, but she's intelligent enough and I was willing to believe quilting might reveal unexpected things. I didn't ask her to go and get anything from my bedroom, because I couldn't decide what I might want her to fetch, so I lay on the couch willing myself to go into a restful mood.

Around seven, there was a knock on the door. I knew perfectly well that the doorbell was in plain view and functioned admirably, so I had just a funny feeling that Endymion had stopped by and was avoiding disturbing my not-easily-disturbed landlady. I limped to the door. He and Rory, one of his band members, stood on the doorstep.

"Gadzooks, you've mutilated yourself," he observed when he saw my feet. "You're all multicolored."

"We brought you some things," said Rory, the youngest member of the band. Rory was about nineteen and had long straight brown hair and an expression of invariable, beatific sweetness. I always had the feeling that he regarded me as a kind of miraculous creature, a unicorn or the like. Or perhaps he regarded me as the moon goddess. At any rate, he liked me and appeared to think I was a valuable influence.

"Stop standing on your feet," said Endymion. "Get back on your couch. We've got analgesic salve, a *small* bottle of whiskey, and a nice book for you. We've also got a reusable ice pack."

I gave him a big hug, and gave Rory one as well, and retreated painfully to the couch, where Endymion applied the salve and ice pack, poured me a glass of whiskey, and set down the book.

"We've got to run, but we'll be thinking of you," he said.

They let themselves out, and I lay back and marveled. They had brought me a copy of *The Hitchhiker's Guide to the Galaxy*, which I had been meaning to read for years and which kept me laughing all evening. How had I come to be so lucky? How had I come to meet such people?

SARAH

"I think Kari has a boyfriend," said my aunt one afternoon, in a sprightly, confidential way. She gets this way from time to time, usually when she's gotten a little too interested in one of our renters.

"A boyfriend?" I said. "Why would you think that?"

"She looks happier. She has that special *glow*. Besides, she doesn't always come home at night anymore." My aunt looked disgustingly smug as she said this.

I hadn't, somehow, noticed any of these things about Kari. This annoyed me; I didn't want to be nosy, but all the same I thought I should be aware of things that might affect us, like boyfriends.

"When did all this start?"

"Oh, I don't know exactly. It's been a while, though. Kari's gone a lot these days. She still works in her room for hours, but she's out as much as she's in. You've been out a lot lately, too; I suppose that's why you haven't noticed."

"Oh," I said. Had I been out all that much? I hadn't thought about it, but maybe I had. I'd started all those new ensembles; I had about four of these going in addition to my usual lessons, practice, and orchestra rehearsals. It meant I was gone for all of that, plus now it was more convenient to do most of my practicing away from home, between rehearsals. My aunt's comment made me feel contrary, though. I said, "Maybe it's not a boyfriend. Maybe she's got a girlfriend."

"Maybe," said my aunt, "but I don't think so."

"I can imagine her having a girlfriend," I said. It seemed possible enough to me. It wouldn't have surprised me if Kari Zilke had had girlfriends at some time in the past.

"Yes," said my aunt, "but I don't think this is a girl."

My aunt has the idea that she can rely on all sorts of strange intuitions she has about people, which often gets on my nerves; she's right often enough to bolster her belief in her powers, but whether she's right much more than fifty percent of the time, I really couldn't say. She thinks she is, but I think the law of averages works in her favor. If you guess right half the time by accident, like flipping a coin, and then add on a few instances of really knowing something, that gives you enough correct guesses to feel like you're almost a psychic.

"Okay, so you think Kari has a boyfriend," I said. For some reason I found this idea mildly depressing. I had always liked the idea that Kari was not reliant on men or on finding a mate; it was one of the things that made her appealing to me in ways that most of our other renters were not. It was restful to have a renter who wasn't always whining about the opposite sex and the deficiencies of singles groups or online dating. I liked having a renter who showed no sign of being obsessed with sex yet who was unlikely to turn out to be a secret fan of kiddie porn or some other awful thing.

"I think Kari is going to be very happy," said my aunt. "Maybe she's even going to get engaged soon."

This assessment made me even more annoyed and depressed. *Engaged?* What planet was my aunt on? Kari did not strike me as at all the kind of person who got engaged. I didn't think we were going to be opening the local paper and seeing her picture over an engagement announcement. That would just be unnatural. At the same time, I had to admit that my aunt is intuitive enough that if she thought Kari was about to get engaged, Kari must at least be in a pretty good mood, and so maybe Kari really was getting laid frequently and relatively satisfactorily. This notion did depress me, because it made Kari a different person than the one I thought I knew something about. I didn't imagine I knew Kari well, or knew very many details about her life as a whole, but I did feel as though I had a sense of her, and this whole boyfriend thing conflicted with my impression of her.

"Have you even seen any boyfriend?" I asked.

"No, never," said my aunt. "But I'm sure he exists. Kari just doesn't bring him to the house."

"You're imagining him," I said, even though it sounded as though my aunt had sufficient evidence for her hypothesis. If Kari was staying out all night, the likelihood was certainly stronger that she had a lover than that she had begun working the night shift.

My aunt sighed and apparently decided not to pursue the topic further. "How are your rehearsals going?" she asked instead.

"Oh, fine," I said. "They keep me pretty busy."

"How are things going with that guitarist you were working with?"

There she was, picking out the one male in the lineup. All the cellists I was practicing with were women, and so were the violinist and the pianist. I hadn't planned it that way; those were just the people I had ended up grouped with. I suppose there are just as many men playing cello, violin, and piano as women, but they weren't playing with *me* just then.

"It's going all right," I said. "He's good." To my horror, I felt myself blushing slightly. This was all Joey's fault, for prodding at me to reveal myself more in conversation. Now there was something between us that didn't exist with my other partners—a weird tension.

"Is he cute?" inquired my aunt. No amount of disgust on my part had ever managed to expunge this word from her vocabulary.

"Um—no, I wouldn't say so," I said. Of course, I didn't regard *anyone* as "cute," except possibly as an insult. Joey wasn't round and fluffy, or anything else that might qualify as cute. He didn't have grotesquely big eyes like some awful doll. I supposed I had better say something more informative in a hurry or my aunt would go on and on. "He doesn't always comb his hair."

My aunt burst out laughing. "He doesn't always comb his hair! Sarah, that has nothing to do with whether he's cute. Really, Sarah, I don't know where you come up with these things.

Why do you have to have *everything* perfectly in place? The world won't end if your guitarist has messy hair."

"I never said it would," I said hotly. "You asked if he was cute, not whether his hair was a world disaster. He's a good musician, he's smart, he's a nice enough person, but he's not cute in any sense of the word. His hair looks all tangled, he wears old T-shirts with the lettering cracking off, and he plays concerts wearing jeans with big holes at the knees. He wears sandals and those high-top sneakers. I mean, really."

"He sounds like he's your age then," said my aunt.

"*I* don't go around like that and neither do most of my friends!" I exclaimed.

"Sarah, you can't expect your whole generation to be like you."

"Lots of it is."

"Yes, but I don't suppose you're the majority." My aunt sighed again. "If you had gone into the business world like I did, you'd probably feel like you were in the majority there, but you're a musician. I doubt that all the musicians your age, even the classical musicians, are constantly combing their hair and shining their shoes."

"No, of course not. Lots of musicians are disgustingly grubby. At least Joey bathes. I know one guy, a violinist, who always smells like old sweat. It's gross."

"Well, let's not talk about *him*," said my aunt. "You've never liked anyone who smelled sweaty. But you like Joey, even if he wears old clothes and doesn't comb his hair."

"He's all right," I said. "But stop trying to make him into some kind of love interest. He's just a guitarist."

My aunt looked at me as if I were out of my mind. "Whoever he is, he's not just a guitarist," she said.

KARI

My feet bothered me for several days, much longer than I had anticipated. After a few hours, and with the aid of the ice, the analgesic cream, and the whiskey, I was able to crawl upstairs and into bed, but I didn't emerge often. I needed to stay off my feet and read books that made me laugh. I wasn't incapable of sitting up and editing awful self-help books, and I wasn't incapable of working on our production from home, but it felt like time to give these things a short rest, especially the editing, and baby myself a little. Reading books that made me laugh took my attention off my physical pain, and if I had any other kinds of pain left tormenting me, those were certainly evaporating. I might not know exactly where I was going in my life, but I felt like I was in motion again, going somewhere interesting and worthwhile (even if at the moment I was largely trapped in my bed).

Endymion was, obviously, a major factor in this. Would I be doing any of the things I was now doing if not for him? It seemed unlikely. At the same time, it was not as though I was doing things that I would exactly have been unable to do without his help. I had envisioned and put together theater pieces long before I had met him—even, I suspected, when he was a small child. I still knew people who could have helped me—people like Steven and some of Marty's friends. But *would* I have done any of this? I didn't know. I didn't know whether I would have been motivated, or had an idea that insisted on being developed. I had distanced myself from all of this for years, for nearly the whole of my thirties. I had gone very far from the things that had mattered to me in my teens and twenties.

Endymion, I recognized, was a remarkable person. My friends were, in general, intelligent and creative, sensitive and kind. A few of them even managed to make me laugh, and I love to be persuaded to laugh. But I had met very few people who had anything like Endymion's combination of intelligence, creativity, wit, and generous humanity. I certainly couldn't think of anyone else his age who had these traits, although I was willing to believe the members of his band might prove to share them.

What sort of luck or providence had led me to the table next to his the evening of Marty's memorial? What curiosity and compassion had prompted him to speak to me? What strange openness had enabled us to embark on our first conversation and develop it in such a manner that we could both find one another worth knowing? I knew little about his past or upbringing beyond that he was one of several children and that at some point in his childhood, his mother had decided to go back to school and get her MFCC, whereupon she had gotten a job working with some very troubled people; he said she seemed to be unusually good at this, and I supposed he must have picked up some of her knack and skills.

Looking at things realistically, by which I might really mean pessimistically, it seemed implausible to me that this relationship could continue for long. It seemed too perfect and wondrous for real life. Real life was the province of my marriage, which had had many fine and admirable things about it and yet had been much too much of a compromise on both sides. My parents and all my successfully married relatives claim that marriage requires much compromise, not independence, and I had always assumed they knew what they were talking about, because clearly it had worked for them. Endymion and I did not compromise, because we had not run into anything that required it. We led our largely independent lives, collaborated on our project, and enjoyed a passionate friendship. We did not claim to be monogamous, although we probably were, and we did not inquire into each other's finances or wash each other's clothes or make plans for a future together. This worked very well for us in the present, but how could it continue to work? Would my domesticized bourgeois side return to the fore and gum up the works, or would I leave it forever behind only to discover that Endymion had a great desire to find a wife and raise a family?

At another time in my life, such questions would have caused me great anxiety and pain, but at this point, as I read through *Hitchhiker's Guide* and some other comic novels and laughed away the pain in my feet, I simply felt grateful that I had such a wonderful person in my life here and now, making me laugh and inspiring me and prodding me to do interesting things and be my full self or something approaching it. The fact that I also found him astonishingly attractive, and that we enjoyed deeply satisfying sex, was important and perhaps miraculous, but I still felt that no matter how important this was to me, it remained an additional wonder, not the fundamental root of our partnership.

And so, as I mulled these things over in between laughing and icing my feet, I gave thanks and sent the wish out into the ether that the future would bring whatever was best for both of us.

Sarah

I found my aunt's comments about both Kari and Joey quite irritating. They nettled me. Why was she so anxious to assume Kari was not just involved with someone but on the verge of getting engaged? Why did she have to seize upon Joey, of all my musical partners, as a person she could imagine I would find "cute" and even as someone she apparently hoped I would fall for? I supposed that you could say, with some truth, that Joey was good-looking in his way, but why should that matter to me? He did seem to take more of an interest in me than my other partners did, but there was no indication that his interest was at all romantic. He had various friends, and apparently he thought I should be one of them, only he thought I was hard to get to know. I didn't understand quite what he wanted from me, but I was pretty sure it didn't include pairing up. He hadn't even wanted me to go hear his band.

That night I had another nightmarish dream. I seemed to be having a lot of unpleasant dreams lately, often about driving straight up narrow roads and willing the car forward, and often dreams in which I had to go back to grade school or high school to relearn something I ought to already know, like social studies or health. I also had the occasional dream in which I went on-stage with my cello and was about to perform when I realized I was naked, which was unsettling. The first time I dreamt that, I asked Wanda if she had ever had such a dream, and she said no, but that back in the late sixties an avant-garde cellist named Charlotte Moorman had performed topless in Nam June Paik's *Opera Sextronique*, so maybe I was channeling her spirit. I said I really didn't think so, as even if it was possible to channel some-one's spirit, Charlotte Moorman was more likely to pick Wanda than me as her conduit. She wouldn't want to pick someone like me who had never heard of her and thought performing topless sounded stupid. Wanda had laughed and suggested that Moorman was actually *more* likely to pick me for exactly these reasons. She thought this would probably appeal to Moorman's sense of humor, which would undoubtedly (said Wanda) have survived Moorman's physical death.

Of course, I didn't think any of my dreams of finding myself naked onstage involved channeling Charlotte Moorman; they were merely embarrassing, and Charlotte Moorman certainly wouldn't have performed topless if it had embarrassed her. Apparently she had followed up the topless stunt with one where she wore little TVs as a bra, which surely must have contributed to giving her the breast cancer that killed her. You have to be careful about being too close to all those electronic devices and their EMFs. I'm sure my generation will be decimated by cancers caused by computers and cell phones.

But my dreams after my conversation with my aunt didn't involve any of the usual anxieties. No steep slopes, no returns to grade school, no public nakedness. Instead, it was like a follow-up to my earlier nightmare about Joey. Now again I lay on a table, unable to escape, while both he and Julio were forcing hallucinogens on me by rubbing a cream into my skin like crazed masseurs, assuring me it would enlighten me and make me very sexy all at the same time. Again, I felt as if I were starting to lose consciousness and fall into a coma with the intensity of the drugs; my skin crawled from all that horrible rubbing as the toxic cream became absorbed, and I began to go into convulsions as if there were strychnine in the cream. I woke up thrashing and sweaty and nearly fell out of bed; why were they doing this to me?

After I began to come to my senses, I had to wonder why I was dreaming such awful things. I could understand having dreams about steep slopes and going back to school and being naked in public; while they were stressful, they were understandable. Even if Wanda wanted to pretend I was channeling Charlotte Moorman, I knew that lots of people do have dreams about suddenly realizing they're naked in public, so my dreams were just a cellist's version of a common type of bad dream. Going up a steep slope and going back to grade school didn't seem that hard to interpret, either. But these dreams about Joey forcing drugs on me, and in such sexual ways, were very disturbing. I had no such fears about him when I was wide awake. I wasn't sure I knew how to deal with him as a person, but I thought he was ethical. I might not understand what he wanted from me, or why he liked some of the music he did, or why he dressed the way he did, but in my waking hours I was sure he was a good person. Why, then, did I dream that he forced drugs on me? I found myself crying hot tears as I took my morning shower, and was glad that the sound of the water covered up the sound. At least I wasn't crying as intensely as I had that day in the practice room; these were mostly quiet tears.

KARI

I was very pleased with the way our rehearsals were shaping up. I am less experienced as a director than as a writer or designer, but with some assistance from Steven and Susan, the blocking—where the actors stand or move on stage—was getting worked out. We were developing a choreography for the dancers over on the mythic side, and working out the nuances of phrasing. Both the actors and the dancers proved adept and professional, speaking up if they had ideas but otherwise not wasting time arguing about how things should be done. A larger cast develops its own often rambunctious energy, which is usually more fun offstage than productive in rehearsal, but these four struck me as unusually focused, perhaps because two were dancers and dancers have a very different way of approaching theater than actors, who usually like to clown around a good deal. Bryce and Meryl were, I thought, typical dancers in their seriousness about their work; Siobhan and Nick were sometimes playful but this surfaced more in their ability to enliven the characters and come up with useful bits of stage business than in any tendency to engage in excessive hijinks. There were a certain number of jokes about Bryce's entrance pulling a line of wheeled sheep behind him, especially once we added "Beautiful Dreamer" sung to ukulele in a mildly kitschy manner; this joking was natural and to be expected. Likewise, when Matt brought out a large cardboard cutout of Piazzetta's very eighteenth-century Diana minus her Endymion but with one leg obscured so she could birth a long line of identically archaic-looking daughters to be pulled downstage, none of us could restrain our laughter or ribald remarks.

"I'm afraid the audience is going to laugh too when they see that," I said, wondering whether we were going too far with our more humorous bits of stagecraft.

"Let them," said Rhiannon, the designer. "They won't laugh as hard as we are, 'cause the lighting will cast a whole different mood on things."

"Exactly," said Endymion, who had been a strong proponent of representing the birth of the Menae.

"The highlights are done in just a touch of glow-in-the-dark paint," said Matt. "Only a touch, mixed with white. It should give a little bit of ghostly moonlit gleam to the fifty daughters. And to the crescent moon on Mama's forehead."

"That Piazzetta Diana is almost too much for me," I continued, still a little stunned at seeing the physical object we had so lightly imagined. "She brings to mind Hogarth's engraving of Mary Tofts giving birth to a litter of rabbits."

I should have known not to mention anything as complicated as one of Hogarth's satirical prints. Everyone wanted it explained. "Hogarth's version is more fun than the original story," I said, "because Hogarth showed the rabbits alive and hopping around, which they weren't in real life. I'm not sure how Tofts convinced anyone that she had given birth to a passel of dead rabbits."

"Wild," said Siobhan.

"Anyhow, I suppose the Piazzetta Diana looks a little more decorous than Hogarth's Mary," I said. "We'll just have to see how the audience reacts."

"It'll be fine, it'll be fine," said Endymion, who never showed the slightest fear that we would take anything too far and lose our audience. And I assumed he was right, because I always do come up with wild ideas, look them over with trepidation, and then conclude they're just what I want and nothing like so crazy as I had thought at first. And there was that big cutout of Piazzetta's Diana, with her crescent moon on her head and her skirt lifted above her knee, calmly giving birth to a row of fifty archaic accordion-fold-paper-doll daughters. Archaic? They looked quite a bit like the "La Parisienne" fresco fragment from Knossos, so that put them well before Archaic and even before Geometric. Rhiannon and Matt had made them look positively Minoan, minus the bare breasts. The Enlightenment or Rococo was birthing the truly Ancient. Okay, I liked it. Let the audience laugh if they wanted.

SARAH

I continued to practice the duets with Joey and to go over to Julio's to learn improvisation, although now I was aware of a certain sense of strain and discomfort in my dealings with Joey. He seemed more absentminded, less likely to offer to lend me CDs he had discovered. I had told him his band was interesting, but he had wanted me to define what I meant by "interesting," and when I mentioned the use of polyrhythms, he seemed unimpressed, or at least not satisfied. Maybe polyrhythms were everyday fare for him, but if so, I couldn't tell what he hoped was interesting about what his band played. Their use of additional instruments? The fact that they didn't sing? I didn't know what he wanted to hear, and I wasn't going to say something I didn't actually think was true.

Overall, he seemed a little preoccupied, though still friendly, and indicated that he had a lot of rehearsals and things to go to. I thought his mind was not fully engaged with our duets anymore, although he said he was thinking about where and when we could do a recital of them; he was more his usual self over at Julio's, although I sometimes thought he was sorry he had brought me into the improvs. While I was getting the hang of playing with them, I didn't feel as though we were a trio so much as a duo with an added support player; on a personal level, of course, Joey and Julio continued to know each other in a way that was impossible for me to attain with either one, so I felt like I knew Joey in the way I knew Joey, and that I was getting to know Julio almost in a separate way, although I didn't know Julio so well as Joey. Julio and I had hung out a bit at the gallery gig; we hadn't stayed to hear the group that played after Joey's band, because instead Julio had persuaded me to go get a snack with him—initially he suggested going to the corner bar for beer, but when I rejected that idea, he proposed cookies and mineral water a block or two away, which sounded acceptable enough.

I felt mildly ill at ease with Julio, but not for any reason other than that I didn't know him well and he was becoming in some sense my teacher although we didn't actually have lessons and I didn't pay him for his time. I didn't know what our exact relationship was supposed to be or to what extent he was willing to have me become part of his sessions with Joey, so I thought I had better try to find out what he wanted. Julio, on his part, expressed no clear plan regarding what he thought my role should be. Instead, he seemed to want to scope me out as a person, but in a manner that made Joey's questions seem like interrogation by comparison.

"So Sarah, Ms. Sarah," he drawled when we sat down with our mineral water, "you like to play the cello, huh?"

"Well, yes," I said. "I thought you knew that. You see me play it, after all."

"You play it, but do you *like* it?"

"Of course I do," I said. "I wouldn't play it if I didn't like it."

"Some people do," he said. "Maybe their parents like it or something like that. I thought, you don't always look like you like it, so maybe I should ask."

"Well, I like it. If I look like I don't, I guess that just means I'm concentrating or something. I don't know. I don't watch myself play to see what I look like, after all."

Julio thought about this answer for a while. Then he said "Maybe you think too much."

"Think too much? That's unlikely. Thinking isn't my thing, I play music. Besides, what's wrong with thinking? A person shouldn't be some kind of dummy."

"You gotta think," said Julio, "but not too much. You gotta think the right amount, in the right ways."

"Joey thinks a lot," I said. "He's a pretty intellectual person for a musician."

"Joey knows how to think," said Julio. "He doesn't let it get in the way of his music, not usually."

"He's very smart," I said.

"You said it," said Julio. "The boy is smart. He knows how to make his thinking work for him. He knows how to listen, how to feel the music."

"He's very talented," I said.

"He knows how to *play*."

I wasn't sure what he meant by that. It was obvious that Joey knew how to play, even though there's always room for improvement.

"Do *you* know how to play, Ms. Sarah?" Julio asked.

I felt a little insulted. "I play as well as I know how," I said. "I want to learn to play better."

"Yeah, yeah, but can you *play*? Do you ever let go of your thinking and fool around until the music just takes over your soul?"

Now he was sounding kind of like Joey, only not as pressing. Joey had emotion behind his questions; he was invested in the answers somehow, while Julio was more detached. Julio hadn't put any time into me yet, to speak of. He could always tell me not to come back, if he didn't like my answers or didn't think I was worth spending time with. Was this an interview to see whether I was worth teaching? I could tell that while Joey called Julio his friend, Julio was the master teacher and Joey the student. Joey had told me, after we left Julio's that afternoon, that Julio was famous. You didn't just knock on his door and ask to jam with him. Or maybe you did, and that marked you as the kind of person he liked. Joey didn't explain how he had gotten to be friendly with Julio. Maybe he would have if I'd thought to ask. Maybe Joey had knocked on his door out of nowhere. Joey had that kind of nerve.

"I don't know," I said. "I think I know when it feels right. I don't know if that means the music's taken over my soul."

"You're thinking too much," said Julio. "You should listen to how it feels. What's some of your favorite music?"

"Well, I like lots of classical music. You know, like Bach and Beethoven and so on."

"Yeah, I know those guys. *Favorite* music, I said. What you love. Maybe it's something you play, maybe it's something you wish you could play, maybe it's something you could never play."

I went blank for a moment. I try not to have favorites, in a way. Then I remembered some of what made me choose the cello instead of violin or clarinet or, god help me, the tuba. "Maybe Schubert's 'Death and the Maiden' and that Elgar cello concerto, the one Jacqueline du Pré played. Have you heard those?"

"Sure," said Julio. "I know those." He thought about it for a minute. "You like music with passion. How come you don't play that way?"

He and Joey might have different styles of presenting themselves, but they were starting to sound a lot alike. It was easier to get this kind of question from Julio, though. Maybe it was because he was older than we were. Maybe it was because Julio didn't have such an educated way of expressing himself but obviously knew a lot. Joey seemed pretty sure of himself, but Julio really *was* sure of himself. Julio wasn't badgering me and making me cry.

"I don't know," I said.

"You don't know, huh? Well, I don't know either. You like music about passion, you must have passion in you somewhere."

"Doesn't everybody?"

"I'm not talkin' about everybody, Ms. Sarah."

I devoted myself to peeling the label off my bottle of mineral water. "Do you think there's something missing in how I play?"

"Maybe. Kind of depends what you want to play, doesn't it?"

"I don't think much about passion," I said.

"You think too much," Julio repeated. "Feel it." He picked up my hand and pressed his thumb to parts of my palm and the pads of my fingers. "Feel it in your hands. Let it come out your fingers when you play."

It was a strange sensation to feel Julio press my palm and fingers. The pressure on my hand was firm and assured, as if my palm and fingers were guitar strings. Something surged in me, but quietly, like a very low electrical current. I didn't think it was passion, but I didn't know what it was. Maybe something was flowing from his hand to mine. I don't believe in mystical transferences of power, but I let myself imagine that some type of skill or understanding could come to me through Julio's fingers.

"I feel like you're reading my palm," I said, trying to make a joke of it.

"Maybe I am," said Julio. "You know, I can do a lotta things."

"You don't read palms," I said.

"You don't know what I can do," he said, and began to look at my palm.

"Bull, you don't read palms."

"I'm reading yours right now. You don't like people to know too much about you, do you."

"You're just bullshitting me."

He traced a line on my palm. "There's your lifeline…"

I pulled my hand back. "Stop it. That's enough."

"See, like I said, you don't like people to know too much about you."

"What're you trying to find out? Maybe I'd just tell you if you asked."

"Nah, you don't tell people things. Not with words, anyhow. So, you like my friend Joey?"

"What do you mean? Like him, how? Sure I like him, he's a good person."

"See, you don't tell people anything with words, you just hide things with words."

"Sometimes there's nothing to tell. You're making things up."

"Joey's kinda worried about you, but right now he's got a lot on his plate."

"Joey doesn't have any reason to worry about me. Nobody," I said more loudly, "has any reason to worry about me."

Julio sat back in his chair and regarded me calmly. "Hey, I'm just making a few observations."

"I don't know why some people think it's not enough that I want to be a good musician. I don't know why some people have a lot of other expectations."

"Well, you know, Ms. Sarah, nobody's just a musician."

"Yeah, yeah, I know we all have to make a living somehow."

"You gotta be a conduit."

"For what?" I asked. This was getting to be too much.

Julio grinned at me. "Don't ask me, ask yourself."

"Aw, you guys—"

"Passion, divinity, light, darkness, hey, I don't know, you gotta look inside and find out for yourself. You gotta look and you gotta listen."

I peeled the last shreds of label off my mineral water bottle. These guys were weird.

"Why do you care?"

"Me? Maybe I do, maybe I don't. You're Joey's friend, a nice girl…Joey's friends are my friends. Come over sometime. Get your head together. Ask yourself a few things. Stop walking in circles unless you want to get dizzy. Anyway, I gotta go now, I got some work to do."

"What, at this hour?"

"Sure." He got up and blew me a businesslike kiss. "See you later, alligator."

I didn't know what to think, but later I did go see him. More than once. After he started showing up in my dreams.

KARI

We were getting very close to opening night. Things were coming together, as they should after a good series of rehearsals.

Endymion and I had both become so wrapped up in the play that it felt as though we did little else. I had taken on less editorial work, which was necessary in order for me to have the time to write and rehearse, and Endymion had cut back on some of his other rehearsals. For the first time in at least a couple of weeks, we met for dinner and an evening of dancing.

In a curious way, I had the sensation that we were reprising our first encounters. We sat at the same table, although with more elaborate food in front of us, and there was an excitement hovering in the air between us.

"It's really coming together," I said, a little awed.

"How does it feel?" said Endymion.

"It feels—oh—it feels amazing. Exhilarating. Sure, I'll do something better someday, maybe something deeper, but right now this is what makes me happy. It flows along, it falls into place."

"Not everything has to be deeper than Lake Baikal or the Marianas Trench," said Endymion. "We won't be performing for an audience of anaerobic bacteria or whatever it is that lives in the depths."

"Fish with built-in lanterns," I said. "Hey, let's do our next show about *them*, or something that involves them. We could have streamers of blue and green tissue paper hanging from over the stage. Burbly, liquid underwater music sort of like Smetana's *Moldau*. But that's not what I was going to say. How does it feel for you?"

"I think you've already described it," said Endymion, and I was struck, not for the first time, that although he valued other people's feelings and had a knack for eliciting descriptions of them, he often seemed unaware of the degree to which he failed to describe his own. I did not think he did this intentionally, and indeed I usually had a pretty good idea how he felt about things, but he did have a bit of the professional therapist's habit—perhaps picked up from his mother—of keeping the focus on the other person's feelings and experiences.

"No, no," I said, picking up his hand and kissing each of his fingertips, "I described how *I* feel. Now it's your turn."

He grinned at me. "I love when you kiss my fingers. It's so sexy I can hardly stand it."

"And how does the show feel?"

"Mmm, it's very sexy too. Exhilarating, as you said. It's a new experience, putting together something this big. Well—I've told you before that I'd done a little sound design for theater, but nothing so ambitious. The things I did were afterthoughts. Successful afterthoughts, but not fundamental. This is like dreaming in tandem. You say things, and ideas spark in my mind. Like—you bring up the *Moldau* and instantly I hear it and think yes-and-no, it's brilliant water music but it's river music, not deep ocean current music. So we'd use it somewhere but not for ocean depths. Ocean depths are full of heavy currents and intense pressure, so something slow, almost with a touch of the elephant's dance in *Carnival of the Animals*. Something dark and ponderous, with gongs. I have to think about it. But we're not even there yet and it's already starting up. We're dizzy with seeing the Endymion show come together and it sets off new ideas. It's great. I like living like this. I'm not sure it's so great for all my other musical commitments, but it's one of those things that gives me that feeling of being part of the divine energy, of the ideas coursing through me."

"Flowing through your fingertips to my mouth," I said.

"Or your mouth to my fingertips, either way. The energy flows. It's attuned. It's there vibrating in the air."

"The music of the spheres," I said.

"Exactly. Okay, that goes in with the ocean depths. Same play. As above, so below."

"What's that, the title?"

"No, I don't think it's catchy enough. It's too alchemical. Call it *Music of the Spheres*. We can say 'as above, so below' somewhere in the text. *Music of the Spheres* is more intriguing and I think more people have heard the phrase."

"I think I love you."

"Well, maybe you do," he said. "Maybe I love you. Let's not worry about that. We love what we do together."

"Yes," I said. It was true. We were dreaming in tandem.

SARAH

Julio and I were sitting on his couch smoking a joint. I wasn't sure why I was willing to toke up with him and not with anyone else I knew, but after giving in that first time, I found it didn't bother me, somehow. Maybe in part it was that Julio was a jazz musician, not a hippie type, even if he was probably old enough to have been a hippie and did wear a ponytail. Jazz musicians, after all, were smoking weed long before hippies and had a whole different way of going about things. I don't know. I can't really explain it. I would still have refused to do it with anyone else. I didn't inhale very much even with Julio, although I wouldn't have told anyone that because of all the jokes about not inhaling.

Joey wasn't there; he had a rehearsal somewhere else. I hadn't even brought my cello. We were just sitting there toking and watching what we could see of the sunset out the window. I doubt, actually, that Julio smokes all that much grass regularly, because as a rule he is clear-headed, but he seemed to bring it out when I came by.

"What's that funny-looking plant you've got next to the aloe vera?" I asked to make conversation. "It looks like a lump."

"That one?" said Julio, pointing. "That's no lump, that's peyote."

"It's *what?*" I said, shocked.

"You know, peyote. Sacred cactus."

"You grow that in your house?"

"Sure, why not?"

I was about to say it was illegal, when I remembered that it wasn't necessarily, whereas the pot we were smoking definitely was. I rethought what I was going to say. "You use that stuff?"

Evidently I didn't keep the disdain out of my voice. "Be a little respectful," said Julio mildly. "This ain't Drano we're talking about, that kills fish somewhere if you put it down your sink. It's not heroin either. People have eaten peyote for thousands of years." He opened a small decorated box that sat on the coffee table. "You harvest the buttons very carefully, then you dry them. It's not for every day. It's very special. It's for wisdom and healing."

I looked at the dried buttons in the box. I thought they looked mummified and disgusting. I thought about how my mother probably used to eat this stuff. I doubted she thought it was sacred or for wisdom and healing.

"You can put it away," I said. "I'm sorry I asked. I don't want to know any more about it."

"You know, Ms. Sarah, Sarasota, there's a lot of things you don't want to know any more about," observed Julio.

"That's not true," I said. "I want to be an educated person."

"Huh," said Julio. "You think you're more educated than I am?"

Even a little stoned, I could tell that was a trick question. "No," I said.

"You think I'm more educated than you are?"

"Probably."

Julio laughed.

"Well, you know lots of stuff I don't," I said.

"There's different kinds of education, but hey. You're a sweet young thing trying to be a musician, right, Sarasota?"

I was annoyed by this description. I could tell it was meant more satirically than condescendingly, but it still pissed me off. "Quit insulting me."

"Just seeing if you stand up for yourself."

"Damn right I stand up for myself," I said.

We sat for a while not talking, but it didn't feel especially uncomfortable. Julio didn't make me uncomfortable in the way that Joey sometimes did. After a while, he lit another joint, then passed it to me.

I was away in my thoughts, but took it. "I had some strange dreams about you," I said suddenly.

"How strange?"

"Horrible."

"Scary ones?"

"Yeah. Nightmares."

"Are you scared of me?"

I accidentally inhaled heavily and went into a coughing fit. It was so violent I lost my balance on the couch and hit my head against his leg. I sat up again quickly. "I'm—not afraid." The coughing wasn't over, and I wheezed between words. "I'm—only afraid—in the dreams."

I sat there for a moment waiting for my lungs to recover. I couldn't imagine why anyone inhaled on purpose. You'd think it'd be enough to get a contact high and not bother to inhale.

"I dream creepy stuff, like that you and Joey put a weird cream on me that made me have hallucinations and go into convulsions," I said at last.

We sat for a while in one of those long pot-smoker silences. Time slowed; now that I had really inhaled, I was really stoned. As time stood still, I thought about how very stoned I was and how this wasn't such a terrible state, just a very different one.

"Cream, huh?" said Julio. "Where'd we put this cream?"

"My arms and legs. All over, I guess. It was awful. I couldn't get away. I was going out of my mind. I woke up when I nearly fell out of bed."

Julio considered this. "Why do you want us to do things you're afraid of, Sarasota?"

"I don't." I drew my knee up under my chin and wrapped my arms around it; I was barefoot, so I didn't think he'd mind my foot on the couch. Why would I want anyone to do things I was afraid of?

"Sounds to me like you want us to," he said. "What d'you think about us when you're awake, huh? You're not afraid when you're awake, right?"

"No, no. Come on, I don't hang out with people I'm afraid of."

"You like us, right?"

"Yeah, I like you."

"Well, sounds to me like you're not afraid of *us*, you're afraid of what you *want* from us. Whaddayou want from us, Sarasota?"

"I don't know—I want to learn stuff, I guess."

"And why does that scare you so much?"

"Aw, I don't know." I felt gloomy and troubled.

"Well, whaddayou want to learn from us that's so scary?"

I didn't say anything. I felt my blood pumping through my body. What was I supposed to say?

Julio said, "Seems to me you want something. You desire."

I still didn't say anything.

Julio picked up the edge of my skirt and touched it gently to my cheek. "You desire. You want passion and enlightenment, right?"

I said nothing.

"Well, you know, nobody can give you those things. You gotta find them somewhere inside. All anybody else can do is give you a little help along the way." We sat there for a while saying nothing, and then he ran his hand slowly and gently down the inside of my thigh. I didn't stop him. He looked into my eyes as he did so, watching for any sign of refusal. He stroked my thigh again and curled some escaped hairs around one finger. We looked at each other.

"Maybe you wanna lie back," he suggested, his hand pressed against me, warm and firm. Slowly, I lay back. He stroked me quietly through my underwear, then raised my skirt above my waist. "You're all wet," he said, and took my hand to feel where. "That's from you, not me," he said. Still looking into my eyes, he lowered his head until our faces were no longer visible to one another, and kissed the insides of my thighs.

I closed my eyes and let him kiss all around the edges of my underwear, then let him remove it and let him kiss me some more, very gently. I could have made him stop at any time, but I let him go on, and on, opening my legs further. I didn't think I was still stoned, but time was still languid and slow. I felt tears seep out of my eyes and drip down the sides of my face, but I wasn't unhappy, they seemed to be tears that echoed the wetness between my legs. Then I felt myself moving uncontrollably, even thrashing, but he didn't stop, not for a while longer.

Julio sat up and looked at me. "Are you okay?"

I had to bring my mind back from wherever it had gone. "Okay?"

"Yeah, are you all right? How do you feel?"

"I don't know." I lifted my hand and reached over to feel where he had kissed me.

"You don't know much, Sarasota. You don't feel bad, do you?"

"No."

"And you aren't afraid, are you?"

"No."

"Maybe you even feel good?"

I thought about it, laboriously. "Maybe."

"Maybe! If it's only maybe, how come you're smiling?"

"I don't know." Was I smiling? "I feel different."

"Put it in your music, Sarasota. There's more to passion than sex, but sex is part of passion."

I lay there thinking about the whole thing. My body was throbbing from all that kissing. I knew I could get mad at him and claim he took advantage of me, but I didn't think that was really true. I knew, inside, that I had wanted to find out.

He reached over and put my skirt back down over my knees. "You gonna lie there all evening?"

"No."

"Well, this part of the program's over."

I sat up and put myself back together. "I guess I should head home," I said.

Julio looked at me in a serious but friendly manner. We got up and walked to the door. He opened it, then took my hand. "Don't have any more bad dreams about me and Joey, okay?"

"I'll try not to," I said, though I couldn't see how trying would make a difference.

"Just don't," he said.

KARI

The audience entered the theater to find a dark stage lit only by a projection of Girodet's *Endymion*, gleaming dimly on the scrim. Quiet, unearthly music played: a pairing of flute and panpipe wandering aimless as a cloud (or so it seemed) above a dulcimer accompaniment. Gradually, when everyone had settled themselves and the house lights had gone off, a faint dappled pattern began to be visible on the stage floor, but it was very faint.

Bryce, garbed in a version of ancient Greek attire, his hair done in dark classical-looking ringlets (a wig, if the truth must be told, but a good wig) began to make his way toward the stage from the back of the house, pulling his sheep and lit by an amber follow-spot. He walked simply and slowly, and alert listeners would have noticed that a tom-tom or some similar drum had been added, but at a very low level, like a heartbeat or a footstep. When he came to the stage, which was several feet above the aisle, he had to coax his sheep up a ramp situated at right angles to the aisle—in other words, crossing in front of the stage—which was a trick that had involved a good deal of practice. The pull-toy line of sheep not only had to round a sharp corner, but could not be allowed to fall off the ramp. Bryce led his sheep to the beginning of the ramp, and here we had set things up so that there were a small number of ridges along the ramp so that Bryce could pull the first few sheep carefully around the corner and up, and then park them with the lead sheep's wheels over the first ridge. He could then gesture to the remaining sheep to follow, find that they did not, and step down and help them up until the entire lineup was higgledy-piggledy either on the ramp or aligned to start up it. Around this point, the lamb-baas started up; we had five or six of these toys and they baa'd all the way up the ramp as Bryce continued to pull and lift them on their way. Once onstage, he had another turnaround trick to get them facing the other direction, but this one was a little simpler as it merely involved getting them off the ramp and pointed the other way. Bryce was solicitous of his sheep and their difficulties, as any good shepherd ought to be, and even pointed the way for them. And, like any good shepherd, he had a dog; the dog brought up the tail end of the procession and could be unhooked and led with a separate string.

The baaing settled down a bit once the excitement of the ramp was over; Bryce led the sheep across the stage and into the wings back and forth several times until at last they all reached the rear of the stage, near the scrim. Meanwhile, the level of the lighting onstage had risen, revealing a light scattering of stage shrubbery—stylized painted plywood plants on stands—and a hillock sitting just in front of the scrim. The image of Girodet's *Endymion* had disappeared and was replaced by a dark sky punctuated with stars and the outlines of tall conifers.

Bryce helped his flock into a comfortable little arrangement in front of the hillock, unhooked his dog, and, planting the dog at the base, seated himself upon the hillock, which was built on the remains of a decrepit sofa. By this time, the flute, panpipe, and drum had faded away, leaving only a bit of dulcimer.

Now came a voice out of the darkness; a woman's voice reciting the opening to Keats's "Endymion:"

A thing of beauty is a joy for ever:
Its loveliness increases; it will never
Pass into nothingness; but still will keep
A bower quiet for us, and a sleep
Full of sweet dreams, and health, and quiet breathing.
Therefore, on every morrow, are we wreathing
A flowery band to bind us to the earth,
Spite of despondence, of the inhuman dearth
Of noble natures, of the gloomy days,
Of all the unhealthy and o'er-darkened ways
Made for our searching: yes, in spite of all,

Some shape of beauty moves away the pall
From our dark spirits. Such the sun, the moon,
Trees old and young, sprouting a shady boon
For simple sheep; and such are daffodils
With the green world they live in; and clear rills
That for themselves a cooling covert make
'Gainst the hot season; the mid forest brake,
Rich with a sprinkling of fair musk-rose blooms:
And such too is the grandeur of the dooms
We have imagined for the mighty dead;
All lovely tales that we have heard or read:
An endless fountain of immortal drink,
Pouring unto us from the heaven's brink.

Nor do we merely feel these essences
For one short hour; no, even as the trees
That whisper round a temple become soon
Dear as the temple's self, so does the moon,
The passion poesy, glories infinite,
Haunt us till they become a cheering light
Unto our souls, and bound to us so fast,
That, whether there be shine, or gloom o'ercast,
They always must be with us, or we die.

Therefore, 'tis with full happiness that I
Will trace the story of Endymion.
The very music of the name has gone
Into my being, and each pleasant scene
Is growing fresh before me as the green
Of our own vallies: so I will begin
Now while I cannot hear the city's din…

At the end of this recital, a slide composed of an engraving of the Roman Luna with crescent moon, conveniently filched from *The Illustrated Bartsch* and superimposed onto a gigantic color photo of the moon, appeared on the scrim. Bryce then, in a pose vaguely reminiscent of Rodin's *Thinker*, inquired:

No rest, Endymion? Still uncertain how to settle
thy steps by day or thy thoughts by night?
I will see if I can beguile myself
with sleep; and, if no slumber will take hold in my eyes, yet
will I embrace the golden thoughts in my head and wish to
melt by musing, that as ebony, which no fire can scorch, is
yet consumed with sweet savors, so my heart, which cannot
be bent by the hardness of fortune, may be bruised by
amorous desires. On yonder bank never grew anything
but lunary, and hereafter I will never have any bed but
that bank.

Bryce spoke fairly well for a dancer, which was one reason
we had wanted him, and with a little coaching, he had gotten
the Lyly lines into a pleasing bedtime speech. Having said his
piece, he settled himself in more of a slumberous posture.
Lights dimmed on most of the stage but remained gleaming on
his figure, and the same offstage female voice—it was, in fact,
my own—began to sing a slightly altered (gender-appropriate)
version of "Beautiful Dreamer" to the accompaniment of a
ukulele and an occasional lamb-baa:

Beautiful dreamer, wake unto me,
Starlight and dewdrops are waiting for thee;
Sounds of the rude world, heard in the day,
Lull'd by the moonlight have all pass'd away!
Beautiful dreamer, prince of my song,
List while I woo thee with soft melody;
Gone are the cares of life's busy throng,
Beautiful dreamer, awake unto me!
Beautiful dreamer, awake unto me!

A black-garbed stagehand then pulled a divider across the
stage to delineate the modern area, separate from Bryce and his
mythic hillside. Other stagehands removed the plants from the
modern area and brought out a few items of furniture, such as a
small table and two chairs, and the lights went up, in a relatively
prosaic fashion, on the half of the stage where Nick and Siobhan
were to enact their modern encounters.

I had taken a few elements of my first encounter with Endymion for this scene, but for the most part I had fashioned a new version of the pair's meeting. I did use the woman's failure to ask the man's name, and the general outline of our sparring about that, leading to his being termed Endymion. I had hesitated between naming the woman Diana and naming her Cynthia, but went for Diana on the grounds that while both names are used today, Diana is both more common (unless every Cindy is a Cynthia) and more recognizable as a form of moon goddess. In this, I let go of my objections to references to chaste goddesses, as no one especially associates living Dianes and Dianas with chastity.

When the time came, we represented their sleep with dimmed lights, the entrance of a stagehand holding a melodrama-style placard reading "They Sleep," and some gentle guitar arpeggios. After this first modern scene, which ended with the naming of Endymion, the lights went down on that part of the stage and we returned to the mythic Endymion, sleeping under the image of Luna and the moon photo. The slide changed to the image we had placed on the program cover, an old print of Selene throwing up her hands in astonishment at the sight of Endymion. There were more guitar arpeggios, but dramatic ones; Meryl appeared onstage in flowing garments (the magic drapability of rayon knits!) with a crescent moon in her hair, and stole toward the sleeping Bryce, kissed his forehead, and performed a brief pantomime of surprise and adoration. Then she ran off and the slide returned to Luna with the moon photo.

Bryce stirred and, rising slightly, stretched. Gesturing toward the projection, he remarked:

"My thoughts [...] are stitched to the stars, which being as high as I can see, thou may'st imagine how much higher they are than I can reach."

Offstage, I said:

"If you be enamored of anything above the moon, your thoughts are ridiculous; for that things immortal are not subject to affections. If allured or enchanted with these transitory things under the moon, you show yourself senseless to attribute such lofty titles to such low trifles."

Bryce continued:

"My love is placed neither under the moon nor above."

In my role as an offstage, impersonal voice of reason—though using the words of a character Lyly had oddly called Eumenides—I said, "I hope you be not sotted upon the Man in the Moon."

Bryce murmured, "No, but settled either to die or possess the moon herself."

At which point music intervened, and I inquired, "Is Endymion mad, or do I mistake? Do you love the moon, Endymion?"

Bryce replied, inevitably, "The moon."

A species of chorus, consisting of Nick, Siobhan, me, and Susan then entered downstage doing a simple version of a Balkan line dance, chanting:

"There was never any so *peevish* to imagine the moon either capable of affection or shape of a mistress; for as impossible it is to make love fit to her humor, which no man knoweth, as a coat to her form, which continueth not in one bigness whilst she is measuring. Cease off, Endymion, to feed so much upon fancies."

Bryce gazed up at the image of Luna, gesturing rather melodramatically to her, and exclaimed:

"O fair Selene, why do others term thee unconstant whom I have ever found unmovable? Unkind men, who, finding a constancy not to be matched in my sweet mistress, have christened her with the name of wavering, waxing, and waning! Is she inconstant that keepeth a settled course, which since her first creation altereth not one minute in her moving? There is nothing thought more admirable or commendable in the sea than the ebbing and flowing; and shall the moon, from whom the sea taketh this virtue, be accounted fickle for increasing and decreasing? Flowers in their buds are nothing worth till they be blown, nor blossoms accounted till they be ripe fruit; and shall we then say they be changeable for that they grow from seeds to leaves, from leaves to buds, from buds to their perfection? Then why be not twigs that become trees, children that become men, and mornings that grow to evenings termed wavering, for that they continue not at one stay? Ay, but Selene, being in her fullness, decayeth, as not delighting in her greatest beauty, or withering when she should be most honored. When malice cannot object anything, folly will, making that a vice which is the greatest virtue. What thing (my mistress excepted) being in the pride of her beauty and latter minute of her age, that waxeth young again? Tell me, what is he that, having a mistress of ripe years and infinite virtues, great honors and unspeakable beauty; but would wish that she might grow tender again, getting youth by years and never-decaying beauty by time, whose fair face neither the summer's blaze can scorch nor winter's blast chap, nor the numbering of years breed altering of colors? Such is my sweet Selene, whom time cannot touch because she is divine nor will offend because she is delicate."

Bryce sighed audibly, and continued,

"I am that Endymion, sweet Selene, that have carried my thoughts in equal balance with my actions, being always as free from imagining ill as enterprising: that Endymion whose eyes never esteemed … anything fair but thy face, whose tongue termed nothing rare but thy virtues, and whose heart imagined nothing miraculous but thy government."

At this juncture, we returned to the modern side of things, where Nick and Siobhan began to invent pretexts for lunar fantasy.

Back in mythic Greece, we began to move on to Endymion's dreams. First he returned to Keats—I hoped that no literary specialists in the audience would lambast me for interweaving the words of the Elizabethan Lyly and the Romantic Keats in the monologues of but one character—and Bryce, who was really quite a satisfactory actor as well as a dancer, looked up wonderingly and said:

"On I thought,
Until my head was dizzy and distraught.
Moreover, through the dancing poppies stole
A breeze, most softly lulling to my soul;
And shaping visions all about my sight

Of colours, wings, and bursts of spangly light;
The which became more strange, and strange, and dim,
And then were gulph'd in a tumultuous swim:
And then I fell asleep. Ah, can I tell
The enchantment that afterwards befel?
Yet it was but a dream: yet such a dream
That never tongue, although it overteem
With mellow utterance, like a cavern spring,
Could figure out and to conception bring
All I beheld and felt. Methought I lay
Watching the zenith, where the milky way
Among the stars in virgin splendour pours;
And travelling my eye, until the doors
Of heaven appear'd to open for my flight,
I became loth and fearful to alight
From such high soaring by a downward glance:
So kept me stedfast in that airy trance,
And lo! from opening clouds, I saw emerge
The loveliest moon, that ever silver'd o'er
A shell for Neptune's goblet: she did soar..."

He rubbed his eyes as if to awake, but instead lay back again
with an arm over his face; Meryl again stole in and kissed him,
but this time, lit by a pale follow-spot, she took his hand and
pulled him up and led him into a lovers' dance.

"Methought I fainted at the charmed touch,
I was distracted; madly did I kiss
The wooing arms which held me, and did give
My eyes at once to death: but 'twas to live,
To take in draughts of life from the gold fount
Of kind and passionate looks; to count, and count
The moments, by some greedy help that seem'd
A second self, that each might be redeem'd...
Why did I dream that sleep o'er-power'd me
In midst of all this heaven?"

And so it went. We had slides of daffodils and ferns; slides of various paintings and prints on the theme of Endymion; slides of the cosmos. We had lighting effects. We had music. Bryce told of Endymion's dreams in a language less loftily poetic than that of Lyly and Keats, since as a late twentieth-century person I did not have their style of linguistic abundance ready to hand, but it was still in what I hoped was an ecstatic and marvelous mode, for which I had primed myself by reading surrealist love poetry. We wanted to bring things, eventually, to an intoxicating, almost hallucinatory, frenzy of music, visuals, language, and movement, but not too quickly; after all, Endymion had to have several intensifying, erotic but poetic, dreams and Nick and Siobhan also had to bring their characters to a suitable degree of wild abandon in which their personas overtook their ordinary identities (something that had not occurred, and was not really wanted, in our own lives).

While things had to intensify to some form of climax, I was entirely opposed to the idea of bringing any serious discord into the thing, which would have been the norm for most plays. The average playwright would have reveled in destroying the lives or love of the modern characters—there would have been infidelity and jealousy, or someone would have gone mad, or someone's mother would have entered to wreak havoc, or all would have been blightingly revealed as a pathetic illusion. But this did not appeal to us. For one thing, the myth was not a tragic one. We weren't retelling *Oedipus* or the *Oresteia*. No haemartia came into the thing at all. Instead, what I had discovered in my research was that while there is no extant Greek drama or epic poem on the topic of Selene and Endymion, the myth of the sleeping, deathless, beloved shepherd had come to be understood as a reference to eternal life. In late antiquity, then, when Christianity, Orphic cults, the Eleusinian mysteries, and other death-and-resurrection religions grew widespread, the love of Selene and Endymion became a popular theme for sarcophagi. And so, at the close, after considerable dance and shadow performance lit by the whirling Milky Way, up went an image of a Gallo-Roman sarcophagus out of which appeared to emanate George Frederick Watts's dazzling Pre-Raphaelite vision of the lovers.

SARAH

I was alone in the house when the doorbell rang; my aunt had gone out with one of her friends, and Kari was out somewhere as well. For once I had no rehearsals to go to; my only plan for the day was to practice at home and then attend a play Joey had done some music for, which was opening that evening.

I was tempted not to answer the doorbell; I wasn't expecting anyone, and I didn't feel much like turning away newspaper salesboys, political canvassers, Jehovah's Witnesses, or Mormons. I thought we ought to have a sign up saying "No Solicitors," but my aunt thought that was unfriendly, as she sometimes liked talking to the miscellaneous people who came through the neighborhood, even though she had no intention of becoming a Mormon or Jehovah's Witness, and was not a big contributor to any of the causes that employed door-to-door workers. However, I had been taking a break by dusting the living room, so I thought I wouldn't be distracted from anything very *important* by answering the door.

A tall bearded man, probably in his forties, stood on the mat. He was casually but neatly dressed, as a political canvasser might be, but he had no clipboard, and besides, those jobs are usually done by college students. He looked a little nervous.

"Are you Sarah?" he asked.

I was taken aback. "Who are you? How do you know my name?"

"I'm sorry," he said, "I'm not starting this right. You're Lee Ann's daughter, aren't you? My name is Eli. I'm probably your father."

I stared at him. "*Eli?*" I said. "The poet?"

"More of an English professor than a poet these days. I guess you've heard of me, then. Do you remember me?"

I really didn't know what to say. After a moment I said, "I don't know why I would remember you. You went away."

"Not until you were about three," said Eli. "You don't remember me?"

"I don't think so," I said. "I've heard of you, of course. But I remember my mother having lots of boyfriends. Weren't you just kind of one of the flock?"

"Well, maybe," said Eli, looking a little hurt. "I didn't think so at the time."

"I could be wrong," I said. "I don't remember all that much from when I was a little kid. I know people thought you were probably my father."

"I've always thought I was," said Eli. "I don't know for sure, but I was pretty sure."

I realized it wasn't very polite of me to be holding this conversation on the front doorstep, but I didn't really want to invite him into the living room. "Would you like to come around to the back yard and have some lemonade?" I offered as a compromise. We had a little table and some lawn chairs back there, and my aunt always has a nice flower garden.

"I'd be delighted," said Eli.

We went round to the back, I installed him at the table, and then went in to get our lemonade. I thought it might give me time to think, but it really didn't. I simply felt dazed and confused. Eli, who might be my father, had sought me out! Why? Why wait all this time? Why wait until I was twenty-two years old? What did he care? I felt lightheaded and unsure what to do, so I concentrated on getting the pitcher.

Eli thanked me for the lemonade. "You must be wondering why I've suddenly come to see you."

"Well, yes," I said. "Where have you been?" I let it out. "I'm twenty-two years old. I don't need a father now."

"I'm sorry," said Eli. "I can't know what you need now. I'm sorry I wasn't around when you were younger."

"Well, here I am. What do you want?"

"I'd like to get to know you a little, and for you to get to know me. But I suppose you might not want to, and I can understand that."

I was, actually, pretty curious about this character Eli, who was probably my father but didn't seem to be any surer of it than anyone else. At the same time, I felt like he really deserved to be given a hard time.

"I live here with my aunt and I study cello. That's about what there is to know about me," I said. "What about you? Where have you been?"

"I've been a lot of places," said Eli. "I was depressed after Lee Ann and I broke up. I wandered around. I loved your mother, but we were both immature. I didn't know what to do with myself, so I just bummed around for a while doing odd jobs. You could do that in the seventies and early eighties without exactly being a homeless person. I'm not sure you can now. Anyway, after a while I went back to school. I decided I liked it, so I stayed in academia. I tried to get back in touch with Lee Ann a couple of times, but first I heard she was locked up in the mental hospital, and I wasn't sure I could take visiting her there."

"You couldn't," I said coldly. "We used to visit her. She was awful. A big fat half-catatonic lump. You couldn't talk to her. Imagine having that for your mother."

I noticed a tear escaping Eli's eye. This interview wasn't going too easily for him. "How did she get that way, though? She was a lovely, sweet, generous girl."

"They don't know. I think I remember someone saying it was because somebody put PCP in a joint, but my aunt says she doesn't remember hearing that."

"PCP was weird stuff. I heard strange things about it," said Eli. "I didn't think it sounded good. Well, I didn't visit her, and maybe I should have. Or maybe I was right. I don't know what's right in a situation like that. But later I checked with the hospital again to see if she'd recovered, and instead she'd died."

"That was awful too," I said. "She fell and hit her head the wrong way. The hospital was probably negligent, but we didn't sue."

Eli put his head in his hands and looked down at the table. My mother's bad end seemed to bother him more than it did me, but I was used to this story and evidently he wasn't.

"She was a bad mother," I added, just to make sure this was clear.

"I'm sorry you feel that way," he said. "She was very excited when you were born. Very happy. She wanted—we both wanted—to be good parents. Maybe not in the traditional way, but to be good parents anyway, in a new way."

"She was a terrible parent," I said. I wanted to make him feel worse.

"I have a hard time believing Lee Ann could have been a terrible parent," said Eli. "A bad one, maybe, but not terrible. She was a kind person, after all. She was gentle. She helped others when she could. Are you saying she was cruel to you?"

"Cruel? Oh no. But how would you like to grow up in a nasty old commune?" I realized as I said it that this might not make any sense to him, as evidently he had thought it would be just great.

"We wanted you to have a good life," said Eli, "one full of people who loved you, not just Lee Ann and me. We didn't want you to grow up with a lot of bourgeois hang-ups and people limiting your growth and creativity. We wanted you to be a free spirit."

"Hah!" I said derisively. "Life with a bunch of dirty dope-smoking hippies, that's just great." Again, as soon as I said this, I realized that this was not a smart thing to say, that now that I had taken up smoking dope with Julio, it was even a hypocritical thing to say, but I assured myself that I still wasn't a dirty hippie.

"I'm sorry you feel that way about it," said Eli. "We were hippies, sure, but I don't think we were all that dirty. I grant we smoked a lot of dope, but we didn't think that made us bad parents. It's not like we were stoned all the time or never washed."

Eli's recollection did not exactly jive with mine. I didn't remember him being around till I was three, although I supposed he might have been, and in my recollection the adults—if they were truly adults—were pretty much always stoned. Which of us was right?

"Maybe I should tell you a little about my side of the family," Eli went on. "My parents—your grandparents—live in Chicago. My dad's an engineer and my mom got a degree in French; they weren't very happy when I dropped out of college and joined the counterculture, but we get along fine now. My sister Ruth was a Maoist for a while, but now she does art therapy with the disabled, so I guess no one can really complain about that."

"I guess not," I said. At least, I didn't see how I could. Working with the disabled sounded like a reasonable way to atone for having been a Maoist.

"I can see where you would get the music from," Eli went on. "We always had music playing when I was growing up; my parents listen to a lot of classical music and jazz, and Ruth and I listened to that and a lot more as well. I really wanted to learn to play the sitar, but I didn't have much of a chance to get good at it. Or I didn't know how to go about pursuing it. I still think it's a neat instrument, and I love Indian classical music."

Things went on from there. I didn't want to hear all about Eli's family and life history, and at the same time I couldn't help being curious. Part of me wanted to shut him out, tell him to go away and not come back, and part of me wanted to know all about him so that I could fill in this blank. He also irritated me. He gave every indication of being a perfectly nice person in his way, but did he show any real comprehension of what it must be like for me to suddenly have a probable—not even certain— father show up out of nowhere? No! Not at all. Sure, he paid lip service to the idea that I might not be overjoyed to meet him, but it was clear that underneath, he really imagined that I would quickly throw aside any resentments and turn into his happy new daughter. You could see that this man hadn't brought up any children of any kind. He apparently thought children are automatically grateful for having been born or something.

I tried to be polite throughout the visit, but it was a strain. He clearly wanted an enthusiastic reunion, and there was no way I could provide one. I also wanted him to leave before my aunt came home; she would probably want to have a further long conversation and invite him to dinner or who knows what, which seemed completely undesirable. I wasn't entirely unwilling to see him again and get to know him a little better, but I really couldn't stomach the thought of him hanging around all afternoon trying to create a family tie that had never developed before. Maybe I was harsh, but it does seem to me that most people would have the same reaction to an unfamiliar parent who appeared without warning, out of nowhere.

Once he was finally gone and I had washed up our glasses, I flung myself onto the couch and banged on the cushions until this began to seem ridiculous and stupid. I didn't know what to think or what to do; I paced the living room for a while, but nothing in my mind seemed to settle.

Late in the afternoon, my aunt called to say that she wouldn't be home for supper. At that point, I gave up trying to make sense of his visit. I ran up to my bedroom and dug through my purse until I found my most senseless possession: some bits of dried peyote that I had stolen from Julio's box in a moment of insanity. Why I had stolen them, I couldn't really say; I had had no conscious plan to do anything with them. But now I had them, and I had a mad impulse to do something extreme, so I ate them.

I knew very little about how people took peyote other than that they ate it; *how* they ate it was mysterious to me and not something I had given any thought to. The dried pieces were quite small, so I simply expected to swallow them like pills.

The taste was abominable. I nearly spat them out right there. But having gotten this far with my mad act, I was determined to take it all the way. Gagging, I forced them down with the help of a glass of water.

I continued to feel nauseous, but I wasn't about to give in. It amazed me that anyone would take this stuff for fun—surely I wasn't the only one who found it noxious. Maybe Julio wasn't fooling when he said it wasn't for everyday use, that it was for wisdom and healing. Maybe it brought the wisdom not to eat it a second time, or it healed people by helping them vomit up toxins. I rolled around on my bed trying to keep the stuff down. I couldn't have said why I wanted to do this, except that I felt a compulsion to do something extreme and out of my normal bounds.

I did vomit once; I rinsed my mouth thoroughly and splashed cold water over my face and stumbled back out of the bathroom. I had no notion what to do next; the nausea began to pass and I began to feel better, possibly even a little exalted—I had swallowed this stuff and it hadn't killed me. Not that I expected it to be fatal, because I knew better than to think peyote is dangerous in the usual sense of the word, but all the same I thought I was brave to have downed the nasty stuff. I felt a little peculiar physically, which I didn't like, but I supposed that at least it was an improvement over the nausea.

I didn't know what I wanted from this experience, or what I expected. I knew a bit about peyote—I had heard a little over the years and then I'd looked it up after seeing it at Julio's—so I knew that it's a type of cactus native to the Southwest and that Native Americans had used it in their religious practices for thousands of years, well before people like my mother and Eli came along looking for ways of getting high. But I didn't really have a clear sense of what people experienced, other than that they generally had some sort of hallucinations.

Now, I can't really say I wanted to have hallucinations. If you had asked me at any point in my life whether I wanted to hallucinate, I would most certainly have said no! It would have struck me as one of the most undesirable, disagreeable, horrible things that could happen to a person, and seeking out such a state seemed like a completely crazy and stupid thing to do. And so, a person might reasonably want to know what possessed me to steal peyote, which I knew to be hallucinogenic, and then to go ahead and actually eat it instead of throwing it in the trash.

I have no very sensible answer for this. Certainly I wasn't behaving rationally either when I stole the peyote in the first place or when I proceeded to eat it. But I don't think there was a complete breakdown of my ability to think straight, either. Julio had told me the peyote was for wisdom and healing, and he had said I seemed to be afraid of what I wanted from him. Well, maybe some part of me was thinking in a different way than usual, thinking without thinking, in a sense. I didn't like it when he said maybe I thought too much, but I knew that he didn't mean I ought to be stupid and not think at all. I think it's very important to be a rational, sensible person, but I do know that not everything in life involves reason. You can reason out music to a certain extent, but if music were purely reason, hardly anyone would care about it. And of course that's true of most other things as well. So I assume some other part of my mind was operating when I had the notion to steal the peyote, and again when I took it into my head to swallow it. Some other part of me that wanted to bypass my usual thoughts and behaviors, just like when I lay back on Julio's couch.

I went outside and looked around. It seemed kind of bright out for the time of day and I had the impression that perhaps things were pulsating around me. I wasn't entirely sure; I wanted to be very careful about what I did and be very aware of whatever I might experience so that I could protect myself if necessary. I didn't want to do something stupid like walking into traffic. But I looked around for a while, at the trees and shrubs and houses and so on, and tried to figure out if I really saw them pulsating, or if I was just imagining that I saw this because I expected to have some kind of hallucination. If they were pulsating, it wasn't very strongly, although I did think I heard a buzzing in my ears, which reminded me of cicadas for some reason even though cicadas don't buzz.

After a while, it occurred to me that I had told Joey I would go see his play. In a more sensible frame of mind, I would probably have decided that it wasn't wise to try to go to a play after eating pieces of a hallucinogenic plant, but this never crossed my mind; I only remembered that I'd said I would go, and I felt somehow that if I didn't go now and put it off, he'd be upset and something awful would happen. What awful thing would happen, I couldn't imagine, but I was sure it would, so I got my jacket and purse and locked the front door and went off to the theater. I still thought everything might be pulsating a bit, but if it was, it wasn't enough to disorient me or even seem all that interesting. I thought maybe I just wasn't much affected by the peyote or that it wasn't working. Or, for that matter, that nothing would happen until later, although that should have been an argument against leaving home. As it was, I simply focused on which bus I needed to catch and on not doing anything complicated; I knew where the theater was, so that wasn't hard. It had been closed for years and then been renovated and there had been lots of news coverage of the renovation in the local arts press.

But I hadn't been paying attention to the time. Of course, I got to the theater early. The box office wasn't open yet and the doors were open for the cast and crew, so I walked in as if I were one of them, not even thinking twice about it. The air was starting to shimmer around me and the edges of things looked sort of grainy and odd, but I wasn't really paying attention; part of me thought maybe I ought to be keeping track of any unusual sensations, or at least paying attention to them, but mostly my mind was focused on how I had told Joey I'd be at the theater that night. Whether Joey was even there yet was immaterial so long as *I* got there.

I had never been inside this theater before, so it didn't seem all that strange to me that the walls of the lobby glowed and gleamed with unexpected colors. I stood there looking around, when suddenly a voice said, "Sarah, what are you doing here?"

I didn't recognize the voice at first; then I turned and realized that Kari Zilke had come in. I certainly wasn't expecting her to be at the theater, so I was tempted to respond by asking what *she* was doing there, but instead I decided to keep things simple. I said, "I'm here to see the play."

"Well, that's nice of you," said Kari, "but it doesn't start for another hour."

I said I could wait.

Before either of us could say anything else, Joey appeared as well and threw his arms around Kari, appearing to give her a kiss and saying, "How does it feel, O Lunar Deity?"

I was baffled, because why was he hugging Kari Zilke and

who was he asking? How did *what* feel? He couldn't mean the peyote, could he?

I must have made a noise without realizing it, because then Joey looked at me and said, "You're awfully early. Did you write down the wrong time?"

I didn't know what to say, since Kari and I had already covered this topic, or so it seemed, so I shrugged.

"Do you know Sarah?" Kari asked Joey.

"Sure," he said. "Do you?"

"Well, yes, we live in the same house," said Kari. "Her aunt is my landlady."

Their voices were more interesting to me at that moment than what they were actually saying; it sounded to me as though their voices were bells, although I couldn't have explained how their voices could sound like bells and yet remain recognizable. They said a few more things that I didn't quite catch because I was paying attention to the timbre of the bells instead of the meaning of the words, although I was surprised that they seemed to know each other.

Then Joey said, "Sarah, Kari and I have a lot of things to take care of right now, so maybe you can just sit in the audience while we get things set up." He must have realized I wasn't quite my usual self, because he came over and took my hand and walked me into the theater proper, out of the lobby, and settled me in a back-row seat. And from there on things became very unpredictable. My hand tingled from being held, making me feel much as I had after the events on Julio's couch, and it seemed to me that after settling me down in the theater seat, Joey sat down next to me and began to kiss me, but in retrospect I think this must have been a hallucination. I know I didn't hallucinate Julio laying me down on his couch, but I am pretty sure that I was hallucinating Joey's kisses after we walked into the theater, because I had the idea he kissed me for a long time and then ran off down a long tunnel shouting Kari's name.

I suppose stagehands came in and out of the theater during the setup, but I didn't really notice, because I closed my eyes not to be distracted. Instead, I imagined I heard Julio asking me again what I wanted from him that I was afraid of, and I heard some vast nonverbal part of me saying, "I want everything, because I'm afraid of everything." But that made me angry because I didn't think I was afraid of everything, by any means, and even if I *was*, I didn't want to go around *announcing* that I was. I tried to say that actually I wasn't really afraid of anything, but I had the feeling that Julio started laughing and telling me that I was afraid of lots of things.

I didn't actually hear him say it, but I knew, as if in a dream, that he said, "You're afraid of me and of Joey and of my guitar and your cello and of sex and drugs and rock and roll. You're afraid of the moon and stars. You're afraid of good feelings and bad feelings and funny feelings and sad feelings."

Then I had the sense that Joey was there and joined in, telling me in the same fashion that I was afraid of him and afraid of liking him and afraid of Scott Joplin and Benny Goodman and, of course, afraid of sex and drugs and rock and roll.

As if this wasn't enough, then Kari Zilke arrived as well and started listing things that she thought I was afraid of too, starting with Günter Grass and Mario Vargas Llosa and going on to James Joyce and dildos and lesbian bars.

And all this made me mad, but it was worse because I knew some of it was true and I didn't want to sit down and figure out which of these accusations were truthful and which ones were just mudslinging, so I ran—or imagined myself running—off down a long hall, which might have been the same one that I thought Joey had run down after kissing me, but which after all might have been a completely different hallway, and I found that the hallway was dark and full of quite a few scary-looking and scary-sounding and scary-feeling things that made me wonder why anyone would think I could possibly be afraid of Scott Joplin or Mario Vargas Llosa when after all there I was in this nasty icky tunnel full of mucus and weird stuff. Whether the peyote was making me see things or just loosening up my imagination, I wasn't sure.

At which point it occurred to me that if I was in a tunnel full of mucus and whatnot, maybe I was back in my mother's vagina in the process of being born or escaping or some strange thing, since while that might be bizarre, it made more sense than thinking I was in somebody's nostril or intestine. So was I being reborn or was I trying to return to the womb? I didn't know, and while I was wondering about this, I realized that my mother herself was walking toward me. At first it seemed that she was the young, pretty hippie mother I remembered from my early childhood, and she smiled at me encouragingly and said, "Wow, Sarah, I can't believe you're so big! My little mouse grew into a giraffe!"

I didn't really like hearing this, but it was relatively neutral, and she looked friendly, so I let her come closer. She was wearing one of her favorite embroidered Mexican blouses and a long skirt with shisha work. The shisha mirrors glittered and sparkled, and although the mirrors were tiny, I found that I could see my reflection in them—but rather than reflections of how I looked at that moment, I saw reflections of how I had looked at all sorts of moments in my past, from infancy to grade school and high school and concerts and even a reflection of myself lying on Julio's couch with my skirt up and my knees disappearing somewhere over his shoulders. The reflections were all moving and some of them were speaking as well, and I found that if I listened closely, I could hear some of what I had said at different times in my life. But I didn't really want to hear all sorts of things I had said long ago, or even recently, many of which sounded mean or unhappy or stuck up, and I heard myself now saying, "Mama, why are you doing this to me?"

"But Sarah," said my mother, "I'm not doing anything to you. I'm only showing you a few little pieces of yourself. Don't you like yourself?"

"Why should I like myself?" I heard myself say. "Why should I like anybody?"

"Why?" said my mother. "Why not, Sweetie? I like nearly everybody. It's easy. People are good, aren't they?"

"I don't know where you get that idea," I said. "Look at how they make war and commit serial murders and pollute the earth and all kinds of horrible things."

"Well, we're not all good all the time, Kitten," said my mother gaily. "But why focus on the bad? If you don't like yourself, why don't you change who you are? Look, you can change in the blink of an eye!" And with that, *she* changed, but into the mother I remembered from the mental hospital, a dull, listless, fat woman with greasy hair and ugly clothes that didn't fit right.

"You're not my mother," I said.

"Oh, yes I am!" said this apparition. "I've always been your mother and I always will be!"

"You're horrible," I said. "You're a troll."

"Yes!" giggled my mother. "I'm a troll mother and I gave birth to a troll brat!" She held up a big mirror and I saw myself looking just like her, only still somehow recognizably myself. "You couldn't resist all that good weed and you couldn't resist the magic cactus either."

"I'm not going to be like you!" I said. "I'm different."

"The apple falls close to the tree!" hooted my mother. "Doper, doper, sanctimonious little doper!"

Well, I didn't want to listen to that, even if it was pretty much true. I ran at her and shoved her over, except that she bounced right back like those awful toys, usually made to look like clowns, that keep flying back upright no matter how many times you hit them. Then all of a sudden she was my pretty mother again, wanting to know why I was hitting her.

"Don't you love your mama, Sarah? Why're you hitting me when I love you more than anything else in the world?"

"More than Eli? More than Tom, Dick, and Harry and all the rest of them?"

She started laughing again. "No, I love myself the very best. Don't you?"

"Why are you here?" I countered. "Why are you bothering me?"

"I'm here because you want me. You called me out of my sleep."

"No I didn't."

"Oh, Baby Girl, you called me and I came. You want me and you hate me and you fear me. Am I really all that bad? You want me to beat you and feed you drugs and make you have sex with me. I can do it if that's what you really want."

"No, no, I don't want anything like that from you, I wanted a nice normal mommy!"

"You don't know what you really want," said another voice. It sounded like Joey's. I turned, and there he was, only dressed like a rapper and starting to launch into some kind of long rap song about all the things I didn't know about myself and my wants. Then Julio and Kari joined in like some kind of weird backup vocalists, singing, "You don't always know what you want, and you can't always get what you need," adding in just a little "Sha-na-na-na-na" and "Shu-be-do-be-do" just to make the song sound really wacko.

This sort of torment went on for quite a while, and then Joey said, "It's time for you to play with us."

I assumed he meant play music, so I said I didn't have my cello along, but he said, "No, no, no, that doesn't matter, you're going to be the cello."

This alarmed me, and I realized that I had turned into a weird hybrid creature that was simultaneously Charlotte Moorman and her cello, naked and festooned with small televisions that played all sorts of bizarre scenes of people being killed in wars and natural disasters, interspersed with scenes of my childhood and scenes of what I could only guess might be my future, everything vibrating and making distorted sounds as Joey and the others moved the bow across my strings.

"Who are you?" they chanted. "What do you want? Who do you want to be from now on?"

I felt utterly stupid and incoherent as all this was going on; how could I get out of this oppressive situation and return to normal? Then it occurred to me that this was all just in my head, like a dream.

I opened my eyes and realized that I was still sitting in a theater seat; Julio was sitting next to me, or so it appeared, keeping an eye on me. People were sitting all around us; it was dark except for what looked like a guy with long curly hair pulling a row of toy sheep toward the stage. Well, I thought, now I'm really hallucinating, if I dreamt up all this crap and now I'm imagining that Julio and I are sitting in a theater watching a guy dressed like an ancient Greek pulling a string of toy sheep. I closed my eyes again and when I reopened them, something more like a play seemed to be going on, though I couldn't really bring myself to listen to what the actors were saying after everything I had already been imagining hearing people say. I was baffled. I remembered that I had, in fact, come to a theater to see a play that Joey had done some music for, and that Kari Zilke appeared to be involved in it in some way too, but was this the play I had come to see or was this just a more vivid, open-eye hallucination?

I began to try to pay attention to what was occurring onstage, although as I had missed the opening, I was utterly unclear what was going on and what I could rely on as being the actual play and what was merely in my head masquerading as a play. Joey hadn't really said anything about the nature of the play, but had merely mentioned it as a reason he couldn't rehearse as often for a while, and as something that I might want to see.

I had a vague idea that it all had something to do with Greek mythology, but while I know some of the basics—Zeus was the king of the gods and threw thunderbolts, and Apollo had to do with reason and Dionysus was the god of wine—I really wouldn't say I knew any of the stories or minor characters, so there was nothing in my education to help me figure out what anything here meant. Characters seemed to be in the throes of love or attraction, but why that was or what they were up to was pretty opaque to me, especially since one side of the stage seemed to have one set of lovers and the other side seemed to have a different set, with no interaction between the two. I didn't think the ancient Greeks staged their dramas like that; I thought they held their dramas in big outdoor amphitheaters. But these days people stage things in all kinds of strange ways; I'd seen Shakespeare's *Richard III* made to look like it took place in a Latin American dictatorship. There's no accounting for what theater people will do, and I guess sometimes it works, although I would have preferred *Richard III* to look historically appropriate. After all, people wore interesting clothing back then which I'd much rather look at than twentieth-century military uniforms.

But there it was. Something or other was going on onstage, and maybe most of it was actually being performed by real people rather than by figments of my imagination, even though I found it terribly hard to follow. The language, for instance, sometimes sounded like Shakespeare, which made me wonder whether Shakespeare had written about the ancient Greeks; but then sometimes the language sounded like real live present-day people, which couldn't be Shakespeare. And the music consisted of strange bits and pieces, flutes and drums and guitar and miscellaneous other things fading in and out so that I wasn't sure, again, how much I was hearing and how much I was making up, because who knew what Joey might think was suitable music for a play, and how much music does any given play need to have when it isn't a musical or an opera? Sometimes this one didn't seem to have any music, and then other times the music seemed to take over.

And at times there was dancing and pantomime, or I supposed there was; and the longer things went on, the weirder it all got, because either the play got very strange or the peyote was taking hold again, and all sorts of swirling lights and starry galaxies appeared, and photos of gigantic, intensely colored flowers, and a man's voice describing his dreams, all of which seemed to involve what his girlfriend or maybe the moon had done to him while he was asleep. The lights were unsettlingly bright. And the dream descriptions began to be very disturbing precisely because all of that description, wherever it came from, prompted more illusions in which it seemed to me that all sorts of people I knew, but particularly Joey, Julio, Kari Zilke, and Wanda, were trying out these different things on me, which was embarrassing because I was aware at some level that I was sitting in a theater surrounded by lots of people, and what if I did something inappropriate that made them notice me? I was very nervous about this and anxious for the whole thing to stop.

KARI

I think that, in the excitement of launching into a life of renewed purpose, full of putting together the Endymion play and going dancing and plotting new projects, I have not paid sufficient attention to those aspects of my life that lay outside the realms of love and imagination. Specifically, that is, to whatever was going on with my landlady's niece, Sarah.

I could argue that Sarah's life was tangential to my own; we didn't see much of each other, and while I could tell she was rather intrigued by me, she was a bit prickly and made herself hard to get to know. But I've been wrapped up in my own woes and my own new happinesses, and I thought that she was equally wrapped up in her own life, which I supposed had next to nothing to do with my own.

I was surprised when she showed up at the theater an hour or so before our opening performance, but it seemed that she knew Endymion from the conservatory, so although she looked a little less poised than usual, I didn't pay much attention. If he had given her a comp ticket and she sat quietly in the audience while we finished our preparations, what difference did it make? She's a professional musician, or planning to become one, so she ought to know how to behave at someone else's show. But I wasn't thinking about all the wild emotions that roil under the surface when people are in their twenties, even though my own twenties were filled with wild feelings that both spurred me on and devoured my time in useless anxieties and despair. Perhaps like my older friends, when I saw Sarah around the house or got into a conversation with her, I had encouraged myself to see a person who apparently knew what she wanted in life and was busy working her way toward getting it. Someone who seemed calm and relatively mature, whose attention was focused on a reasonable yet ambitious goal, not a person one would imagine to be prey to wild extremes.

In my oblivious, first-night excitement, then, it seemed perfectly reasonable to invite her to our cast party. It was a small
party—people connected with the production plus a very few
others, mainly Endymion's band members since the party was
at his apartment and they had helped out with some of the
music. A typical sort of small-cast party, in other words. A few
six-packs, some bottles of wine, cheese and crackers, chips and
dip, pita bread and hummus, a veggie platter from the store,
nothing fancy because none of us had the time or money to do
anything special. Well—a bottle of champagne on general prin-
ciples. I don't even like champagne, but there have to be toasts.

Sarah was quiet most of the time. It didn't seem odd, because she's not a very talkative person in the first place and she
didn't know most of the people there, who were, after all, eager
to replay all the best and worst moments of the performance.
She mostly sat, apparently listening, sometimes talking with
Endymion's friend Julio, whom I knew very slightly and also
knew to be a respected jazz guitarist.

So there were toasts to our success (the audience had been
of respectable size and had clapped at the end), jokes about
the script and the props and anything else one could make a
joke about, talk of how the lighting seemed to work well, all
the usual. Eventually, of course, people began to wander home,
and I looked forward to wrapping myself around Endymion
and drifting off to a well-deserved night's sleep.

But after everyone else had gone, we were left with Julio and
Sarah, and I realized that an argument was underway, which
had been hushed and unobtrusive while the other guests were
still on the scene, but which was now able to burst forth in full
force.

"I can't believe you'd let this happen!" exclaimed Endymion.
I don't think I had ever before seen him really angry, but now
he was letting loose. "I can't believe you would be so irresponsible…"

"Not irresponsible, man, she has to make her own choices,"
Julio was saying, by no means as worked up.

"Her own choices, bullshit," said Endymion. "Does she

seem to be making intelligent choices lately? Sarah, do you think it was such a brilliant decision to show up tonight tripping out of your fucking mind?"

"Well—" Sarah began.

"Come on, give her some slack. She has to make her own mistakes," said Julio. "She's a grown-up, it's not nursery school. She's gotta learn. Sarah, you're not complaining, are you?"

Sarah looked generally pissed off, as well she might with two guys arguing over her ability to make her own decisions. "I have a lot to complain about," she announced.

"What the hell is going on?" I demanded, but nobody paid any attention to that.

"What," said Julio, "you're not mad at me about anything, are you?"

"And why wouldn't she be?" said Endymion. "She can be mad at you, you're not perfect."

"Are you mad at me, Sarah?" said Julio.

"Umm…" said Sarah at length, "no, I'm just mad in general."

"That's just fucking great," said Endymion. "You're on planet Saturn, you've never let on what your problem is—"

"She has to find her own way, and it's not your way," said Julio. "You like women who like to talk, like Kari here."

I wasn't sure whether I exactly cared for being categorized as a woman who likes to talk, but clearly this was not the time to worry about that.

"Of course I like women who like to talk, if they have something intelligent to say," said Endymion. "That's beside the point. We're not talking about my taste in women. My taste in women has nothing whatsoever to do with Sarah."

Judging by the look on Sarah's face, this phrasing was perhaps overly blunt. I hoped she hadn't fallen for Endymion, but even if she hadn't, he made it sound as though she was simply beyond the pale, attraction-wise. Nobody likes to hear that about themselves.

"What the hell are you guys arguing about?" I demanded. "If you're arguing about Sarah, why're you leaving her out of the conversation? What's this all about?"

"I'm trying to find out what it's all about," said Endymion, "and as usual Sarah has next to nothing to say for herself and it turns out that my friend Julio, who I thought might be a good person for her to know, is letting her get all messed up."

I had the feeling Endymion was censoring this account considerably, since it is not usual for him to be so vague.

"I'm not letting her get all messed up," said Julio. "She's gonna be just fine. You're gonna give her a bad trip if you keep yelling at her."

"I'm *already* having a bad trip," said Sarah. "It's been bad all the way."

"Well, what'd I tell you," said Julio, "peyote isn't for everyday kicks. I didn't tell you to take it, I didn't tell you it was something you should try, I just told you what it was. But something in you said you had to do this, and I'm not gonna say it was smart or stupid."

"Well, I say it was stupid," said Endymion, "and you, Julio, are to blame for not keeping an eye on things."

"It sounds to me," I said to Endymion, "as though *you* are feeling guilty and shoving the blame off onto Julio. And isn't Julio right that Sarah's old enough to make her own decisions? She'll be done tripping tomorrow, right?"

"I *do* feel guilty," said Endymion, "because I wasn't paying attention after I took Sarah over to Julio's, and because I think all of us are responsible for one another's lives."

"You're taking this too far," I said. "Responsibility has its limits. Sarah, you're not suicidal or anything, are you?"

She shook her head.

"Well, okay, then I don't see what the big deal is unless there's a lot more to this."

"Oh, there's more," said Endymion.

Things went on from there. Between what was said then and what I heard later, I gathered that Endymion had introduced Sarah to Julio out of an intuition that she needed to broaden her horizons both musically and personally, but that the experiment had gone haywire—in terms of his expectations, I should say, and not necessarily in any real sense—and now Endymion was alarmed that not only had Julio gotten Sarah to loosen up musically, which was desirable, but he had—supposedly—made a pothead out of her, seduced her, and now she had stolen Julio's stash of peyote and was having a bad trip on that.

Oho! So Miss Straitlaced Classical Musician did have a secret life! How very naughty of her.

I knew Endymion admired Julio both as a musician and for other, harder to define, personal qualities; thus Endymion was convinced that this was a great betrayal of trust. He appeared to see Sarah as a person of fragile personality, strong only on the outside but likely to fall apart if led in the wrong direction

I did not fully buy this assessment, and neither, obviously, did Julio. I didn't think Julio should be let off the hook, because he could be said to have abused, or at least tested, the trust of a much younger woman who perhaps did not have significant prior experience. But on the other hand, I agreed with Julio that Sarah was a grown-up person who should certainly be able to decide for herself about all of these things. It was not as though Sarah had been leading a life devoid of temptation; if Julio was the first person who had successfully tempted her, and was an admirable person overall rather than some kind of evil or deranged or stupid one, then it seemed to me that this all came under the heading of Things One Does in the Process of Growing Up. If coercion and serious danger were not involved, and there seemed to be no hint that they were, then maybe it would all turn out to be one of those things that has its good and its bad aspects but that ultimately promote growth and self-awareness. I didn't think Endymion needed to take this as either a personal failure of his own or as criminal behavior on Julio's part.

I was, admittedly, startled when Sarah revealed that during the peyote trip she had imagined she was having sex with all three of us as well as other people unknown to me, but I supposed that this was some sort of wish-fulfillment dream gone wild, and not anything she actually thought she had to try in real life, so I didn't comment on it. If she decides that her future will involve a round of orgies, I will decline to participate, not being much drawn to severe young women who have to be shaken out of their self-imposed narrownesses and who then go plunging in the opposite direction.

The discussion went on most of the night, and I was relieved when Endymion finally announced that he had had enough, a conclusion I would have thought Sarah should have voiced considerably earlier, except that I remembered myself at her age and how one can simply batten on disputes and emotionality and endless talk about people's behavior and feelings about it. It can feel so grown-up to go on endlessly about feelings and nuances of relationships and who said what and why, but I am no longer nearly so fond of that as I once was and I did not get the impression that Julio had *ever* been one for endless talk.

So, finally, Endymion had to bring out his extra bedding and settle everyone for what was left of the night, and in the morning we all had to go out to breakfast together, although I had long since had enough of the whole problem and didn't want to hear any more about it or devote any more of my thoughts to Sarah's life and development. Perhaps it was selfish of me, but we did, after all, have another show to do in the evening.

It seemed clear to me that the time had come to move out of the room in Sarah's aunt's house.

SARAH

After I began to come out of the peyote trip and think about things more rationally, I had to admit that Joey and Julio were right, it was stupid of me to take the peyote when I was all stressed out and also when I had prior plans for the evening. Joey thought I was stupid to take it at all, and he was probably right, although Julio insisted that under different circumstances I'd get very different things out of the experience. He didn't seem to blame me for stealing his stash and claimed it was just part of my education, not that I was supposed to become a kleptomaniac or go into a life of crime, of course.

I was kind of upset to discover that Joey was involved with Kari Zilke, of all people, who despite being an interesting person is much older than we are. It's true that Julio is also much older, but I don't really see anything very similar in the two situations. I don't have any intention of having an actual liaison with him. I learned some things from spending time with him, and if Joey is going to flip out about this, then he should look at why he's so enamored of Kari Zilke.

The trip did make me think about a lot of things once I got back into my right mind. I don't know how to interpret all the things I saw and heard, but I'm trying to go over it all and see what I can learn, even though it's not very agreeable. People said that everything I experienced was something from my own mind, my fears and desires, and not things that happened externally, so I think I have to take it as being somewhat like a dream, in which things that bother me come up in new forms. So I have to think about my relationship to various people, and especially to my mother.

I suppose that in a way I don't know what my mother was really like—what she would have thought of me today, for instance, or what she would have liked to read or what music she would have liked to listen to. After all, the fact that when I was little she listened to Jimi Hendrix and to sitar music and other trendy things, and that she read Kahlil Gibran, does not mean she'd still be into those same things now. She was very young in those days—about my age, but she seems so immature to me—so you'd think that she might have changed over time if she'd had the chance. Most people did, even Eli. When I think about this now, I sometimes feel that I've been too hard on her, that if she hadn't had me at the age she did and hadn't done whatever it was that made her crazy, then she might be leading a normal kind of life today like most of her old friends. Probably not a life like my aunt's, but she would probably have a job, and maybe a husband and kids, or at least a dog and a garden. She might have gotten back in touch with all those high school friends who had good memories of her. I suppose she would probably have stayed a little bit of a hippie, which lots of people have, but in a harmless way. It wouldn't matter if she kept doing the *I Ching* or wearing Mexican blouses. There are thousands of people who do things I associate with being a hippie which are, in fact, completely benign. But she made choices that took her too far in that direction, and this is hard for me to forgive. How can I know what I would have thought of her if she had led a different life and had me in different circumstances?

When I try to wrap my mind around these ideas, these possibilities of other outcomes—which I find myself doing now and then these days—I get all confused and moody. When Kari Zilke was living at our house, I'd sometimes look at her and ponder how she seemed to regard our choices in life as all continuing to exist on some level, out there in space or something (well, maybe not in space, but existing), that having gone in one direction didn't automatically close off access to other directions, but instead perhaps created a trail from which you might, if you decided it didn't work, depart and go tracking through the landscape in search of some other better trail that you might have abandoned years ago, or that you might not even have known was there waiting for you. Kari, and even our other renters, I suppose, had left whatever paths she and they were on, and our house was in some fashion a small path or a way station or even just a bench that they encountered in their journey to an alternate path. This idea of alternate paths was both unsettling and exciting for me. Once I thought about it, I realized that it was hardly a new concept, but it was new to me. It's not always important whether an idea is new, but whether it comes to you at a time when it can be meaningful, which is another thing that was beginning to strike me during the time Kari Zilke lived with us. It's obvious that you can't, for example, learn algebra until your mind is prepared to grasp it, but we don't always think that way about other things. I might, for example, try to play a piece that was beyond my skill, but more from optimism and a desire to test myself, not because I really expected to be able to perform it—but at the same time I wouldn't knowingly choose such a piece unless it was something that already spoke to me musically. I don't think I'm a very deep person, but I hope I am not a shallow one; I feel that I don't understand much of life very well yet, but I hope that someday I will. I would like, I think, to stop hating my mother and begin to understand who she was.

And I confess that although I was brought up not to steal and I don't think I ever stole anything more significant than cookies or small change before taking Julio's peyote, I did steal one more thing. After Kari Zilke told my aunt she was moving out, I went through her papers and stole her account of her life with us and her affair with Joey, and when she asked me if I had taken it, I denied it.

I don't think I'm a bad person, but I realize that she might not forgive me.

Kari: Epilogue

In recent months, I find myself thinking back on what my life was like during the year after I left my husband. It's not a time I had thought much about for some years, perhaps because my life went on in relatively exciting ways and that year was simply the beginning, but perhaps also because once I decided to make the second move, the one out of Sarah's aunt's house, I found I no longer had the pages I had written about my life after my marriage.

I knew who had taken them, but she wouldn't confess, and I wasn't going to imitate her by searching her bedroom. For one thing, if she wanted that piece of me so badly, I knew she was going to hide it somewhere I didn't have good access to. It was probably in her cello case or in some sheet-music-filled locker at the conservatory. Perhaps, then, I was precipitous in my decision to move out of Sarah's aunt's house. If I had stayed a little longer, Sarah might have settled down a little after her adventure with the peyote, which I didn't even regard as all that big a deal. She would probably have gone back to obsessing about her rehearsals and stopped regarding me as an object of fascination and, perhaps, as someone who took up with a guy she was interested in. Although, actually, I couldn't tell whether she was more drawn to me or to Endymion; she wasn't particularly close to either of us, but I had the feeling that she fought against attractions to both of us.

But I don't know what she's doing these days; my own life leaped forward after the Endymion play and I haven't inquired in several years. I kept in touch with Sarah's Aunt Joan in a sporadic, Christmas-card manner, because I rather liked Joan and her garden and had gotten interested in quilting after she showed me her first piecework and took me to see a show of modern quilts down at the store where she took her classes. Joan said Sarah had eventually gotten involved with a cellist named Wanda and moved out, but that the relationship hadn't lasted all that long because both girls (she called them girls, though I wouldn't have) were headstrong and difficult and annoyed each other constantly. Joan thought Sarah had a way of latching on to people who were more intellectual and better talkers than she was, and that while Sarah was smart, she didn't contribute enough to these friendships to hold people's interest. I thought that might be true. It fit my experience with her. And I could imagine her fighting with this woman Wanda, whom Joan described as a sexy, bratty intellectual type who kept up on all the latest developments in contemporary music and art. Endymion knew Wanda slightly, and he said she was an interesting, intense character who could pick a fight over whether Yoko Ono was brilliant or whether video art was going to die in the computer age. There was no way the Sarah I knew was going to suit a person like that. Maybe she'd changed a bit, though. People do.

I moved in with Endymion—I did learn his name, but we don't use it—for a short time, in a stopgap way; we both thought I should get out of Sarah's life for a while, or at least out of her aunt's house. But I didn't think it made any sense for me to perch in Endymion's apartment for long either. I liked him too much to want to risk territorial disputes and petty irritations. So I got my own place in the same neighborhood and we continued our collaboration.

Some of the reviewers liked the Endymion play, and of course others thought it was formless and self-indulgent and too reliant on Lyly and Keats. We knew there would be people in the latter camp; the good thing was that some people were excited and praised the piece. So after its run, we went on and did other shows with the same theater, helping build its reputation as an experimental venue. It took us a while to work up *Music of the Spheres*, but it pleased us to work on a more philosophical project after the pleasures of one more primarily erotic, although both were very sensuous theater.

As for our personal relationship, I still say its basis is in friendship and collaboration, which continue to function pretty well. At its outset, I sometimes wondered what would happen as time went on; I still don't know what will happen, because it's never possible to know these things. I think, for example, that Endymion would like to have children, which is hardly likely to happen with me at this point. A more conventional person might say, "I want children, therefore I must leave you and find someone else," but he is not all that conventional, and we have our own way of negotiating life, which has not shipwrecked us yet. So I don't know what he'll do. Attractions come and attractions go, but I haven't seen him prefer anyone else in any real way. Something always pulls us back together before we get too far apart.

Last night I suddenly had the notion of looking up a person we may call X, whom I loved miserably so many years ago, before my marriage. He was the cause of my marriage, we could even say. And ah, the wonders of Google. He is the most prominent person of his name, so my curiosity was soon satisfied. He was headed for an academic career when I knew him, so I was not surprised to learn that his university has given him tenure. He teaches, gives conference papers, wins awards, advises TV shows—and apparently looks almost unchanged from when we first met. It is true he's secretly a little vain about his looks, so it's possible the photos aren't quite current. On the other hand, there are YouTube videos of him lecturing in which he looks just the same. YouTube is relatively new; ergo, he probably really looks like this. Is it heredity? Good diet? Low stress? Regular exercise?

But I digress. What would my life be like had he really fallen for me? Not bad, I suppose, but all the same I never had any yen to be a faculty wife. I am glad X is doing well (at least in his career) but I do not yearn to join him.

And then there's my husband. We got our divorce and we now exchange holiday cards and wish one another well.

I think I will see what happens in the unforeseeable future, what happens with collaboration once Endymion gets nearer forty and has, perhaps, anxieties about the things he hasn't done yet. We've done a lot of theater with some dazzling music and design; will it continue or will it turn into something else? It could be a new adventure for both of us.

I'm asking the universe to give us whatever is best and not merely what we think we want.

ACKNOWLEDGMENTS

Thanks are due to many friends along the way, but particularly to Dirk van Nouhuys and the late Betty Dietz for their comments on the manuscript back when it was very new.

It has been a long road from the writing to the publication, during which I finished my PhD, became a professor of art history, published a book on the Czech surrealist Toyen, and even (as this book went to press) retired. Yet eventually the stars aligned for this project, and the enthusiasm shown by Jaynie Royal and the rest of the Regal House team has been all that an author could wish for. Their efforts to build a community of writers supporting other writers are exemplary, and so I want to thank them and my fellow Regal House authors for making the process of publication and promotion a largely pleasant one. I also want to thank the 2022 Debuts! group, which (privately on Facebook and publicly on Instagram and Twitter) has been another great group of writers supporting one another.

I'm glad to finally see this tale, which was so much fun to write, go forth.